'I want you!' Viscount Emery roared.

Thea blenched. 'Emery, really...!'

Charles coughed discreetly. 'I say, p'rhaps I should leave. Not the right thing to be present when a fellow makes love to a female.'

Thea sniffed. 'You needn't go, Charles! Emery is not making love to me.'

'No,' the viscount agreed. 'I had rather thought I was making you an offer.'

Thea gasped, then reached for the nearest object—a pitcher of cream—which she dashed full into Emery's face.

Clarice Peters was born in Honolulu, Hawaii, where she still lives with her husband, Adrian, a high school principal and her son, Jeremy. She's worked as an advertising copywriter, freelance curriculum writer and substitute teacher. She enjoys golf and tennis and has a weakness for Italian food.

Thea is Clarice Peters' second Masquerade Historical Romance, the first being *The False Betrothal*.

THEA

Clarice Peters

MILLS & BOON LIMITED
ETON HOUSE   18-24 PARADISE ROAD
RICHMOND   SURREY   TW9 1SR

First published in Great Britain 1989
by Mills & Boon Limited

© Laureen Kwock 1985

Australian copyright 1989
Philippine copyright 1989
This edition 1989

ISBN 0 263 76355 2

Set in Times Roman 10 on 12½ pt.
04-8903-64754 C

Made and printed in Great Britain

CHAPTER ONE

BREAKFAST at Chumley Field was ordinarily a quiet affair. Occasionally a passing footman overheard a muffled laugh or groan, the latter usually issued from Lord Marlow after a night of too many glasses of his favourite port. But on this May morning of 1816 it was not a groan that was heard but a shriek, and emanating from the lovely throat of Lady Marlow.

'Charles, Hadrian is getting married!' Lady Marlow gasped as she pushed aside the letter she had just completed reading.

Her shriek had caught her beloved husband just as he had been about to swallow a generous portion of ham, half of which he sputtered on to his plate, the other half lodging in his throat.

'My dear Amelia, do you want to give me the apoplexy?' he protested when he managed to speak. He began to wipe his mouth with a napkin, checking that movement when he realised what she had just said.

'What's this about Hadrian?' he demanded.

'He has offered for a Miss Beaseley. Look for yourself.' Amelia waved the letter distractedly under his moustache. 'You remember telling me to write to him last month about visiting us here? I told him the streams were *teeming* with trout, and since he is so fond of the sport, he has agreed to come. And then in the very last line of the letter he mentions that he is planning to offer for a Miss Beaseley, and that if all goes well, she may accompany him here.'

'It can't be,' Lord Marlow murmured, laying down his fork with a look of profound bafflement on his ruddy face. Of all the fellows in the ton, Hadrian, Viscount Emery, was the least likely to take a leg shackle and had frequently railed against the entire institution of matrimony.

'Hadrian would never write such a thing if it weren't true,' Lady Marlow countered. Her benevolent head was encircled by a crown of blonde curls, which shook now with her mounting excitement. 'I wonder who Miss Beaseley is.' Her forehead wrinkled in thought as she tried in vain to recall which of the pretty girls launched year after year had at last succeeded in winning her brother's heart.

'Perhaps she was that pretty brunette he was dancing with at Almack's earlier in the Season.'

'I was always of the mind that Hadrian favoured blondes myself,' Lord Marlow said with a contemplative look in his eyes. 'I seem to recall several of his female friends...' The rest of his words withered on his tongue as his wife dealt him a measuring look from across the table. 'Well, well, enough of that.'

'*More* than enough,' Amelia agreed, not unacquainted with her brother's forays into the petticoat line. While no rake, Hadrian was not impervious to female charms.

'She'll probably be a beauty,' she said now of the unknown Miss Beaseley.

'To be sure,' Lord Marlow agreed. 'Nothing but the best would do for Hadrian. And she'll be a lucky chit at that. Why, he might have his pick of the ton beauties. I just wonder why he set his mind on marriage now.'

'He is one-and-thirty, and that disposes a man to think. Or perhaps'—Amelia's voice broke slightly—'he may have decided it time to set up his nursery.'

Lord Marlow, who shared his wife's disappointment at not having a child after ten years of marriage, patted her on the hand. 'Amelia, my love...'

'Oh, Charles, I am fine,' she said stoutly. 'And don't let me turn into a watering-pot at my age.'

'Your age! Bosh, woman, you ain't in your dotage yet.'

She giggled at him and picked up another letter from the silver platter in front of her. She frowned slightly, then broke the seal, and for the second time that morning shrieked in surprise.

Charles, who had renewed his attack on the ham, sputtered it once again on to his dish.

'Amelia,' he implored, 'is this to be a new habit of yours? If so, perhaps you could take breakfast in your room.'

Amelia paid not a jot of attention to his complaint. 'Charles, Thea is coming for a visit.'

'Thea? Who's she?'

'Theodora Campion. Don't you recall meeting her five years ago when we were passing through Vienna? She's the dearest friend, only of course I haven't seen her for years since she *will* live on the Continent. Her parents were divorced,' she reminded her spouse. 'Such a shocking scandal. Thea went away with her mother, who died, I recollect, about a year and a half ago. Now Thea writes that the Continent bores her, and she plans to visit her uncle Andrew Campion, who lives close by and who is laid up with gout. She asks if it would be all right to visit us. Isn't that delightful?'

'Yes, yes, very nice,' Lord Marlow agreed. Some pleasant female company might be just the thing to cheer up Amelia, who lately had been increasingly despondent over her childless state.

'It is more than nice,' Lady Marlow declared, her eyes dancing with excitement. 'Only think how busy we shall be! First Hadrian coming to visit and bringing his new bride-to-be, and now Thea.' These words had no sooner left her lips than she shrieked a third time, causing Charles to drop his fork resignedly on his plate.

'I suppose if females can take a tray in their bed-chambers in the morning, we males can do the same. Man might starve to death eating here with you.'

'Oh, Charles! Do stop thinking of *food* at a time like this!' Amelia commanded. 'We shall have Hadrian and Thea descending on us possibly within days. And that means I shall have to order the beds turned and the chambers aired, not to mention the provisions to be or-dered. And what shall we do for entertainment?' She rose without giving him a chance to reply and quitted the room, leaving her long-suffering spouse to finally finish his morning meal.

While Lady Marlow occupied herself during the week that followed with the many preparations necessary for her impending visitors, her brother in London was busy with his pursuit of Miss Louisa Beaseley, who was not the pretty brunette Lady Marlow had recalled him dancing with at Almack's. True to Lord Marlow's thoughts on the matter, Miss Beaseley was a blonde, quite in the Immaculata style, with huge blue eyes and a porcelain doll complexion. Her appearance only a month earlier had taken the ton by storm with no fewer than a dozen eligible bachelors languishing at her feet. The wags at White's had given Emery the advantage in the race for her hand. After all, in the last week he had driven her daily in the park, squired her to the opera and Drury Lane, and stood up with her three times at the Sefton ball. Four times would undoubtedly have caused talk.

On this particular morning the viscount had just finished his toilette and cast an oblique eye into the pier glass his valet held out for him, satisfied that he looked none the worse for having spent a good portion of the early morning at the green baize tables of White's.

The hazel eyes that gazed good-humouredly back at him were clear and undissipated. Not too bad-looking a chap, Emery thought, lifting a self-deprecating brow. Indeed several females had once called his head of shaggy brown curls 'Adonis-like', a remark that still caused him to wince when it was repeated to him by the Bow window set.

'That will have to do,' he said, laughing and picking up his malacca cane. He stepped leisurely down the Adam stairs and out on to Berkeley Square, looking every inch the top-of-the-trees Corinthian he was.

His coat of Bath-blue superfine hugged a torso that showed clear evidence of his addiction to sport. His snowy white cravat tied flawlessly *à la mathématique* was complemented by the palest of biscuit pantaloons.

Emery took the reins of his high-perched phaeton in one hand and drove off for Green Street and the town residence of Miss Beaseley and Mrs Chester, the aunt who was sponsoring her in London. He felt in the best of good humour.

But a mere ten minutes later that mood took a turn for the worse as he stared dumbfounded into the eyes of the young female plying a Chinese fan on the croco-dile-legged couch.

'What did you just say to me?' Emery demanded wondering if at the ripe age of thirty-one his hearing had suddenly deserted him.

'I said that I'm sorry, but I must refuse your offer,' Miss Beaseley replied with a sunny smile.

The viscount continued to stare at her. She had to be roasting him, and yet a sense of humour was not one of her chief attributes. But could she be serious? Refusing him?

'Forgive my confusion, Miss Beaseley,' he said now, gathering his wits together. 'I've been of the opinion that my attentions were not *unwelcome* to you.'

'Oh, they haven't been,' she agreed quickly. 'I've enjoyed you ever so much, and I do like you. You are one of the most dashing and handsome gentlemen I know, but...'

'But?' he prompted, one eyebrow raised like an imperious question mark.

Miss Beaseley folded the fan in her lap and blushed slightly. 'There's Appleton,' she said finally. 'He, you must own, is every bit as dashing as you, my lord, and just as handsome, although his colouring is fair and yours is dark. But he also boasts the most romantic moustache!' She punctuated this remark with a little squeak.

'*Moustache?*' the viscount muttered. Was the chit such a wet goose as to refuse him on account of a moustache?

'And,' Miss Beaseley confided, 'he is a marquis.'

This reason the viscount could readily understand. His lips curled ever so slightly. 'I see. Appleton has tendered you an offer?'

'Not yet,' she confessed. 'But he did say he had something pressing to discuss when we ride in the park later today.'

'I wish you happy,' Emery said politely. 'But before you settle for Appleton you might wish to cultivate the friendship of Lord Fallingsworth.'

Miss Beaseley puckered her face in pretty confusion. 'Fallingsworth? I don't believe I know him.'

'You can remedy that at once. I own he's twice as dashing as either Appleton or myself, and he boasts not only a moustache but a beard.'

'A beard?' Miss Beaseley appeared to waver somewhat.

'And,' Emery went on to deliver the facer, 'Fallingsworth is an earl.'

On that Parthian shot he departed, almost bowling over Mrs Chester, who was lurking in the hall. Once in his phaeton he ran his fingers speculatively over his cheeks, wondering what he might look like with a moustache. But that was utter nonsense. Miss Beaseley was a ninnyhammer! And so was he for even offering for her.

He returned to his Berkeley Square residence, wearing a visage so far from his normal good humour that his butler, Chadwick, avoided enquiring what sort of morning his employer might have passed. Chadwick, a most superior butler, did not need to ask the obvious. His lordship had been refused, and by a schoolroom miss!

The viscount, ruminating later on his rejection in the comfortable solitude of his bookroom, and fortified by a tray of restoratives that Chadwick had sent in, found little pleasure in the idea of remaining in London. A widgeon like Miss Beaseley could be relied upon to make his offer and her subsequent refusal known to all her bosom bows. The word would spread like the plague and he would soon be the butt of the Bond Street beaux.

Of course, he thought grimly, Miss Beaseley might be served with her own sauce if she did try and cultivate Fallingsworth, who, despite being an earl with a magnificent beard, had nearly sixty years in his dish. He was also the premier misogynist of the kingdom.

Emery chuckled. Miss Beaseley would have her work cut out for her if she tried to lure Fallingsworth to the altar. Feeling cheered, he emerged from his library to encounter his butler hovering close at hand.

'Ah, Chadwick! I shall be closing up my residence here a week earlier than expected.'

'Very good, sir.'

'Should anyone enquire after me, I shall be in Wiltshire with my sister, Amelia.'

He mounted the Adam stairs and gave the order to prepare a satchel of his things. By the time he sat down to luncheon his mood had improved so much that the foremost thought on his mind was not Miss Beaseley's refusal but the trout that Amelia had promised him.

*   *   *

Some twenty-four hours later Miss Theodora Campion gazed out of the window of the vehicle that carried her away from her uncle's residence, wishing with all her heart that her companion would order the groom to give the horses the office. This, however, was as good as wishing for snow in July. Sir Percy Boyle would have perished before allowing a female to racket about the kingdom at anything other than a snail's pace.

'Can't these horses go any faster?' Thea implored.

Sir Percy attempted a deprecating shake of his head, a move that triggered ripples of fat from his chin down his throat and on to his broad belly.

'Patience, Miss Campion. Far better to have you arrive safe and sound at Lady Marlow's than wind up with a broken neck.' He paused, which allowed his chin to catch up to the rest of him. 'I can't believe you were considering riding to Chumley Field,' he chided.

'But I've always ridden there. It's only five miles. I dare say Amelia shall think it odd of me to arrive in a carriage. Not,' she added hastily lest she appear unappreciative of the ancient team and vehicle they were riding in, 'that it wasn't civil of you to offer your services to me when you came to visit Uncle Andrew.'

Sir Percy smiled indulgently. 'Always glad to be of service, my dear. One can never be too careful, especially with the threat of highwaymen lurking. It was a stroke of good fortune that I happened to call on your Uncle Andrew today. I generally call on him on Wednesdays, but I had some business nearby and thought I'd pop in and surprise him. I know how lonely he can get, burdened with the gout.'

Thea murmured an appropriate sound of appreciation, knowing full well that her uncle considered the baronet's visit a waste of his precious time. Mr Andrew Campion was of a scholarly persuasion, and being confined with the gout gave him an excuse to turn to his beloved books.

Indeed, Thea suspected that her uncle's suggestion a half-hour earlier that Sir Percy escort her to Chumley Field came not from fear for her safety but as a method of removing the baronet from his parlour.

'Lady Marlow is expecting you, I trust?' Sir Percy asked now, a question that had been asked and answered at least twice before during the ride.

'Oh, yes,' she repeated now, adding hastily, 'and you must not let me delay you once you have dropped me at her doorstep.'

'Tut-tut, Miss Campion. A visit to Chumley Field shall not be too displeasing to me. I have not visited her ladyship for several days, not since Friday, I do believe.'

Thea stifled a groan. Poor Amelia would have every right to slay her for inflicting the greatest bore in Christendom on her unsuspecting head. She sank back resignedly on the hard seat, wishing that Sir Percy might have had a more comfortable conveyance. Perhaps it was a good thing they were moving so slowly. A faster pace would have caused it to shake loose from the frame.

She turned her face away to hide a yawn and began to think of Amelia. How good it would be to see her! For several minutes she was lost in pleasurable thought about the reunion ahead. A discreet cough from her companion caused her to start guiltily.

'Er, yes, Sir Percy?'

'I wonder what you think of my suggestion, Miss Campion,' the baronet said.

Embarrassed at being caught in an air dream, Thea blurted out that she thought the idea splendid. He looked pleased.

'Good, good. I shall call on your uncle tomorrow, then, with my translation of Virgil.'

Too late, Thea realised that Sir Percy's splendid notion was to present her uncle with a translation of Virgil, one that Mr Campion, a high stickler in matters of scholarship, would probably take issue with. She was trying to find a way of dissuading Sir Percy from this path of folly when the vehicle suddenly lurched to the right and then to the left before falling over to the side, sending her flying across the seat to land with a resounding thump on Sir Percy's stout chest.

CHAPTER TWO

IT WAS difficult to say just who was more surprised: Sir Percy, at receiving Miss Campion on his chest, or Thea, at being there. Since she was the younger, she was the first to recover her breath and pull away.

'What happened?' Sir Percy demanded.

'We have been ditched, I fear,' Thea said, deducing as much from the precarious tilt of the vehicle, which tottered alarmingly.

'Sir Percy, are you all right?' The voice of the baronet's groom, Albert, could be heard from outside.

'Albert, I shall have you whipped,' Sir Percy bellowed.

'Heavens, Percy. There's no necessity to resort to such violence,' a voice drawled as the door opened and a slender hand was extended. 'And don't whip your groom, for it was my fault, even though I do think your carriage was a trifle slow. I'd forgotten the road narrowed around this bend.' A second hand joined the first and together they clasped Thea lightly around the waist and lifted her out of the carriage and safely to the ground.

Thea could not but appreciate the strength in those hands as well as the rest of the body, which included a head of tousled brown hair half-hidden beneath a beaver felt, brown eyes twinkling appreciatively at her, an aquiline nose and sturdy chin.

'Emery, as I live and breathe!' Percy's exclamation cut Thea's scrutiny short as the viscount turned and held

out a hand to the baronet, whose head was just peeking
from the carriage.

'I don't need your help,' Sir Percy said stiffly.

'Very well,' Emery said amicably, having more interest
in Percy's companion than in the baronet, who as a rule
did not travel in the company of females blessed with
auburn hair and sparkling green eyes.

'I don't think I've had the pleasure of meeting your
companion, Percy,' the viscount said now.

The baronet, who had been busy surveying the damage
to his vehicle, looked over his shoulder. 'This is Miss
Theodora Campion,' he said distractedly. 'And she ain't
accustomed to riding into ditches!'

'No, of course she isn't,' the viscount murmured
soothingly. 'How very *peculiar* of her if she were!'

Thea swallowed a giggle.

'Enchanted to meet you, Miss Campion. I am Viscount
Emery!'

A heartwrenching wail forestalled her response.

'My chaise! Just look at it!'

Thea obligingly turned her eyes towards Sir Percy's
vehicle, which did look in a very poor way. Two wheels
had come off, the door on the far side was crushed, and
the roof appeared to have caved in. It was a small miracle
that the horses had escaped injury.

'And it's a miracle we weren't crushed to death,' Thea
commented.

'If you had, I should have held myself entirely to
blame,' Emery said promptly. 'And I would have done
an appropriate penance.'

'Do you mean sackcloth and ashes?' she quizzed, her green eyes meeting his hazel ones, which twinkled at her good-naturedly.

'At the very least. And quite possibly a hair shirt as well.'

She laughed, delighted to find his love of the ridiculous equalled hers.

The same, unfortunately, could not be said of Sir Percy, who found nothing remotely amusing in the prospect of being snatched within an ame's ace of mortal injury, which presumably not even the adoption of sackcloth and ashes could rectify.

'You've no business riding at such breakneck speed,' he expostulated now. 'Just look at the damage to my carriage. It will cost well over five hundred pounds to repair, and I wouldn't be surprised to find it a total loss.'

The viscount held his quizzing-glass to one eye. 'I shouldn't be surprised either, Percy.' He put down the glass, yawning. 'Would you like a new one instead?'

Thea, who was standing between the two men, blinked at such generosity. Sir Percy's carriage had been falling apart from old age. The price of a new one would far exceed the value of the old.

Sir Percy, however, knew a windfall when it fell into his lap, and he pounced eagerly on Emery's words, adding his own ideas of just which carriage-maker in Wiltshire might be engaged to construct the new vehicle.

The discussion, which Sir Percy was in danger of monopolising, came to an abrupt halt when a shot rang out. A masked figure on horseback advanced with a pistol levelled at the four of them.

The faces regarding the highwayman held a variety of expressions. Thea, who had never seen a highwayman in the flesh before, stared at the figure with keen interest. She was a bit disappointed, all in all, to find him not the heroic figure imagination might have sketched, but a thin person almost dwarfed by his black cloak. The handkerchief he wore over his mouth made it almost impossible for her to determine just how handsome his features were.

Sir Percy had no interest in the robber's features, handsome or otherwise. The day for him had gone from bad to worse. To be ditched was one thing—and since Emery was planning to buy him a new carriage he couldn't really regret it—but to be accosted in broad daylight was something else! Not that he knew precisely what he could do about it.

The viscount shared neither of his companion's sentiments. He merely gazed ahead, a bored expression on his face, which nevertheless held a wary appreciation of the pistol in the robber's hand.

'This is all your fault, Emery,' the baronet hissed.

The viscount turned an astounded countenance his way. 'My fault, Percy? You are all about in your head.'

'No, I ain't. If you hadn't run us into the ditch we wouldn't be easy pickings for the likes of him.'

'Oh, I don't know about that, Percy,' Emery demurred. 'Your vehicle was moving devilishly slow, you must own.'

'All the same...' The baronet's voice trailed off as the highwayman, growing obviously impatient, moved his pistol in the direction of Sir Percy's pudgy chest.

'Don't shoot,' Sir Percy said, lifting his hands.

'Don't be a coxcomb, Percy,' Emery said bracingly. 'If the fellow had wanted to shoot us I dare say he would have done so long ago. Like most highwaymen he is after money, or perhaps jewels?' He dealt a questioning look at the mounted figure, who nodded.

'See, I am right.'

'How do you know so much about highwaymen?' Thea asked, unable to repress her curiosity. 'Have you perchance fallen victim to them before?'

Emery shook his head. 'It merely stood to reason that a robber would want money, Miss Campion.' He turned to Sir Percy. 'Let's begin by having you hand me your purse, Percy.'

The baronet recoiled as though stung. 'I say, Emery.'

'This is a robbery,' the viscount reminded him. 'The sooner we turn the funds over to him the sooner we shall see the end to it. I shall include my own purse with yours, Percy.' Observing the baronet's hesitation, he continued. 'Dangerous sort of fellow to keep waiting, Percy.'

'He shan't get away with it,' the baronet hissed, digging into his pocket.

'I don't see why not,' Emery replied reflectively. 'His steed certainly appears swift enough, and he has that pistol.' His eyes widened as Sir Percy reluctantly handed over a roll of bills. 'What a large roll of bills!' He clucked his tongue. 'And here I always thought you devilishly hard-up.'

Sir Percy choked.

'Now, then.' Emery addressed the masked figure. 'Shall we divest the lady of her jewellery?'

'Unfortunately,' Thea replied as she threw herself into the spirit of the crime, 'I am not wearing any. But then,' she confessed, 'I possess few to begin with.'

'Well, you should be grateful for that,' Emery said.

'Enough!' the highwayman cried out.

Emery turned toward him. 'Do you wish the lady's purse as well?' He turned back to Thea. 'I assume you carry a reticule somewhere about.'

The highwayman shook his head grimly. Emery beamed.

'You see, he is a good sort after all. He just wants our purses, Percy.' He started forward with them but halted as the pistol swung his way. 'Don't you want the money?' the viscount asked exasperatedly.

'Let him bring it,' the highwayman said, his voice muffled by the handkerchief he wore.

'M—Me? Why me?' Percy stammered.

Emery shrugged. 'Oh, he must have his whims when it comes to such things. Go ahead,' he urged, handing him the bills and giving him a little push. 'Then we can return to our discussion of your new carriage!'

'Don't be frightened, Sir Percy,' Thea said encouragingly.

Recalled by these words to the presence of a member of the weaker sex, Percy drew himself up to his full height and stepped gingerly forward. It was just like Emery to stand there laughing, as though it were a grand joke, but he was not about to take such things lying down.

Sir Percy threw back his shoulders—a task made difficult due to the amount of padding his valet was obliged to use to hide the deficiency of his shoulders—and walked towards the highwayman. As the robber leaned over to grasp the money, Percy made a wild lunge for the pistol. The horse, which had been docile throughout the encounter, reared sharply at the sudden move, and the robber, cursing, struggled for control.

Percy, seeing his chance, dropped the money and grabbed the bridle. 'I've got him!' he shouted, a slight exaggeration, for all he had at the moment was the bridle.

Emery, recognising in a trice the micefeet that Percy had made of a perfectly simple robbery, reacted swiftly. The highwayman's horse, nostrils flaring and legs kicking, was out of control. The robber was still struggling with the reins. He swung the pistol now, which was levelled at Miss Campion.

'That fool shall get us both killed,' the viscount murmured as Percy continued to wrestle at the bridle. Sizing up the situation, Emery pushed Thea down hard on the ground just as a shot rang out.

'I've got him! I've got him!' the baronet crowed exultantly.

'You've got no one,' Thea answered, her exasperation rising along with her face. Her annoyance with Sir Percy disappeared, however, when she saw a trickle of blood oozing from a small hole in Emery's shoulder.

'You're hurt!' she exclaimed.

These words acted like a restorative to the highwayman, who took advantage of the attention drawn to Emery by kicking Percy with a boot and fleeing.

'Follow him!' The baronet commanded Albert, who ignored such a foolish idea and lent Thea his assistance in looking to the viscount's wound.

'It is a veritable scratch,' Emery protested, attempting to fend off their ministrations. 'My good Miss Campion, don't make me out an invalid.'

Thea placed one hand squarely against his broad chest and pushed him down to the ground. 'Scratch or not, it is bleeding profusely!' she pointed out. He was obliged to endure a few minutes' wait as she wrapped his handkerchief on the wound and then tied hers about it.

Although loath to admit it, Emery did feel a trifle lightheaded. He was conscious of her deftness and lack of missishness in treating the wound. Most females he knew—Miss Beaseley flitted into mind—would have swooned on the spot.

'A doctor should look at this,' she informed him as she gave the bandage a final pat. 'I should hate for you to contract a poisoning of the blood.'

'It was just a nick. The ball passed cleanly,' he said.

'Is it very painful?'

'I think I shall live,' he drawled.

She gave a quick smile of relief. 'And I shall live as well, thanks to you,' she replied.

'Thanks to him?' Sir Percy, who had been waiting impatiently while she tended to the viscount, could not believe his ears. 'I'll have you know, Miss Campion, that 'twas I who saved us all from that highwayman!'

'Oh, Sir Percy, *really!*' Thea's exasperation knew no bounds. 'There would have been no danger at all if you had merely given him the money in the way the viscount told you to. Instead of which you staged such a misguided attempt. That's what caused the horse to rear. And if the viscount does die, which I think highly improbable, for despite the bleeding, the wound looks minor, I shall hold you accountable.'

The baronet's mouth opened, then shut, as though engaged in the act of catching flies.

The viscount, his good shoulder shaking, attempted to soothe Sir Percy's ruffled feathers. 'You may rest easy, Percy. I promise you, I shan't die from this.'

The baronet had no interest in such assurances. He had just finished performing the heroic deed of rescuing a female in distress, and she, the dratted female, had not even noticed.

'I suppose there is no understanding females,' he said now with rigid courtesy. 'Scaring off a highwayman would have occasioned thanks from any other female.'

'I cannot hope to speak for my *entire* sex,' Thea acknowledged, 'and I suppose a few might be demented enough to thank you. But I shan't. You very nearly got us killed, and all on account of your purse!'

What the baronet, who was very attached to his purse, might have said to this was left in the air, for the viscount deemed it wisest to intervene, saying that while his wound was minor, it was a trifle uncomfortable.

'Of course it's uncomfortable,' Thea exclaimed. 'We must get help for you and all of us.'

'Thanks to Emery,' the baronet pointed out stiffly, 'my carriage is not fit to be ridden in.'

'But my horse is ready and able,' Emery replied.

'You can't ride it, injured as you are,' Thea protested immediately.

'I assure you, Miss Campion...'

'Let me ride it,' she said.

His brows lifted. 'I fear that Pompeii may be a trifle difficult for a lady to handle.'

'I have ridden horses before,' she assured him.

'I am certain of that. But even the most prodigious of riders would have trouble with a mount like Pompeii.'

'Then Sir Percy must ride him,' Thea declared, an assertion that caused Sir Percy to blench noticeably.

'I don't think that would be a good idea either,' the viscount answered, loath to inflict the likes of the baronet on his hardworking mount.

'Then Albert shall go,' Thea said.

The groom coughed. 'Begging your pardon, miss, but that horse is a touch above me, so to speak.'

'I will go,' Emery insisted, 'and I shall send help back for you.'

He got to his feet with help from Albert and started towards his horse, a little surprised at his lightheadedness, which he attempted to shrug off.

'You are in no condition to ride,' Thea said, going to his side at once while Albert supported the other.

'I am fine,' he repeated. 'I merely need some assistance into the saddle.'

'And what if you should faint during your ride?' she asked as Albert helped him up. 'I shall go with you.'

'Go with me?' He looked down at her, feeling even more dizzy than before.

'What other recourse do we have?' she demanded. 'You are injured, and neither Percy nor Albert seems anxious to mount your great beast.'

'Aren't you afflicted by such qualms yourself?'

'Indeed I am, for I am no fool. But you will be with me to calm Pompeii, and I shall be at hand in case anything dire happens to you. We shall send help for you, Sir Percy.' She turned to reassure the baronet. 'Albert, if you would kindly help me up?'

Minutes later, Emery, with his good arm round Thea's waist, touched his heels to the flanks of his horse. Instantly it took off, leaving Thea scarcely time to collect her breath. As they rode off, she did catch a glimpse of the baronet's scandalised countenance. After the first dizzying minutes on Pompeii she was more than happy that the viscount was at hand.

'Albert was right,' she murmured. 'Your horse is a touch above me.'

Emery smiled. 'In truth, he's a touch above me on occasion. Pure Arabian. Quite different from Sir Percy's cattle.'

The wind brought the sound of her laugh back to him. '*Poor* Sir Percy! He undoubtedly thinks me sunk beneath reproach for riding off with you in this brazen way!'

'If he does, you have only to remind him that you are on an errand of mercy lest I suffer a fatal collapse.'

She wrinkled up her nose. 'That's true,' she said, much struck, 'but you certainly appear sturdy enough.'

'Poor Percy does have his uses. Only think of his courage in foiling the highwayman!' Emery said.

She caught the ironic gleam in his eyes and bubbled with quick mirth. 'Foiling? I call it folly myself. He nearly caused you to be killed. And if it weren't for you, I surely would have been.' She turned round in the saddle to gaze at him, unaware of a smudge of mud on her upturned nose. 'Have I thanked you fully for that?'

Emery could not help smiling down at her. 'Not yet,' he acknowledged.

'Well, I do now, most sincerely. To be shot must be disagreeable.'

'Having endured that experience more than once, I concur with your opinion.'

'Have you been wounded before?' she asked, interested. 'I suppose it was probably a duel?'

'My dear Miss Campion,' he protested mildly, 'I'll have you know that of the two duels I fought in my salad days, I was not on the receiving end of things. I am alleged to be a fair shot.'

She appeared properly impressed by this and would have questioned him further on the details of these affairs of honour when she suddenly realised that they were headed through the gates of Chumley Field. Emery with no direction from her had headed a course straight for Amelia's.

'Why, we're at Amelia's!' she exclaimed now.

'Yes,' he acknowledged, somewhat surprised. 'Do you know her?'

Thea laughed. 'Know Amelia? I should say I do. She is my great friend.'

'And my great sister!'

'Your sister?'

No further investigation on this issue could be had, as the great friend and sister who was just enjoying a ride with her spouse spied them coming through the gates on the same horse. Her shock at seeing the makeshift bandage adorning her brother's shoulder—at great cost to his coat of Bath-blue superfine—and smudged face of Thea necessitated a good number of questions, which the two attempted to answer as they were being led through the front door of Amelia's establishment.

CHAPTER THREE

WITHIN moments of ushering Emery into the Crimson Saloon, Amelia began to pelt him with questions. Since Thea had pleaded for a chance to wash and been dispatched abovestairs, Lady Marlow seized the opportunity to acquaint herself with the particulars of her brother's upcoming marriage.

Emery was a bit fagged from his long day of travel and would have preferred to attend to the sherry Charles was pouring across the room than to any of Amelia's queries concerning Miss Beaseley.

'I'd assumed you would bring her with you, and instead you appear with Thea.'

'Yes, but I thought I explained all about the accident as we rode up.'

'Yes, yes. Sir Percy's carriage was ditched. And while I don't mean to pinch at you, my dear, perhaps you might restrain yourself from riding at your usual breakneck speed hereabouts. We pursue a more leisurely pace in the country. But you haven't uttered a syllable yet about your marriage. I am on pins and needles to learn all about Miss Beaseley. Where is she?'

Emery leaned back in the Trafalgar chair and gazed longingly at the sherry Charles was carrying over. 'I would imagine, Amelia, that Miss Beaseley is in London.'

'In London?' Amelia frowned, and a hurt look came into her eyes. 'Doesn't she wish to come here and see us?'

'It isn't Chumley Field she objects to, but me.' His voice dropped and she was forced to bend over to hear his next words. 'Miss Beaseley refused me.'

Lady Marlow shrieked, startling Charles into throwing up his hands and the glasses of sherry. The sherry flew into his face and down his neckcloth and frilled shirt.

'Oh, I say, Amelia, no more of that, I beg you.' He made a futile dab at drying his shirt. 'I'd better change. Help yourself to the sherry, Hadrian,' he said.

Amelia, after murmuring apologies to her husband, turned quickly to her brother. 'Now that we're alone, Hadrian, do tell me what's about. What's this about the Beaseley chit?'

'I told you, Amelia,' Emery said testily. 'She refused me.'

'She must be mad,' Lady Marlow declared, an incredulous look on her face. She followed him across the room to the tray of sherry. 'What more could she want in a gentleman but you? You are the perfect specimen of a husband, loath though I am to add to your consequence: well-pursed, well-bred, pleasant of features, and titled since Uncle Fester died and left you his heir.'

'Apparently Miss Beaseley prefers her gentlemen moustachioed,' Emery said, taking a swallow of the sherry at last and finding it well worth the wait.

'She must be mad,' Lady Marlow repeated. She lifted her blue eyes suspiciously. 'Or is this one of your frivolous hoaxes?'

'No, to both,' he declared as she waved away the glass of sherry he offered her. 'Miss Beaseley is not mad, merely idiotish and somewhat inclined to the romantic. It seems that Appleton has been paying her court too. He is just as handsome as me but has the added lure of a moustache, and to top things off he is a marquis.'

'Good God, she sounds a perfect ninnyhammer,' Lady Marlow replied, seeing no necessity to mince words.

Emery gave a crack of laughter. 'I suppose she is that,' he agreed, 'but she is also quite beautiful.'

The wistful note reminded Amelia that, regardless how stupid Miss Beaseley might be, Hadrian had suffered his first disappointment, and her manner turned immediately sympathetic.

'Poor Hadrian, it must have been a shocking blow to you. No wonder you arrived a full week ahead of schedule. I just hope you managed to outrun the prattle-boxes as well.'

He grimaced slightly. 'A temporary measure. Miss Beaseley will probably swear each of her friends to secrecy about my offer and refusal. The word will undoubtedly circulate about the ton.'

'Odious, odious female!'

'Yes,' Emery said complacently. 'And why do we speak of her when there are more topics to enjoy, such as your charming friend Miss Campion? And why have you never mentioned her to me?'

'She wasn't here,' Amelia protested. They had made their way back to the Egyptian couch. 'She lives in Vienna, or at least she did before now. I don't know what her plans are. And anyway'—she tossed her hair and fixed her keen eyes on her brother—'even if I had spoken of her, you wouldn't have paid a jot of attention. Up until a fortnight ago you were as confirmed a bachelor as one could find in the kingdom.'

Emery could not dispute the truth in this scorching rejoinder. '*Touché,* Amelia. But do tell me more of Miss Campion now. I noticed you called her Thea as we rode up. Just how well acquainted are you with her?'

'We met five years ago in Vienna,' Lady Marlow replied, relaxing against the scalloped-backed couch. 'I was accompanying Charles on one of his missions. That was when that monster Napoleon was still roaming about. He used to help his uncle in the diplomatic field—Charles, I mean, not Napoleon. Anyhow, Thea was in Vienna with her mother. We met at a soirée there and formed an instant rapport.'

Emery looked puzzled. 'Why does she live in Vienna?'

His sister's eyes clouded. 'It's a long story. Her father was a profligate and the mother's family had warned her not to marry. Of course, nothing could be more stupid than that, for that was the surest way to drive the two into each other's arms. Before anyone could blink an eye, they had eloped to Gretna. After the marriage, all the family's worst fears were realised. Campion was a wastrel, running through Eleanor's dowry and his own small portion as well. After Thea was born, the two divorced. I don't know the grounds, but I dare say she had good reason for it. About a month after the decree was issued he broke his neck in some hunting mishap, and Eleanor went abroad to live with the child.'

'Living on what?' the viscount asked.

'An aunt had taken pity on her and left her an easy competence. She raised Thea in comfort. You mustn't think they were paupers. Thea was brought out in society, and I know she is not without admirers. She once turned down the hand of a German duke.'

'Did she? Perhaps it wasn't washed. They say these Germans have some peculiarities!'

'That's not what I mean, you gudgeon!' she railed, then saw the amusement in his eyes. 'Do stop jesting, Hadrian. She turned down an offer of marriage from the duke.'

'Really? Which one?'

Amelia frowned, trying to think. 'I can't recall his name. Von Ryan? Von Richards. Von Something. Is it so important?'

'Not to me,' her brother averred. 'I was merely curious. She mentioned an uncle to me.'

Amelia nodded. 'That would be Mr Andrew Campion, quite an excellent person and a scholar! There's a son, too, I believe. Jonathon is his name.' She became suddenly aware that Emery was digesting all this news with an avidity that bespoke more than just a passing interest in the family Campion. A wild hope surged in her breast.

'Thea is quite lovely and even-tempered, don't you think, Hadrian?' she asked now.

'Even-tempered, Amelia? Much too modest. I know of no other female who would endure a carriage mishap and being accosted by a highwayman without resorting to the vapours or at least her vinaigrette!'

Lady Marlow thought despairingly that it was just like Hadrian to praise Thea for her lack of sensibility rather than her beauty, but she supposed that compared to the volatile Miss Beaseley her friend might appear a veritable Rock of Gibraltar.

At this point the Rock herself entered the room, accompanied by Lord Marlow, who had exchanged his wet shirt and cravat for dry ones.

'My dear, come in,' Amelia exclaimed.

'You should have told me my nose was smudged,' Thea scolded Emery. 'Imagine coming all this way looking like a gypsy. By all rights I should be mortified.'

'But you're not,' he said with aplomb. 'And while I had noticed the smudge—inevitable, since I undoubtedly gave it to you by hurtling you to the ground— I found it rather charming.'

Lord Marlow, who had never heard such poppycock before from the lips of his brother-in-law, shot his wife a look of disbelief, curious as to why she was looking so pleased with herself.

Thea, however, had laughed off Emery's words and was now addressing Amelia on the matter of Sir Percy.

'Sir Percy!' Lady Marlow stared, aghast. 'Good heavens, I forgot him completely.' Recalled now to a sense of her duty, she gave the bellpull a vigorous tug and ordered the answering footman to seek out Sir Percy down the road and render him whatever assistance was necessary.

'Just don't bring him back here!' she commanded. 'And,' she added when the footman had departed, 'I hope that Percy doesn't feel obligated to call on us to thank us. He visited us only the day before yesterday, and that was quite enough.' She turned to Thea. 'I have been telling Hadrian how we met in Vienna.'

'At Lady Cunningham's soirée,' Thea said with a nostalgic smile. 'Lady Cunningham,' she explained to Emery, 'fancies herself a patroness of the arts. I had been dragooned into accompanying Mama there. Somehow Amelia and Charles had wandered in, thinking it would be a grand fête.'

'And it was no such thing,' Lady Marlow chuckled at the memory. 'They had a poet reading verse, and in German of all absurdities.' Languages had never been one of her strong suits.

'And we encountered each other in the refreshment-room,' Thea concluded.

'Well, you shall find no German poets here,' Emery replied briskly. 'Am I right, Charles?'

Lord Marlow, who had been sampling his sherry, blenched at the very notion. 'Shoot one if he ever came round,' he said, looking as though for two pins he would do exactly that. He gazed over the rim of his glass at his brother-in-law. 'What happened to Miss Beaseley, Hadrian? Will she be joining you later?'

The amusement vanished from the viscount's eyes. Amelia shot her spouse a frantic look.

'No, Charles,' Emery said finally. 'Miss Beaseley remains behind in London.'

Later, strolling with his wife in the gardens while Thea napped and Emery submitted to a doctor's examination, Lord Marlow demanded to know what exactly lay between Emery and Miss Beaseley.

'Thought you were about to bite my head off when I asked him a simple question.'

'Nothing lies between them,' Amelia explained hastily. 'The silly creature refused him.'

Charles nearly stumbled on a garden stone. 'Refused Hadrian?'

'Yes. She must be a perfect shatterbrain, don't you agree? And while it is a blow to Hadrian, it might well be a blessing in disguise.'

'How so?' Charles asked, unable to follow his wife's line of reasoning.

'Because of Thea, of course,' Lady Marlow said, giving his arm a little shake. 'I must own I have been a shatterbrain myself not to have thought of her before. She is perfect for Hadrian and he for her. Of course, she was living in Vienna. And they say, out of sight out of mind, but she is definitely in sight now and definitely in mind.'

'Amelia, you ain't thinking of playing matchmaker, are you?' Charles asked, recalling her previous attempts at playing Cupid.

'No, of course not, my dear,' she said placatingly, 'but a little nudge in the right direction might be just what the doctor ordered.'

The only doctor in the vicinity, however, was more concerned with the viscount's shoulder than with his affairs of the heart.

'You are a lucky fellow, my lord,' Dr Marsh said, looking as grim as his grizzled grey head. 'Another few inches, and you wouldn't be here to complain about this examination. As it is, a little stiffness in the shoulder is all you shall have to endure for a few days.'

'Will it interfere with my riding?' Emery asked.

'It might. You'd best take it easy for a day or two. And you'd have to exercise more caution the next time you encounter a highwayman.' With that, he brushed aside Emery's thanks and departed, leaving behind strict instructions that he be notified if the injury took a turn for the worse.

Alone in the Marlow parlour, Emery muttered a veiled oath on the head of Sir Percy Boyle. For someone who had always enjoyed good health, to be slowed even for a few days constituted a penance of the highest order. But at least he had the pleasure of getting to know Thea better.

An involuntary smile flitted across Emery's face as he thought of the lovely face peeking out from the head of reddish locks and the green eyes that could by turns flash with temper or good humour. A week of recuperation was not such a bad prescription after all. He rose from the couch and walked out into the hall, wondering if perhaps Thea had arisen from her afternoon slumber.

This query, when put to Mrs Jenkins, elicited a negative response as well as a look that made him feel like a schoolboy with his first flirtation. He was relieved to hear his name called and turned to find Lord Marlow at his elbow.

'I thought we might have a round of billiards, Hadrian,' he said. 'Oh, stupid thought! I forgot about your shoulder. What did Marsh have to say about it?'

'I shall survive. And your invitation wasn't stupid in the least. I may not hold a cue myself, but I can certainly admire your prowess with one.'

Marlow, who did pride himself on his skill with a cue, beamed at his brother-in-law and led him into the billard-room.

'Amelia told me about the Beaseley chit,' he said as he selected a cue from the rack. 'Sorry for you.'

'You needn't be,' Emery replied, unperturbed. 'Every man should be refused once in his lifetime.'

Charles laughed. 'Easy to say that. But I know how it feels. I remember once I was top-over-tail in love with some chit. Long before I met Amelia, of course,' he added hastily. 'Calf love is all it was. Sent her roses, strolled with her, and'—he blenched at the memory of his folly—'even composed a sonnet to her.'

Emery's eyes glittered with laughter. 'Charles, really? Poetry from you? Who was this paragon?'

'No one you would know,' Marlow said, sinking a ball in one of the pockets. 'I popped the question, and she refused me. Lucky escape. She led her husband a cat-and-dog life, I'm told.'

'Charles, really! I insist you divulge her name,' Hadrian urged.

Lord Marlow fixed a baleful eye at him. 'You won't tell Amelia?'

'No, of course not. I'm true blue and shall never stain. Tell me at once.'

'Lady Thadham.'

'What?' Emery roared in disbelief. 'That bag of bones!'

'She weren't that skinny then,' Lord Marlow replied, making another adroit manoeuvre with his cue.

Emery leaned his head on his hands and watched Marlow make quick work of the remaining balls on the table. 'Skinny, a quack, and isn't she the one with the passel of brats?'

'Yes, I believe so,' Marlow said quietly, a little too quietly.

Emery, remembering too late the childless state of his sister, a misfortune that grieved both her and her husband, bit his tongue. 'Oh, Charles, I am sorry. Such a blunderhead I am.'

'Don't know what you're babbling about, Hadrian,' Lord Marlow said gruffly. 'Anyhow, Lady Thadham was all long ago. But mind, don't tell Amelia.'

'My lips are sealed,' the viscount promised.

'In all likelihood that Beaseley chit would have turned into someone like Thadham.'

'A reassuring thought for me,' Emery agreed. 'Dare you predict what sort of female Miss Campion might develop into?'

Charles, who was hunched over a new set of balls on the table, looked up, squinting a little. 'Miss Campion, is it? Well, well. That one has a head on her shoulders. Good-looking too, and Amelia is devilishly fond of her.'

'So I gathered,' Emery said meditatively.

Charles, after another questioning look, decided that that was more than enough talk about females for one afternoon and introduced the more agreeable topic of fish, eliciting Emery's views on the matter. Within a half-hour they had agreed on an expedition to his favourite trout stream if weather conditions and Emery's injury permitted.

CHAPTER FOUR

UPON awakening from her nap, Thea lay on the huge four-poster bed, luxuriating in the feeling of once again being in England. It was regrettable that so much of her girlhood had been spent abroad, but such was the cost of having a scandalous past. Not that she considered herself a scarlet woman, but a few people over the years had continued to look askance at her being the daughter of a divorced woman.

A soft knock on her chamber door roused her from the comfort of the bed, and Amelia swept in, carrying a bouquet of freshly-cut roses from the garden.

'Are you fully recovered, my dear?' she asked as she put the roses down on the dressing-table and turned to her friend.

Thea gave a rueful laugh. 'Such a poor guest, Amelia, to be lying here snoring away.'

Amelia answered with a laugh. 'That is only to be expected. After all, you have had a harrowing day.' She sat down on the side of the bed, Thea's hand in hers. 'It is so good to see you again.'

'And I, you. And you must tell me everything that has passed with you in the past five years.'

Amelia made a gallant attempt to fill the order, which would have challenged any master story-teller. Thea heard all about Lord Marlow's attempts to breed champions from his stock, the excellent trout in the streams, and a bit more than one might have anticipated about Emery.

'He received the title last year after Uncle Fester died,' Amelia explained. 'It was such a shock, for he was in the best of health—Uncle Fester, I mean, not Hadrian, who, I might add, always had the constitution of an ox.'

Thea smiled. 'He certainly seems stout enough today, despite the highwayman's shot.'

'Oh, he's pluck to the old backbone,' Lady Marlow agreed, dutifully fanning this small flicker of interest. 'And so pleasant. Not the sort of brother to roast one mercilessly. And when Mama and Papa passed away, he was a tower of strength to me.'

'I'm sure he boasts all manner of male virtues,' Thea agreed.

'And as viscount he now has an income exceeding thirty thousand pounds a year as well as what Papa left him, and the estate in Kent...'

She stopped as she perceived her friend lying back, holding her stomach with laughter. 'Amelia, what are you thinking of?' Thea asked, wiping her streaming eyes.

Lady Marlow shed the last vestige of pretence. 'Thea, you can't blame me for trying. And I do think it was *meant*. You and Hadrian, I mean. As I was telling Charles, nothing would seem more fated than you two meeting on the road and perhaps falling in love and marrying.'

'You may give over that notion at once,' Thea said.

The decisive note in her voice caused Amelia to look across at her friend. Thea in the last five years had left her girlhood behind and was a lovely lady who knew her own mind.

'Don't you like Hadrian?' Amelia asked.

'Amelia, I scarcely know him!' Thea exclaimed. 'Do be sensible. I don't wish for marriage.'

Lady Marlow dealt with this objection with a snap of her fingers. 'Fiddle! Every female wishes for it.'

'Not I,' Thea replied. 'Not after parents such as mine.'

Hearing a despondent note in the usually cheerful voice, Amelia turned quickly sympathetic. 'Thea, you mustn't think that just because your parents' marriage ended disastrously, all marriages will.'

'I know that,' she agreed readily. 'But it does sober one to have a bill of divorcement in the family. Believe me, Amelia, I know how difficult a matter it is to resolve. And Mama, God rest her soul, never forgave herself for it. I suppose that makes me shy away from the altar.'

'You just haven't met the right man, that's all,' Amelia protested. 'Until now, that is.'

Thea could not help laughing again at her friend's audacity. 'No more of that, I beg of you. I'm sure your brother is a paragon without question, and I confess I found him quite enlivening, but I certainly entertain no notion of marrying him! And I'm quite sure he entertains no notion of marriage either.'

Amelia toyed fleetingly with telling Thea about the Miss Beaseley episode before rejecting it. It would never do to have Thea regard Hadrian as another's reject. The match must progress on its own merits with just a little assistance from her quarter.

'I'm sure that you are the best judge of what you want in life,' Lady Marlow said, adopting a change in strategy.

'But no female I know wishes to dwindle into an old maid.'

Thea shrugged. 'Better that than to be wretchedly unhappy with some male.' Knowing that what she had just uttered would undoubtedly be taken for heresy in certain quarters, she ended the matter by asking whether Sir Percy had finally been assisted home.

'Yes, indeed, and one would think he vanquished the highwayman single-handedly. Your trunk is downstairs. I didn't wish to disturb you while you were asleep. I shall have Walter bring it up. Dinner is in an hour, which gives you plenty of time to change.' She got to her feet, but could not resist one last word. 'Hadrian is very partial to the colour yellow.'

A laugh bubbled up in Thea's throat as Amelia skipped out of the room. Her dear friend, Thea decided as she took a sniff of the roses, was incorrigible. But there was no denying her brother was very handsome.

Marriage, however, was an entirely different kettle of fish. And it was, she decided as she dressed for dinner, a very good thing she had no yellow dress in her trunk, for if she did deign to don it, Amelia would soon be posting the banns!

Lady Marlow had no intention of posting the banns, an activity coming under the jurisdiction of the Church. She was loath to interfere in matters of faith. Only think of the bumblebroth Henry the Eighth had bestirred when he dabbled in it. She did, however, reveal to her doting spouse that she had dropped word into Thea's ear that might possibly induce her to look favourably on Hadrian.

'Good Jupiter, Amelia, it ain't as though Hadrian was pining away,' Lord Marlow ejaculated, a gloomy feeling spreading about him at the idea of witnessing his wife's matchmaking abilities.

'Oh, I know that,' Amelia agreed. 'But a little help never hurt anyone.'

Lord Marlow was not convinced. 'Cupid would need no other helper with you in the vicinity. And while I hesitate to interfere, I think you had best leave the matter alone.'

'Hadrian will make micefeet of it by himself,' Amelia pointed out.

'If Hadrian wishes to fix an interest in Miss Campion, he will find his own way of doing so,' her spouse replied, and won her meek promise that she would not after all try and push the two together in a darkened room that very night.

In happy ignorance of his sister's strategems, Emery descended the Adam stairs, the first one to appear for the dinner hour. Wondering if he was the only one in the household with an appetite, he made his way to the Blue Saloon for some sherry. It was there that Thea found him five minutes later when she descended.

'Amelia and Charles?' she queried.

'Are still upstairs.' He held up the decanter of sherry. 'Sherry? I can vouch for its excellence, or would you rather ratafia? I think I saw some of it about.'

'Don't bother searching for it,' she said quickly. 'I'd liefer sherry.'

This choice won a quick approving smile from the viscount as he poured some sherry into a glass for her. 'Never could understand why females would drink ratafia. Sipped it once myself on a dare, and found it the vilest concoction imaginable.'

'Perhaps we drink it because someone dictated that that was the drink females should consume,' Thea replied. 'And like so many stupid rules of convention it came to be.'

He watched her lithe figure in a high-waisted blue gown move towards the couch. 'Your rest seems to have agreed with you,' he said, following. 'You look wonderful.'

'I could scarcely look any worse,' she retorted. 'But a change of clothing does wonders for any woman.'

'Blue is my favourite colour,' he told her, unprepared for the flurry of whoops this innocent statement engendered.

'Did I say something amusing?' he demanded.

She put down her glass shakily before she spilled it. 'No, and I hope you don't think me demented. It's just that Amelia assured me that yellow was your favourite colour.'

A flash of understanding crossed his face. 'I see.'

'Perhaps, Lord Emery, it's a good thing we have this moment alone, for I fear we have a problem brewing.'

'A problem that goes by the name of Amelia?' he asked with a sympathetic look.

She heaved a sigh, and nodded. 'You felt it too, I suppose?'

'How could I help it! Amelia means well.' He gazed at the lady next to him. She was twirling the ribbons at the bodice of her gown about a slender finger. He found it oddly distracting. 'Shall I spare us both the discomfort and cut my visit short?'

She weighed his suggestion carefully. 'That would be a pity. I know you are so partial to angling.'

'Amelia again?' He cocked his head at her.

'No,' she giggled, 'Charles! He told me so in passing. Amelia did mention you were a crack whip as well as a member of the Four Horse Club and a lover of a good mill. And even if Charles hadn't told me of your addiction to angling I might have deduced it. What else could lure you from London with the Season on but sport? It is far too early for the hunt!'

The viscount smiled, not about to relate what had compelled him to quit London. 'Did you actually refuse a duke?' he asked, deciding it was his turn to play inquisitor.

She choked. 'Amelia has been busy.'

'Yes, but I'm still curious.'

'Well then, yes,' she acknowledged. 'He wasn't an English duke,' she added quickly. 'A German or Prussian one, I believe. There are so many of them about that they hardly count. And he was a trifle foxed at the time. I'm certain he was relieved the next morning at my tact in laughing off his stupid notion.'

Emery sniffed. 'Do you find the idea of becoming a duchess so stupid?'

'Not in the least. I find the idea of being married stupid.'

He put down his glass. 'A strange opinion for a female.'

'Perhaps I should have said that I find marriage stupid for me,' she amended quickly. 'For others it may be perfectly congenial. I dare say Amelia must have told you about my parents' divorce? If she told you about the duke, she must surely have mentioned the divorce.'

'There was some mention of it,' he admitted carefully.

'Then you must see how intimately aware I am of the disagreeable side of marriage and divorce.'

'I have no knowledge of divorce myself,' he confessed, 'and I must bow to your greater knowledge of its disagreeable nature. But marriage on the whole is not so terrible a fate.'

'You sound like Amelia!' she retorted. 'And if you feel thusly, why aren't you married by now? I shan't believe the females in London have been blinded to your charms.'

She halted, a trifle embarrassed at her own frankness. Emery, however, gazed back unperturbed and a little amused.

'You never know about these things, Miss Campion. Perhaps I came up short of the mark.'

'How absurd! You are a catalogue of male virtues.'

'My sister is notoriously prone to exaggeration,' he drawled modestly.

She choked on a swallow of sherry. 'Amelia has nothing to do with it. I have eyes to see with. You, Viscount Emery, are the answer to any mother's dream. If you don't know that by now, I advise you to look in a mirror.'

Before he could take advantage of the looking-glass in the saloon, a footman entered, ushering in Jonathon Campion, who had come to discover the true nature of the injury his cousin had sustained during the encounter with the highwayman.

Jonathon, just turned nineteen, was fair-haired and stocky of build, with the faintest trace of a moustache he had been trying to cultivate on his upper lip.

'Sir Percy told us it was a very near brush with death. But you don't look knocked up, coz.'

'I'm not,' Thea replied.

His face brightened. 'That's a relief. Father was worried.' He paused, noticing for the first time that Emery had been unable to fit his bandaged shoulder through the sleeve of his coat and was wearing that garment over one shoulder.

'You are injured, sir.'

'Yes,' Thea said. 'Viscount Emery, allow me to introduce my cousin, Jonathon Campion. Jonathon, this is Lady Marlow's brother, Lord Emery. He injured his shoulder in the scuffle with the highwayman.'

The two men exchanged bows. 'I suppose you're grateful to Sir Percy for being along,' Jonathon said.

Emery, who had been lifting a pinch of snuff to one nostril, checked his move. Grateful to Percy? Was the lad bosky?

Thea, aghast at such a notion, put down her glass. 'Grateful to Sir Percy?!' she exclaimed. 'Pray, what put such a demented idea into your head, Jonathon? Sir Percy nearly got us all killed.'

Jonathon scratched the fuzz on his lip. 'But didn't he rout the highwayman?'

'Is that what he has been saying?' Thea demanded.

'I suppose some might call it a rout,' Emery drawled. 'But it was the most curious routing I ever witnessed.' He gazed at Thea with amusement in his hazel eyes.

'It appears that Percy magnified his role a trifle.'

'You are too charitable by half,' Thea exclaimed with vigour. She turned to her cousin. 'Did Uncle Andrew actually believe that Sir Percy could foil a highwayman?'

Jonathon grinned broadly. 'He said he'd eat his copy of Horace if it turned out to be true. That's why he sent me over to discover the truth.'

'Well, you may tell him that his Horace is safe. We did encounter a highwayman, true enough. Sir Percy made the fatal mistake of trying to scuffle with him, and in the ensuing mill the robber's pistol discharged, and Emery was wounded.'

'A quite ignoble way of getting wounded,' Emery pointed out. 'And I own to being a trifle tired of hearing about it—the highwayman and, most particularly, Percy. Shall it bore the two of you greatly if I suggest a turn in the topic? Would you like some sherry, Jonathon?'

Jonathon, after a quick look at Thea, announced that he would, very much. Thea toyed with the idea of uttering a protest, for she knew her uncle's disapproval of strong spirits for one so young, but she decided not to interfere.

In the brief time she had spent with Jonathon and her uncle, she had felt a growing sympathy for the younger man. Jonathon was not quite out of his boyhood or into his manhood, and he chafed under the restrictions his father, the scholar, placed on him. A little sherry, all in all, would not debauch him.

Thea even managed to be absorbed in her examination of a jade horse adorning the mantel when Jonathon choked on his first quick swallow of sherry. Emery, watching, hid a smile of his own, vividly reminded of his own youth. He soon discovered that, like most men his age, young Jonathon was horse-mad and attempting to save enough to allow him the luxury of a carriage and a team of Welsh-breds.

'Father says a new carriage would be the ultimate in folly. We have an old barouche, you see, and I suppose he's afraid I shall break my neck. He says that's what happens when one is too green, but I'm all of nineteen!'

'Practically in your dotage,' the viscount agreed, a comment that won a reluctant smile from Jonathon.

With just a little assistance from Thea, who was gratified by the interest Emery displayed in her young cousin, the remaining minutes passed with Jonathon questioning Emery about life in London, his knowledge of which had been culled from intense reading of the back issues of the *Morning Post* and the *Gentleman's Monthly*.

'What think you of fishing?' Emery asked when they had appeared to exhaust the topic of horses.

Jonathon's face brightened. 'Fishing? Well, I don't mean to boast, but I am very partial to the sport.'

'Good. We will test those abilities soon enough. I had hoped to persuade your cousin here to try her hand at angling. Charles, my brother-in-law, claims the trout are just begging to be caught.'

'But your shoulder, Emery,' Thea protested.

He gave her a reassuring smile. 'It's perfectly up to the challenge of any trout.'

'When do you plan to fish?' Jonathon asked.

'What's wrong with tomorrow?'

'Tomorrow?' Thea exclaimed.

'Yes, Charles mentioned something along those lines to me.'

'Something along which lines?' a voice asked as Lady Marlow entered.

Hadrian turned towards his sister with a smile. 'Fish, Amelia, fish. Charles mentioned we might try our luck tomorrow if my shoulder continued to mend well. I've invited young Jonathon here to join us, and Miss Campion as well.'

'If you're serious, sir, and your shoulder doesn't trouble you, I would like to come,' Jonathon said eagerly.

'And I come willingly enough.' Thea added her agreement to the scheme. 'But on one condition.'

He cocked his head at her. 'Which is?'

'That you stop calling me Miss Campion in that fashion. I am Thea to my friends.'

'Fair enough. Thea it shall be. Would you care to join us, Amelia?'

Lady Marlow sent her brother a look that made clear what she thought of his suggestion. 'Good God, no, Hadrian. I am promised to the vicar and his wife for morning tea.'

'Then perhaps some other time,' he suggested sweetly.

Before Lady Marlow could rouse herself sufficiently to scotch this threat, a diversion came in the form of her spouse, who declared himself famished, and the five of them—Jonathon had been persuaded to stay for dinner—soon adjourned to the small dining-room.

CHAPTER FIVE

'I HAVE always heard it said that the early bird catches the worm,' Thea remarked the next morning to Hadrian as they rode out with Charles and Jonathon, 'but I didn't know that such applied to fish as well.'

'Come now, Thea,' Emery said bracingly, delighting in her struggle with an enormous yawn. 'Don't you know that one should rise early? It invigorates the blood.'

'I suppose you rise early every day of your life?' she asked, throwing him a sceptical look from under sleepy eyelids.

'No,' he acknowledged manfully. 'Once or twice, I own, I slept late.'

She laughed and slowed her horse at Charles's command. Soon they were trudging up the small stone path, leading to what Lord Marlow dubbed 'the most teeming trout stream in the kingdom'.

Teeming or not, it was certainly wet, and Thea, splashing along, was thankful that she had the foresight to don an old pair of Amelia's boots and one of her oldest dresses.

She found a comfortable spot on the slope of the grassy bank and took the pole Charles handed her, casting the line expertly into the water with the barest flick of her wrist.

'You do know how to fish,' Emery said, a little taken aback at this display of angling skill.

'Enough to know we ought to lower our voices lest the noise scare the fish away.'

Obediently the viscount fell silent and busied himself with his own line. After a vigorous discussion, Charles and Jonathon chose to wander further downstream towards Lord Marlow's favourite spot. Emery and Thea were invited to join them, but declined.

'Who taught you how to fish?' Emery asked, stealing a glance at Thea.

He had planted his pole in the embankment and lain back, his head against a tree-trunk. He looked the very image of a lazy country gentleman.

'My father taught me,' she answered. 'We were staying with some friends of his.' She grimaced slightly. 'When money grew tight, we did that. He decided to go fishing and decided I should come along.' She gave her head a shake. 'Curious what ideas fathers will get into their heads about children.'

'I know,' Emery agreed. 'My father, God rest his soul, once decided that I must learn to swim, and thereupon threw me into the lake every day for an entire month. My mother could do little but wring her hands and beg him to stop.'

Thea laughed. 'And did he?'

'Not until I had learned to swim,' the viscount answered. 'Which I do prodigiously well.'

Despite Lord Marlow's assurances that the fish abounded in the stream, Thea and Hadrian had no luck during the first hour. Jonathon, however, was more fortunate. He had snared three good-sized trout, and his good fortune was written plainly in the smile that suffused his young face.

'A nice lad,' Emery commented after they had admired his catch and he had returned to Charles.

'This is a treat for him,' Thea replied.

The viscount was astounded. 'Fishing, a treat?'

She nodded. 'Yes, fishing. You don't know my uncle.'

'Only that he is a man of scholarly temperament.'

'And quite the reverse of my father,' Thea revealed, 'who was, all in all, a fribble.' She had long ago come to grips with having a charming wastrel and profligate for a father. 'And you mustn't think Uncle Andrew an ogre. He has a heart of gold. Besides,' she said wisely, 'he is a prodigious scholar. Nothing gives him more satisfaction than his studies. Unfortunately he is inclined to think that such must be the case for everyone else, particularly his own son.'

A sympathetic look crossed the viscount's face. 'Young Jonathon doesn't strike me as particularly bookish.'

'He's not, and yet Uncle Andrew will insist he pursue a scholarly path.'

'An unfortunate misreading of his son's character.'

Thea nodded and bit her lip. 'I fear that it may lead to a breach between them.'

'Perhaps not,' Emery said, looking down into the worried face. 'Young Jonathon may yet develop a taste for book learning.'

This, however, struck Thea as likely to happen as the Prince Regent's sudden embracing of Hinduism, but before she could venture this opinion they were interrupted, and by a fish!

'You have a bite!' Thea exclaimed.

Her words brought Emery from his comfortable position on the grass and down to the edge of the bank, where his pole had been firmly planted in the ground. Taking hold of it now, he began to pull the fish in. The trout, however, had other ideas and fought furiously, so furiously that Emery felt a twinge of pain in his bad shoulder. He was beginning to make a little progress when the line abruptly snapped. The fish escaped.

'No doubt laughing all the way,' he lamented to Thea, who commiserated with him on the loss. 'Quite a good-sized specimen, too, more's the pity. A full three feet.'

'I, of course, did not have the excellent view you did,' Thea teased as he hooked his line again. 'But are you certain it was three feet?'

'No, of course not,' he replied. 'As I think back now, it was much nearer to four feet.'

'It always seemed odd to me that the fish that elude capture are those of huge dimension. Indeed, I can't think of a single instance when anything less than three feet eluded capture.'

His laugh echoed hers, and he threw his line out just as she felt a nudge at hers. 'It's your turn,' he said, having glimpsed the fish's activity.

Thea eagerly began to pull the fish in, a task that required considerably more strength than she possessed.

'Let me help you,' Emery said. He had already seen her predicament and slid nimbly behind her. His hands met hers on the pole.

In order to pull in the fish he directed her to lean back against his chest, a position that caused her heart to beat alarmingly. She felt his breath ever so slightly on the back of her neck.

'Easy does it,' he cautioned, trying to concentrate on the job at hand, a difficult task given the slender form in his arms.

The fish leaped and jumped, leading a merry chase that had them both breathless by the time it was triumphantly hauled in.

'We have done the thing,' Thea exulted. The blood rushed to her cheeks in excitement. She looked, Emery thought, even more enchanting than before.

'Viscount Emery?'

He became aware that he was standing like a stock and quickly apologised for woolgathering. 'I do beg your pardon. You were saying?'

'I was merely wondering what you thought it would weigh.'

He glanced down at the fish. 'I'd estimate about four pounds.'

'That much?'

'Or more. You are indeed an excellent fisherman.'

She seemed pleased by his tribute, but common sense told her she could never have done it without his help.

'Teamwork, that's the thing,' he told her when she said as much. 'You help me, and I'll help you.'

'I don't think you would need my help,' she protested.

He cracked a grin. 'One never does know, Thea. My shoulder, after all, is a trifle sore.'

'Oh, is it?' she asked quickly before recognising that twinkle in his eyes.

'You are roasting me,' she accused.

'Not at all, for I see my line is aquiver. Do lend me a hand with this one.'

Knowing full well that he could land any fish he wished to himself, Thea nevertheless took her place in front of him. Once again he slipped his arms about her waist and on to the pole.

Think of the fish, Theodora, she told herself sternly as his hands covered hers. She felt a trifle giddy at their touch and annoyed at herself for such missishness.

'Stop being a bacon brain,' she muttered.

'I beg your pardon. Did you speak?' he asked, taking his eyes off the fish to gaze down at her.

'Oh, I wasn't speaking to you,' she apologised, glancing up quickly. 'Oh, no... *Look out!*' she cried as the fish took advantage of their lapse in concentration and tugged violently. The pole flew out of their hands and into the water. Thea, who had been trying to hang on to the pole, lost her balance and slid down the bank, followed a second later by Emery himself.

'We seem to have the uncanny habit of finding ourselves on the ground,' he observed.

'Is that a way of telling me my face is smudged again?' she asked as she brushed herself off. 'Thank God I wore this old dress. I trust this match goes to the trout?'

'Along with the pole,' Emery said, dusting his clothes off.

A few stray blades of grass clung to Thea's dress, and he reached out a hand to remove them.

'Hadrian, what on earth are you doing to Thea?' Lady Marlow's shocked face appeared over the embankment.

Emery dropped his hand, a little flustered at seeing his sister's trenchant face. 'Nothing, Amelia. I was merely trying to help her.'

'Well, it didn't look like help from here,' she replied tartly. 'It looked as though you were wrestling with her.'

'Good God, Amelia, I never wrestle! Fond of a good mill, but never wrestling.'

'We have just had an encounter with a fish,' Thea quickly explained to her friend.

'What fish?' Amelia asked sceptically.

'The one that got away, of course,' Hadrian replied testily. 'And do rest assured that I was not attempting to seduce Miss Campion. My methods of seduction may be a trifle singular, but they are not so rough and ready.' He helped Thea up the embankment.

'Emery is right,' Thea said with a laugh. 'We were attempting to land the fish when I stupidly lost my balance and the fish sprang free, startling us both. We tumbled down. That's why we appear now in all our dirt.'

'And why do you appear here, good sister?' Emery quizzed in turn. 'I thought you were promised to tea with the vicar's wife. Can it be you rekindled your interest in angling?'

'Don't be daft, Hadrian,' she responded scorchingly. 'I was having tea with the vicar. That's what brought me home like a shot.'

'That bad, eh?' Emery sympathised. 'When I get back to London, I shall send that vicar some of Mr Berry's finest. Let me see. Pekoe, Souchong, Bohea? What would be the best?'

'That's not what I mean, you gudgeon,' his sister railed. 'The tea was all well enough. Drinkable at the very least. It was what was said over it. Sir Percy's story is everywhere! How he rescued you and Thea from the grasp of the highwayman.' The amusement faded from the viscount's face.

'Amelia,' Thea said, 'surely no one believes such a preposterous tale?'

'As to that, I can't say,' Amelia replied scrupulously. 'But from the curious glances I received, I would say they are inclined to believing it.'

'*Devil!*' her brother ejaculated.

'Indeed Vicar Washington himself said how fortunate for us all to have a man of Sir Percy's courage about.'

'A man of Sir Percy's courage?' Emery repeated in measured tones that were no less awful for being softly uttered. 'Implying, I suppose, that my own courage was suspect?'

'Now, Hadrian, he didn't say that,' Amelia said hastily.

'He didn't need to,' her brother retorted.

'But that's absurd,' Thea interjected. 'Sir Percy acted quite stupidly, not bravely at all. You know that as well as I, Emery.'

'Unfortunately,' he replied, 'that is not the conclusion people are reaching. And while I have no interest in what Banbury tales Percy ordinarily spins about himself, when the issue touches on my own mettle, I *will* concern myself. I hope you won't mind, Thea, if I leave the fish to you.'

'But Hadrian, what do you propose to do?' Amelia asked, putting one hand on the sleeve of his coat. If any blood were spilled—perish the thought—it would be on her conscience.

'I propose to scotch the rumours.'

'How?'

'By scotching Sir Percy,' he said grimly, mounting his horse.

An hour later Sir Percy entered his Blue Saloon to find Emery pacing furiously under the watchful gaze of a Boyle ancestor on the wall.

'Emery,' he said, 'what are you doing here? How is the shoulder? Still winged?'

'I'm surprised you recall that it was my shoulder and not my head or chest,' the viscount retorted acidly.

Percy appeared taken aback by this display of churlishness in the usually affable viscount. 'Of course I know it's the shoulder. Not quite sure which of the two it was. The left?' He raised a quizzical brow.

'The right.'

'Well, I knew it was one or the other. Do sit.' He gestured towards the Windsor chair.

'My visit will be brief, and I'd liefer stand.'

'As you will. But what's this about? Rather early in the day to be up and about, even for the country.'

Emery eyed him carefully. The baronet looked much the same as always: the smug, self-satisfied smile on his vacuous face, his portly stomach bulging ever so slightly through his coat. How in thunderation could anyone think that bag pudding could rescue anyone?

'That encounter with the robber is on my mind, Percy,' he said now.

'Oh, is it?' The baronet glanced up.

'It seems I owe you my life.'

Boyle made a deprecating moue. 'Come now, Emery, that's doing it a trifle brown.'

'Oh, do you really think so?' the viscount asked sarcastically.

'To be sure, I do,' came Percy's stout reply. 'Why, anyone else would have done just as I did.'

'And what precisely was it that you did do?' Emery asked frigidly.

The baronet appeared mildly shaken at this lapse in the memory of one who had not yet reached his thirty-second year. 'I stopped him, of course!' he exclaimed. 'The highwayman, I mean. I don't like to boast, Emery, but I think I did the deed as well as any of Gentleman Jack's prize pupils.'

The viscount, who counted himself among the pugilist's favoured few and who had never seen Sir Percy take instruction in Jackson's Bond Street establishment, was bereft of words.

Percy, however, continued to smile blithely back at him. The baronet actually did believe that he had routed the highwayman!

'There are some who say I behaved in an untoward fashion,' Emery said now, managing to keep his voice down with a heroic effort.

'Now, now, Emery, mustn't say that,' Sir Percy said quickly. 'Mustn't think ill of oneself. Bound to fall into the gloomy fits if you do. Some folks are just braver than others.'

Emery turned his face until it was a rigid inch from the baronet's. 'Are you calling me a *coward*, Percy?' he asked dangerously.

Sir Percy gazed into those threatening orbs and swallowed hard. 'No, no,' he said hastily. 'Look here, Emery, you make too much of the incident.'

'I'm not the one who put the tale about.'

'Well, I didn't do that,' Percy protested, colouring slightly at Emery's raised brows. 'Perhaps I did mention it to just a few friends. We did encounter a highwayman. I did grapple with him. You were shot. And he was frightened off. Correct?'

Emery blinked at this bare bones recital of the incident, and yet in truth, he mused later as he rode back to Chumley Field, Sir Percy's story contained no falsehoods. It did, however, cast an entirely different light on things, not the least of which was the character of one Viscount Emery.

CHAPTER SIX

THE TALE of Sir Percy's triumph over the highwayman sped on to London, where it reached the ears of Louisa Beaseley. Unacquainted with the portly baronet, she was inclined to dismiss the somewhat garbled account, which reached her by way of Sir Percy's fourth cousin, had not the matter also concerned Viscount Emery.

The beauty had in fact been indulging in an orgy of self-reproach, admitting only to herself that she might have acted prematurely in dismissing the viscount before the marquis had been landed. The old adage of a bird in hand seemed particularly apt, especially now with Appleton's ardour on the wane. The marquis within the past week had been attempting to fix an interest in another, a Miss Georgianna Price, who boasted, in addition to an agreeable assortment of female charms, a dowry of some twenty thousand pounds.

To make matters worse, Appleton had shaved off the moustache Miss Beaseley had found so dashing. Clean-shaven, he did not appear half as handsome as she had previously imagined.

She also could not imagine why Emery had advised her to become acquainted with Lord Fallingsworth, whom she had discovered to be a stiff-necked old martinet.

When Sir Percy's cousin had related the tale of the baronet's heroism, touching coyly on the grave injury

Emery must have suffered—a head wound, by all accounts—Miss Beaseley's remorse knew no bounds. Her imagination, fed by lending-library romances, took fire as she thought of him languishing his day away in Wiltshire, his own thoughts perhaps turning to the only woman he had offered for, and who—she could not avoid a guilty pang—had thrown him over for another.

This was enough for her to throw caution to the wind and decide to go to him at once.

'Wiltshire, my dear?' Mrs Chester gazed myopically at her niece, who had just burst into her sitting-room, prattling about the necessity of removing there.

A matron on the far side of forty, Mrs Chester had been blessed with sons but no daughters, and had willingly undertaken Louisa's come-out for the duration of the Season, delighting in the admiration won by her lovely niece.

'What, pray, is in Wiltshire, Louisa?' she asked now, pushing her stitchery to one side.

'Chumley Field, home of Lord and Lady Marlow.'

Mrs Chester wrinkled her brow into a furious frown of concentration, but she could not recall any Marlow among her niece's acquaintances.

'Has an invitation come for you in the mail today?' she asked, trying to piece the puzzle together without appearing unduly inquisitive. 'I had no notion the mail had arrived.'

'It hasn't,' Miss Beaseley said. 'And Lady Marlow didn't send me an invitation, exactly. It came from her brother, Viscount Emery. You remember him, I should hope?'

Mrs Chester nodded, her brow clearing. Here was the clue she had been waiting for. Emery had been one of her prime favourites for her niece.

'He told me he was going to visit his sister this summer, and wished to extend the invitation to me as well.'

Mrs Chester clicked her tongue. 'My dear Louisa, you can't dash off to Wiltshire simply on the strength of the viscount's say-so, however amiable he may be. You need an invitation from your hostess yourself.'

Miss Beaseley wrung her hands. 'But, Aunt, there isn't time. I must go to Chumley Field. I heard the most ghastly news today. Emery is lying mortally wounded and calling for me.'

Any sensible chaperon would have looked askance at such a story, but Mrs Chester, despite the very spare and correct exterior she presented to the outside world, was as featherbrained and romantic as her niece. The notion of any gentleman languishing with a lady's name on his lips thrilled her to the marrow. Her objections died away, and she bent her energies in the next two days towards assisting Louisa in their preparations for the trip to Wiltshire. Dashing off to the country might strike some as a hurly-burly affair, but not even the top-lofty Mrs Drummond Burrell would dare to criticise an errand of mercy.

Unaware that he was lying mortally wounded at his sister's estate, the viscount continued to while away his hours fishing with Charles, enjoying his budding friendship with Thea and attempting to find a way out of the fix of being thought in Sir Percy's debt. He was sorely tempted to call the baronet out on some technicality, but provoking duels had never been his style. He even found himself wishing for the reappearance of the highwayman to put the matter straight; but no trace of the criminal had been found, a circumstance that was also credited to Sir Percy's noble deed.

'I just hope I have a shred of reputation left to me,' he complained to Thea one morning as they rode out together on a visit to her uncle.

'What an odd thing a reputation is,' Thea said, her curls peeking from under the rakish tilt of her riding-hat. 'I never knew gentlemen were obliged to suffer over it, as are ladies.'

'Nor did I,' he admitted, 'till now. I may have to emigrate if the matter is not resolved soon enough.'

'That seems a trifle drastic,' she protested. 'And where would you go? India is so far away and hot. The Indies are rather pretty, or so I have been told, but they are also barbaric, and as for the Americas'—she wrinkled up her nose slightly—'I've yet to meet an American who wasn't half buffoon.'

He laughed. 'Who knows, Thea? Perhaps I shall retire to the Continent and take up residence in your city.'

She looked at him with unveiled surprise. 'Do you mean Vienna? You must be hoaxing me. And if you ever did remove there, you would soon be pining for England.'

'Surely it cannot be so bad?'

'No,' she amended, 'it is far worse than that. The Continent is made up of the French, Germans, Italians, not to mention the Dutch and Danes. And they all look down their noses at one another. Just making oneself understood under such circumstances can be a chore.'

'And yet you lived there for years,' he pointed out.

'I had no say in the matter. It was Mama's doing, not mine,' she said so wistfully that he wondered what regrets she might have been harbouring. He did not press her on the matter, and they soon drew up at Mr Campion's estate.

Mr Andrew Campion was pleased to see his niece, and greeted Emery with a cordial handshake. A tall, handsome man with hair just beginning to grey at the temples, he looked as though he had been summoned from his library.

'I hope we haven't come at an awkward moment, Uncle,' Thea asked, taking a seat in his parlour. 'Were you working?'

'Yes, but not on anything urgent. My eyes were beginning to tire. It is one of the nuisances of ageing. Jonathon was supposed to read to me, but he's never about when I need him.'

'Your niece was telling me you were in the midst of preparing a new translation of Aristotle, sir,' Emery said, turning the topic adroitly from the wayward Jonathon.

'Poppycock!' Mr Campion snorted.

The viscount drew back. 'I beg your pardon?'

'Translations,' Mr Campion explained. 'No one can ever translate anything properly. Much better to read it in the original Greek, don't you agree?'

Thea was amused, as Emery appeared to be on uncertain ground. 'Actually,' he divulged, 'I have little time to read Greek these days.'

'Hmmph.'

'Are you writing, then, Uncle Andrew?' Thea asked, heading off her uncle's inclination to point out the merits of Greek masters to the viscount.

Mr Campion nodded. 'Jonathon is supposed to copy some pages of mine. But he's not here. I told him I would need him this morning, but he's racketing about.'

'It is not surprising that Greek would play a far second to such a fine day as this,' Thea soothed.

Her uncle scowled. 'He will never amount to anything if he doesn't know Greek.' He fixed a baleful eye on Emery sitting innocently across from him. 'I dare say you, Lord Emery, are well versed in the classics?'

'Thanks to the tenacity of several schoolmasters, I have a smattering of the language,' the viscount said with aplomb. 'But I never went to my lessons willingly, as I dare say no boy ever does.'

Mr Campion grunted. 'Jonathon isn't a boy. He's very nearly a man, and he shall be educated.'

'Jonathon is certainly not as great a scholar as you,' Thea protested. 'But he is knowledgeable enough. The other night at dinner he acquitted himself quite well with Lord Marlow and Viscount Emery.'

Mr Campion snorted again, not displeased to hear this. 'But I still won't have him riding when he should be studying.' He turned at a passing sound in the hall, and his voice sharpened. 'Jonathon, is that you?'

'Yes, Father,' came the sheepish reply as Jonathon came into the parlour. He was covered from head to shoe in dirt.

'Good gracious! What happened to you?' Thea exclaimed. Jonathon had a cut on one cheek, a scraped chin, and a torn sleeve.

'We had an accident. Gaylord Boyle, Sir Percy's brother, was showing me the baronet's new rig and'— he gulped—'he ditched it.'

'Riding with Gaylord Boyle?' Emery murmured. 'You don't know how lucky you are, young fellow. He's no more than a whipster. You could have broken your neck.'

'Which is all he would deserve,' Mr Campion observed dourly, 'for sneaking away from his studies.'

Jonathon flushed scarlet. 'I meant to return straight away, Father. I was only out for a short walk myself; the day seemed so very pleasant. But I ran into Gaylord with Percy's new carriage. And he was so pleased with himself, boasting about his skill, that when he invited me to sit with him I couldn't resist.'

'Are you certain you sustained no injury?' Thea asked.

'I'm fine. Of course, Gaylord did suffer a slightly bruised arm.'

'Which will be nothing compared to what Percy will inflict on him when he hears of the disaster,' the viscount said drily. 'Is the carriage a total wreck?'

'Pretty near to it,' Jonathon acknowledged.

The viscount cocked his head to one side. 'Were you so desirous of learning the rudiments of driving that you had to resort to observing young Gaylord?'

'I don't get much opportunity otherwise, sir,' Jonathon replied with a sideways look at his father.

'I am acknowledged to be a creditable whip,' Emery said. 'I should be happy to show you the basics. I think I can persuade Charles to allow me the use of his carriage.'

'Oh, sir, would you?' Jonathon's face, even though smudged with dirt, lit up, all memory of the disaster gone. 'When do you think we could begin?' he asked eagerly.

'As soon as you like,' came the reply.

'Tomorrow?'

Emery laughed.

'Jonathon,' Mr Campion interrupted. 'Stop plaguing the viscount. Before you take him up on his generous offer, you will study your Greek and copy those pages for me after first cleaning yourself up.'

'Yes, Father, I promise I shall. But, sir,' he persisted, turning again to Emery, 'when do you think we could have our first lesson?'

'Jonathon!' Mr Campion declared. 'I ordered you to wash.'

Flushed and apologetic, the young man obeyed.

'I'm sorry to have him plaguing you, Lord Emery,' Mr Campion said after Jonathon departed.

'There is no occasion for apologies,' Emery replied. 'I don't consider it plaguing at all. I should like to teach him how to handle the reins.'

'Civil of you, but I think not.'

Thea, seeing Emery's look of mild surprise and knowing Jonathon's own view of the matter, spoke up at once.

'Uncle, Emery is more than just a creditable whip. You need have no fear that Jonathon shall ditch himself under his tutelage.'

'Jonathon has no time to waste on such frivolities,' Mr Campion said with a stern look. 'I want a serious, hard-working son, not a fribble.'

'Such as myself?' the viscount asked languidly.

Campion's eyes narrowed. 'I didn't say that. Jonathon is just a passing acquaintance to you, my lord, but he is my son. And I have planned his future. He shall be a scholar like me. Perhaps even better than me.'

'Shouldn't Jonathon have some say in his own future?' Emery asked gently.

'Jonathon shall do as I say.'

'From what I understand, Uncle Andrew,' Thea interposed in her unruffled manner, 'those were the exact words Grandfather uttered to Papa that caused him to marry Mama—and then the unfortunate unravelling of their marriage occurred. Although,' she acknowledged, 'perhaps not unfortunate for me, for had they not married I shouldn't be here. And don't think me curious, but can't you see that your insistence on scholarship for Jonathon may cause him to turn from it? Any high-spirited boy with a mind of his own would chafe at being so restricted.'

Mr Campion looked mulish. 'He's my son.'

'I know. I also know how important it is to have him educated. But there is nothing that says a scholar may not also be a crack whip or an expert waltzer or any of the other things Jonathon seems keen on learning about.'

'Waltzing?' Mr Campion's rigidity turned to horror. 'Good God, has he been doing that?'

'Not yet.'

'I don't begrudge him the chance to learn to hold the reins properly,' Mr Campion said thoughtfully. 'But I don't want him turning into a ne'er-do-well.'

'He has too much of your brains ever to do that,' Thea soothed, and seeing that she had planted some food for thought in her uncle's own brain, she thought this the proper time to take her adieu.

Emery was oddly silent on the ride back to Chumley Field, and she wondered if he had taken offence at her uncle's remarks. Frankness, alas, was a Campion trait.

'I hope you didn't take Uncle Andrew's comments to heart,' she said to him. 'Sometimes he speaks before he thinks.'

He smiled across at her. 'It is always refreshing to see how another views oneself. Odd. I never considered myself a fribble before.'

She laughed. 'Uncle Andrew is of a sober disposition. I believe at one time he was even considering a career in the Church.'

'Young Jonathon seems not to have inherited that sobriety.'

'I know. His spirit is closer to my aunt's, if what my mother used to tell me of her is anything correct. She was the liveliest of spirits and loved nothing more than a good party.'

'It would seem a strange combination of scholar and wife,' Emery observed.

She nodded. 'And yet there have been stranger combinations. Only look at the Prince Regent and Princess Caroline!'

'Touché!' Emery acknowledged.

They soon reached the house, and he helped Thea to dismount. Turning to the door, they found it already standing open next to an unusually animated Hopkins.

'Is anything amiss, Hopkins?' Emery asked.

'In the parlour, my lord,' Hopkins said, the faintest of shudders in his voice.

Intrigued as to what horror awaited in the parlour, Thea followed Emery across the black and white lozenges into the room, where Lord Marlow sat in a gilded curricle chair. He turned to them with an audible sigh of relief, but he was not allowed to utter a word of greeting, for the other inhabitant of the room, Miss Beaseley, upon seeing her viscount, let loose with a shriek and hurled herself at his bosom, exclaiming, 'Emery, Emery! I am yours!'

CHAPTER SEVEN

MISS BEASELEY had arrived at Chumley Field a half-hour earlier, accompanied by her aunt, who was feeling all the ill effects of a severe bout of carriage sickness. With Lady Marlow absent on a round of morning calls and Thea and Emery at Mr Campion's, the duty of greeting these unexpected arrivals from London fell on Lord Marlow's broad shoulders.

'Oh, Lord Marlow!' Miss Beaseley had exclaimed. 'I came the instant I heard the news. I only hope Emery has not sustained a mortal injury. I would never forgive myself if he had. And I blame myself for all of this.'

Charles, attempting to decipher these cryptic words, found a new problem demanding his attention. Mrs Chester looked even more unwell now that the carriage had finally stopped. Deducing by the sickly green countenance she turned to him of the immediacy of the problem, he dispatched her abovestairs with the help of Hopkins and prayed that Amelia would be returning swiftly from her calls.

Miss Beaseley, while not insensible to the travails of her aunt, turned back to Emery's condition. 'I dare say he is too weak to come belowstairs. He is probably languishing in his bedchamber. Do you think I might intrude on him there?' She caught Lord Marlow's look of startled confusion, and pressed on hastily, 'I know it isn't proper that females burst into a gentleman's chamber, but we can dispense with the proprieties, for he is injured, and we are practically betrothed!'

'Eh, what?' Lord Marlow was a trifle stunned by this communication, which was at odds with the word he had been given by his wife. 'No, you can't. I mean, he ain't up there.'

Miss Beaseley had been sitting, but she now rose, one hand clasped to the heaving bodice of her blue travel dress. 'Lord Marlow, I implore you! You can't mean that I am too late!'

Charles wrinkled his brow, loath to think any female could be so bosky so early in the day. 'Too late?' he expostulated. 'Too late for what, pray? Didn't even expect you here, so how the devil could you be late?'

Miss Beaseley reached out a hand in agitation. 'They haven't taken him away yet, have they? I should have liked to have attended the service and to have placed something special on the coffin.'

'Coffin?' Lord Marlow was jolted. Before he could take issue with such a besotted idea, he spied Hopkins ushering in Emery and Thea, and breathed a sigh of relief.

Miss Beaseley, upon recognising Emery uncoffined and very much alive, shrieked and flung herself on his chest, murmuring his name. 'Oh, Emery!' She pulled away briefly, but continued to clutch his hand to her chest. 'I came the instant I heard. Indeed Aunt Ellen was rendered carriage sick, so swiftly did I order the groom to drive.'

'Did you really, Louisa?' Emery asked, rather discomfited to find his hand nestled between Miss Beaseley's creamy breasts and unable to extract it without calling attention to them. 'What prompted your haste?'

'I thought you were dying, of course,' Miss Beaseley said naïvely.

'Of course,' Emery said affably, observing from the corner of one eye the amusement afflicting Miss Theodora Campion.

'Charles,' Thea said, 'I think we ought to leave Emery with Miss Beaseley. I can see that the two of them are just pining for a private cose.'

Lord Marlow, who had already seen more than enough of his visitor, leaped upon this suggestion with alacrity, and before Emery could murmur a protest, he found himself alone in the parlour with Miss Beaseley.

'Well, now, Louisa,' he said heartily as he made a vain attempt to reclaim his hand, 'I dare say by now you may have noticed that I am not dying.'

'But you are injured.'

'The merest scratch, I assure you.'

'Oh, Emery, Hadrian.' Tears filled her eyes. 'It took me only a day before I came to my senses.'

'Senses?' Emery echoed, a little confused as he finally successfully removed his hand from Miss Beaseley's grasp.

'How could I have been so stupid even to think of Appleton when you were offering for me? That's why when I heard you were dying here in Wiltshire I came like a shot. I had to be reconciled with you before you passed on.'

These continued references to his death made the viscount a trifle uneasy. 'Your sentiments are touching,' he said now, 'but sorely misplaced. I assure you I am not dying.'

'Furthermore,' Miss Beaseley went on, not appearing to hear his words, 'I vowed that if you were alive and well I would marry you.'

The viscount had been busy massaging the blood back into his hand, but at the word 'marry', he looked up. *'Marry? Me?'* he croaked.

Miss Beaseley's face lit up in a radiant smile, and she threw her arms about his neck. 'Yes, my dear, I shall marry you. I shall!'

'Louisa, Miss Beaseley.' Emery attempted to remove her arms from the stranglehold about his neck.

'Am I hurting you?' she asked.

'No, no. Merely crushing my cravat.'

Ever sensible to the importance of a gentleman's cravat, Miss Beaseley loosened her grip on him and turned her mind to the matter of their wedding. 'We have so much to decide. Not the least of which would be the invitations.'

Emery fought off a mounting panic. 'Louisa, don't you recall our last words on this subject?'

Colour stained her cheeks. 'Pray, don't hold that against me, Emery,' she said in a small voice.

'What happened to Appleton?'

She smiled. 'I changed my mind about him. You do still wish to marry me, don't you?' An anxious look came into her blue eyes. 'It's imperative we do so, for the announcement is on its way to the *Gazette*.'

Emery dropped his jaw. 'What announcement?' he demanded.

'The one I sent in before we left London. Since we were coming here I thought it would satisfy the quizzes, who might think it a brazen thing to do. You had offered for me earlier, you recall.'

He frowned. 'But I thought you believed I was dying.'

'Yes, and if you were, no real harm would come from the announcement. And if you were alive, why, then even better. We could be married as you wished.' She shot him a look of sudden suspicion. 'You did offer for me,' she repeated.

'Yes, I know,' he said, wondering what had possessed him to do so.

Miss Beaseley inhaled a sob. 'I shall be so humiliated if we don't marry. How could I face anyone?' Her sobbing gave way to outright bawling. 'I shall be the laughing-stock of the ton. I just know it.'

Emery made a feeble attempt to comfort her. 'No one will say anything, Louisa. Besides, there are a full dozen gentlemen you could marry besides me. What of Appleton?'

'Appleton.' She almost spat the name out. 'Never! He's practically betrothed to Georgianna Price. All that is left for me is to withdraw into a nunnery.'

'There's no call for any such thing!'

'What do you suggest?' she asked, lifting her face from her handkerchief to display reddened eyes. 'I came here on an errand of mercy, believing you to be dying, and I thought your feelings for me rang true. Little did I know I was dealing with a horrid flirt.'

This untruth stung the viscount to the core. 'A flirt?'

'Acting in the most coming fashion towards me. Dangling after me, and all this time it was a mere game to you!'

Emery snapped the lid of his snuff-box shut, narrowly missing his thumbnail. 'A game? I assure you, I never offered for a female I wasn't willing to marry.'

'Well, good. Then you shall get your wish, for I accept your offer.'

Before he could utter another stupefied syllable she had thrown her arms about his neck again just as Mrs Chester, now fully recovered from her bout of carriage sickness, entered.

'Aunt Ellen,' Miss Beaseley exclaimed, 'Emery is not dying at all! We have just become formally engaged.'

'Have you, my dear?' Mrs Chester asked with an indulgent smile. 'How nice.' She shook hands with the viscount, who was a little dazed by the events that had occurred in the last few minutes. 'You are a lucky man, Viscount Emery,' Mrs Chester clucked. 'More sprigs than I could shake a hand at wanted Louisa for a wife.'

'Mrs Chester...' Emery choked.

'Call me Aunt Ellen,' Mrs Chester urged. 'Practically in the family, aren't you?'

'Hadrian, Charles said something about Miss Beaseley arriving here,' Amelia called, coming through the door of the parlour and halting at the sight of her usually unflappable brother looking rather sick.

'Amelia!' He almost leaped to her side. 'You must meet Miss Beaseley and her aunt, Mrs Chester.'

Amelia dutifully acknowledged the two ladies. 'I'm so glad you were able to visit us,' she said.

From the sudden frown that descended on her brother's brow she deduced that this was not the thing he wanted her to say.

'Pray, don't think us odiously rag-mannered for descending on you this way,' Miss Beaseley told Amelia. 'But I hope you shan't hold it against me, for we will soon be related.'

Amelia's eyes widened. 'Related?'

Miss Beaseley beamed and nodded. 'I have decided to accept Emery's offer of marriage. And you must give us your thoughts on the wedding. There are a thousand things to decide. First I must write to Papa. Why he must go to Paris and take Mama with him during the Season is beyond my thinking.'

'A wedding, did you say?' Amelia asked, breaking into Miss Beaseley's monologue. She dealt a questioning look at her brother.

'Yes, Amelia,' Emery said, manfully meeting her eyes. 'It seems that Miss Beaseley and I are betrothed, with the announcement already set to appear in the *Gazette*!'

'I should never have come to Wiltshire,' Emery lamented an hour later in the privacy of his sister's sitting-room. 'First that set-to with Sir Percy and now this muddle with Miss Beaseley.'

'You and Miss Beaseley. I have never heard of anything so preposterous,' Amelia said. She had just finished informing Charles about Miss Beaseley and Emery when her brother had stalked in, having finally freed himself from his betrothed.

'Preposterous or not, it's the truth,' Emery bridled.

'Then you must unbetroth yourself at once.'

'Oh, I say, my dear.' Charles made a deprecating sound. While it was not unheard-of for a gentleman to cry off, it was still extremely rare, with the gentleman usually considered a cur for doing so.

'I can't unbetroth myself,' Emery said. 'Weren't you listening to me, Amelia? The chit shall be a laughing-stock. Either that or wind up a nun.'

'Bosh!'

Emery stared down at the Wilton rug. 'I'll have ruined her, and I can't have that on my conscience.'

Amelia eyed her brother with curious detachment. 'I assume you are speaking metaphorically about ruining her, and not literally?'

'Of course metaphorically,' he snapped. 'I'm no ogre.'

'I was just trying to get a clear grasp of things,' she retorted.

'Then help me instead of saying things such as how preposterous all this is.'

Amelia accepted this rebuke with almost royal calm. 'I don't see how you can escape now from the en-gagement without a good deal of botheration, which you are determined not to raise. What you might have done was pretend that a jokester had sent in the an-nouncement as a prank. But since you have told Miss Beaseley you shall have her, that puts a different light on the affair. It will be twice as difficult to cry off.'

'Not difficult, impossible,' Hadrian said, cast into the thickest gloom and with no one to blame but himself.

Lord Marlow had his own methods of dealing with a gentleman dealt a fatal blow by fate, and he deemed the affair serious enough to merit the bottle of prized Madeira he kept in his bookroom. While he applied such resuscitating efforts to his brother-in-law, Lady Marlow, unable to sit still in the face of an impending disaster in the family, grabbed a sunshade and went out into the gardens where she discovered Thea busily admiring her rose bushes with the help of a gardener.

'Have you rested, Amelia?' Thea asked.

'No, I haven't. Thea, did you hear what happened to Emery?'

'The whole household has heard,' Thea said frankly as she twirled the parasol she carried. 'I must say that the methods of capturing a husband employed by the current crop of London beauties are far different from those used in Vienna.'

Lady Marlow hooted. 'I've never heard anything so impossible. Have you?'

'Never!' came the cheerful response from her guest. 'It sounds like one of those Walter Scott stories.'

'I wish it were just one of Scott's insipid tales. But this is real. Poor Hadrian. I do feel for him.'

The two ladies had been walking as they spoke, but Thea stopped. Her brow was lifted quizzically. 'Come now, Amelia, I dare say the marriage may be a trifle forced, but that is so with many marriages. And while I had only a few moments with Miss Beaseley, I must acknowledge that she is a diamond of the first water. She and Emery make a handsome pair.'

The truth in this statement found no lasting favour with her hostess. 'I'm not denying that she is beautiful, but such a widgeon! And I could kill Hadrian for allowing himself to be roped in such a fashion merely because she threatened to go to a nunnery.'

'I dare say the ranks of bachelors would be thin indeed if every female of marriage age employed such tactics. Your brother is every inch a gentleman.'

'He shall be every inch a Benedict if he's not careful,' Amelia lamented.

A wicked gleam came into Thea's eyes. 'But I thought you wished him married.'

'So I do, but not to her!' Amelia answered vehemently.

Thea took pity on her. 'Perhaps Miss Beaseley is not the female you wished for your brother, but he himself must be the best judge of what would suit him. And he must harbour some feelings of affection for her, since he did offer for her of his free will back in London. If he were serious enough then, perhaps some of those feelings will be rekindled with the help of Miss Beaseley herself. Cheer up, Amelia,' she implored. 'They may surprise you by being happy together!'

Lady Marlow was not inclined to take as optimistic a view of the matter as her friend, but the issue was out of her hands. Thea might be right. Feeling now partly overcome by the emotions of the past hour, Amelia returned to her bedchamber to lie down, a victim of a crushing migraine.

CHAPTER EIGHT

DINNER that evening was not to be counted among Lady Marlow's grander triumphs. She had emerged from her bedchamber with her temples still throbbing, despite the lavender-scented handkerchiefs that had been laid on her brow. Her vexation had not abated when the first person she laid eyes on, Miss Beaseley, resplendent in a lilac gown with matching trim about the sleeves, took her in hand to begin an immediate tête-à-tête concerning wedding festivities.

Having hoped that the wedding between her beloved brother and this lovely widgeon had been merely a bad dream, Amelia summoned up all her will-power, bit her tongue, and managed to keep a civil expression on her face.

Lady Marlow had thought Mrs Chester a sensible companion to her flighty niece, but that was before a chance query as to her health over dinner revealed that Mrs Chester was inclined towards hypochondria and needed little encouragement to launch into a litany of all the vile ailments she had suffered from through the years—beginning with the bunions that had afflicted her feet and going up to her nose, which was alleged to be sensitive to dust.

In keeping with his duties as a host, Lord Marlow did his best to keep up a semblance of conversation with Miss Beaseley on his right and Mrs Chester on his left.

Never fond of quacks, he found his appetite dwindling in the midst of Mrs Chester's surefire cure for dyspepsia.

Not even the delights of his French chef and his favourite creamed sole could mask the taste left in his mouth at the end of such a recital. And there was worse to come.

Miss Beaseley, confessing with a slight titter that she was rather accomplished on the harp, was coaxed by Mrs Chester into giving a performance. Miss Beaseley had not brought her instrument with her to Wiltshire—her speedy removal from London to Emery's imagined deathbed had made that impossible—but she had seen a very ancient instrument in the back parlour that Lord Marlow's mother had occasionally plucked.

The upshot of the matter was that no sooner had the gentlemen finished with their port than the instrument was resurrected, and they were obliged to suffer through what Lord Marlow called in private the most godforsaken twanging he had ever heard in his life.

During one lull in the infernal racket, occasioned by the fortuitous breaking of one of the harp-strings, Lady Marlow, who had been dozing, intercepted the mute appeal of not only her long-suffering husband but her equally put-upon brother. She roused herself to action.

'My dear, that was simply splendid,' she said, going over to the harpist.

'There's more, if we could just repair this string.'

'But it so old, it wouldn't be of any use,' Lady Marlow said, and turned towards her husband for support. 'Am I right, Charles?'

'Yes, yes, my love, quite right,' Charles said hastily, ready to agree to anything if it would stop the plucking. 'Been meaning to throw it out for years.'

'We are in the habit of playing whist after dinner,' Lady Marlow continued. 'Do you play, Miss Beaseley? Mrs Chester?'

Mrs Chester here revealed that she did not play at cards. Miss Beaseley, however, admitted that she did and was soon persuaded to lay down the harp and take a position as Emery's partner against Thea and Charles while Amelia chatted with her aunt.

This move, however, proved to be no great improvement in the evening's atmosphere. Miss Beaseley appeared more interested in prattling on about London affairs or staring off into space when it was her turn to play a card.

'I believe the turn is yours,' Thea said, rather amused by the fulminating looks Emery shot his young bride-to-be.

Miss Beaseley gave a guilty start. 'Surely you err! Can it be my turn again?'

'Perhaps if you apply yourself, you could try and attend to the cards, Louisa,' Emery said, a note of exasperation in his usually amiable voice.

'Miss Beaseley's distraction is quite understandable,' Thea said, pouring oil on the troubled waters she saw about the table. 'She has much on her mind today.'

Glad for an ally, Miss Beaseley smiled at her. 'I don't recall meeting you before in London, Miss Campion, or have I? I confess to the most deplorable head for faces, particularly female ones.'

'In this instance your memory doesn't fail you,' Thea answered cordially. 'I haven't been to London since I was a child. I've lived practically my entire life on the Continent.'

'Have you really?' Miss Beaseley asked. 'But how could you? Not that I mean to say it's so barbaric now that Napoleon is no longer roaming at will, but still there's nothing like London with its balls and routs.'

'They have balls and routs on the Continent too,' Emery drawled, drumming his fingers impatiently on the table. 'And they play whist there, too, I believe. And it is your turn again.'

'Oh, is it?' Miss Beaseley asked contritely, discarding a card. 'You must forgive me, Emery,' she said as Lord Marlow pounced upon the card she had just discarded to score a decided trick. 'You must think I'll drive you into penury if I play like this in the London card-rooms. Shall I promise not to drive you into a poor house?'

'No poor house, but bedlam for certain,' Lord Marlow murmured under his breath, a remark that Miss Beaseley fortunately failed to hear. By the end of an hour it was deemed best to quit. Emery's patience had worn thin, and Lord Marlow himself wore a somewhat glazed expression.

Pleading fatigue, Thea made her excuses and escaped to her bedchamber, leaving the others to make rapid exits of their own.

'For I couldn't abide another minute at the card table,' Lord Marlow confessed to his wife as he pulled off his cravat in his dressing-room.

'At least you had Emery and Thea to support you,' Amelia pointed out. 'I was obliged to endure Mrs Chester single-handedly. And if she's not a quack, I wish to know who on earth is. I used to think your cousin, Roseanna, was invalidish, but next to Mrs Chester, Roseanna enjoys robust good health.'

'Well,' her spouse muttered darkly, 'I couldn't even enjoy a morsel of food with that female prattling on about every disease known to mankind.'

'Yes, I know,' Amelia sympathised. 'I was hard put to it to consume a morsel myself. But perhaps that is all to the good. I have become a trifle stout of late.'

'Nonsense,' Lord Marlow replied. 'Your figure is every bit as exquisite as it used to be.'

She blushed as he punctuated those words by sweeping her into his arms and kissing her soundly.

'Oh, Charles,' she murmured. 'You can always be relied upon to say the right thing. I dare say you will love me even when I am fat and fifty.'

'Of course,' he averred. 'Not that either of us will have much chance to gain an ounce with those females about us. Might waste away to skin and bone.'

She giggled. 'They are impossible, aren't they? But they needn't concern us at the moment, must they?'

Noticing the sparkle in his lovely wife's eyes, Lord Marlow smiled. 'No, indeed, love,' he said, and bent his head to kiss her soundly once again.

Contrary to Lord Marlow's gloomy prediction, he did not waste away to skin and bone in the following week, but this was due more to his foresight in taking several meals in his rooms than any cessation in the annoying behaviour of Mrs Chester or Miss Beaseley.

At dinner he was duty-bound to put in an appearance, but he took the liberty of seating Mrs Chester as far away from him as possible. The others in the household coped with the new guests as best they could with varying degrees of success.

'But if they stay much longer, I shan't be responsible,' Amelia confided to Thea one morning as they arranged flowers in the vases of the sitting-room.

'You are too severe, Amelia,' Thea said, standing back to admire their handiwork. 'Miss Beaseley means well. And she is quite beautiful.'

Lady Marlow snapped her fingers. 'That for beauty! She's a chucklehead and will bore Emery to tears within a month of their vows.'

Thea shrugged, her slender shoulders moving lightly under the green walking-dress she wore. 'I haven't heard him speak of the marriage with any bitterness.'

'He is resigned to his fate,' Amelia informed her, emphasising her point by sticking a rose in the vase with unnecessary force. 'And what could he do? He won't throw her over even though he knows he'll be miserable married to her. Such a distressingly *honourable* sort!' she said despairingly.

'Emery may not be miserable,' Thea said optimistically. 'Only think of odder marriages that have been contracted. And those who are unhappy, from what I understand of marriage, usually come to an agreement of sorts with the partners spending a good deal of time away from each other, leading inevitably to kindlier feelings.'

'That seems a poor recommendation for marriage,' Amelia observed sceptically. She put down the roses,

careful not to prick herself on the thorns, just as a
footman entered with the morning mail.

'Is that the mail, Walter?'

'Yes, my lady. And there is a letter from London for
you.'

'London!' Amelia exclaimed. 'Let me have it,' she
said, snatching it up from the platter.

'Were you expecting news from someone, Amelia?'
Thea asked.

Her friend looked up distractedly. 'Not exactly. Oh,
that reminds me. We have received an invitation from
Sir Percy for Friday evening. He is giving a ball. Quite
a small one, I'm sure, but it shall make for a nice change.
And while it shall be a trial of sorts, for Percy never
could throw a ball, it shall spare us an evening of Miss
Beaseley's infernal harp.'

Thea giggled. Miss Beaseley, after overseeing the repair
to the instrument, had practised daily on it in addition
to her nightly recitals after dinner.

'At least it is an improvement on her whist,' Thea said
mildly. 'But I think Sir Percy's invitation may be just
the thing to perk up our spirits.'

Amelia had attended Percy's balls in the past and
thought them intolerably boring, but she merely murmured. 'Very true,' and went off to enjoy her letter from
London.

Thea went down to the gardens. The sun shone
brightly above, and she carried a small sunshade to ward
off the rays. Unfurling it, she followed the stone path
down from the house and towards the small gardening
hut where Lord Marlow kept his prized orchids. She
walked idly, picking her way across the stones, before

she noticed Emery working his way up. From the intent look on his face it was evident he wished to be alone, but before she could make a graceful retreat, he lifted his head and saw her.

'Good morning.' His long stride closed the distance between them in a flash.

'Good morning,' she returned. 'I hope I didn't disturb you.'

'I'm glad for the interruption. I was pondering my future and being cast in the thickest gloom.'

'It can't be so bad,' she protested.

He grimaced. 'You're not the one marrying Miss Beaseley!'

'No, such is an impossibility between females, you know. But you must not be so disheartened about your future. Marriage may be the very thing for you.'

'How now,' he quizzed. 'Are you turning the champion of matrimonial bliss?'

'For myself, no,' she admitted with a faint smile. 'But, for others, I see nothing wrong with it and a good deal that is right.'

'Well, I don't, as far as Miss Beaseley and I are concerned. Only I can't find a way to bow out.'

'Why must you?' Thea asked. 'You undoubtedly thought marriage to her quite agreeable before. You did offer for her.'

'That was different.'

'How so?'

He glanced down at her upturned nose. 'Just different,' he murmured absently. He gave his head an abrupt shake. 'It is far too pleasant a day to waste on gloom. I feel in the mood for some exercise. Will you join me in a ride?'

'Willingly and with pleasure. But what of Miss Beaseley?'

He snorted. 'She is busy practising that harp.'

'Well, they say practice makes perfect,' Thea said with a twinkle, and went off to change into a riding-habit.

A half-hour later the two of them cantered briskly across the estate grounds. The wind whipped through Thea's hair, and she felt free and alive as she always did when riding. Emery, too, felt his spirits take wing, but this he laid not on the restorative powers of being in a saddle but to his lovely companion.

He stole a look at her now. An involuntary smile curved his lips at the sight of her cheeks so rosy from the wind. She looked adorable. He had been acquainted with her only a fortnight, but it seemed a lifetime. Thea was different from other females he was accustomed to. She was frank, relaxed, and comfortable. Always before, even with those few females he had boasted some measure of affection for, there had been periods of awkward silence when he had not the least notion of what they were thinking or might say. With Thea this was not true. Often before she uttered a word he had a clue to what she was going to say. It was almost as though their thoughts were in harmony.

She turned his way now and murmured something the wind carried off with it.

'What did you say?' he demanded.

Her horse was a little in front of his and she turned back to look over one shoulder. 'I said, the first one to the lake wins!' she called out, and gave her horse a gentle nudge. It sprang forward at once.

Caught by surprise, Emery recovered swiftly, laughing a little at the challenge she had issued and her obvious earnestness in urging her mare forward. He allowed her a few yards' grace, knowing that she would never accept a crushing defeat, and easily closed the gap, emerging the victor at the lake's edge.

'Now, that was quite unfair of you!' she protested, dismounting and splashing water on her flushed cheeks.

'Unfair?' He tied the reins of their horses to a tree limb. 'May I remind you that you gave the signal to be off when I was several yards behind!'

'Yes, but you could easily have made that up,' she retorted. 'Instead you toyed with me, allowing me to think that I would win, only to snatch it from me at the very last moment.'

'You wouldn't have wanted me to lose deliberately now, would you?' he chided, hands on hips.

'Oh, wouldn't I?' She laughed. 'I have a feeling that I should take my victories over you any way I can, and actually I won this race.'

'My dear Miss Campion, can your eyesight be failing at such a tender age? My horse beat yours by at least five yards.'

'Yes, I know, but I specifically said the first of us to reach the lake,' she pointed out, and splashed her hand in the water. 'And I was the first in the water.'

'Do you always insist on having your way with the gentlemen in your life?' he asked, chuckling and looking at her in a way that caused her heart to beat faster.

'Always,' she answered with aplomb. 'And now I think we had better return to the house.'

'If you like,' he said, reluctant to end the afternoon with her.

'Miss Beaseley will be wondering where you have gone to,' she pointed out, reminding him gently that, as far as she was concerned, he was a betrothed man.

CHAPTER NINE

ON FRIDAY evening two of Lord Marlow's carriages were pressed into service to transport him, his wife and their guests to Sir Percy's ball. Emery had the misfortune of accompanying Miss Beaseley in the barouche while Amelia and Charles endured Mrs Chester's company. As Amelia explained to her beleaguered spouse, one could not in good conscience foist both females on to poor Hadrian.

Thea, garbed in an exquisite pale white satin that was no less becoming for being at least a year old, also rode in the barouche. As for Miss Beaseley, she was forced to don one of Amelia's gowns, an orange crepe, since most of her wardrobe consisted of dour greys and blacks that she had prepared in case of Emery's demise.

'Insufferable though London sometimes is, I have missed it,' she confided now in the carriage.

'What do you miss the most?' Thea asked curiously.

The beauty thought for a moment. 'Oh, I don't know. Everything, I suppose. There is always so much to see and do. One is never bored. There are always excursions to go on, picnics and parties.'

'If the country is so boring, Louisa, you can always return to the city,' Emery said, a hopeful gleam in his hazel eyes.

She gave his knuckles a rap with the Chinese fan. 'How you jest, Emery! I wouldn't do any such thing while you must still recuperate from your wound.'

'I am perfectly mended,' he declared. 'Dr Marsh took another look at the shoulder this morning and pronounced me as fine as fivepence. That was after he looked in on your aunt, who was enduring a spasm of some sort.'

'A spasm?' Thea raised her brows. She had heard nothing of this.

'I do hope it was nothing serious, Miss Beaseley.'

'Oh, no,' Miss Beaseley assured them both with an airy smile. 'Aunt Ellen was merely feeling a trifle under the weather. She is very susceptible to changes in the weather. I am that way too,' she confessed. 'I remember once riding in the park on a cold February morning. I was obliged to seek the comfort of not one hot brick but two under my blanket!'

'If it were so cold, I wonder that you ventured out at all,' Thea said, taking a practical view of the matter.

'But I had to,' Miss Beaseley said naïvely. 'Lord Ackworth had invited me.'

'But you might have taken an inflammation of the lungs,' Thea pointed out. 'I wonder that Mrs Chester allowed you to go out.'

'She had to. I insisted upon it. After all, Ackworth is a marquis.'

'How fortunate, then, that he was not an earl, for you might have been lured out into a blizzard,' Emery drawled.

Thea choked at his insouciance, but Miss Beaseley merely looked puzzled. Directing what she hoped would be a quelling look at Emery, Thea took pity on the other lady.

'Do tell me more about London,' she coaxed.

Miss Beaseley fell in agreeably enough with this suggestion, and the rest of the trip to Sir Percy's was occupied with her recollections of the various treats London boasted. The delicious ices of Gunter's were described in lavish detail, as were the hallowed halls of Almack's.

'Almack's?' Thea looked puzzled for a moment. 'Oh, that is a club, is it not, where parties are sometimes held?'

Miss Beaseley uttered a strangled sound. 'Almack's, Miss Campion, is far more than a place for parties.'

'Indeed yes,' Emery concurred. 'It is the Holy Grail to some and the Marriage Mart to others.'

'What an odious thing to say!' Thea said, unable to stifle a laugh herself.

'It's the truth,' he retorted. 'Almack's is the place where marriage-minded mamas bring their daughters. Gentlemen in need of wives also frequent it, and I warn you not to take refreshment there, for it undoubtedly consists of stale cakes and sour lemonade.'

'Are you so well acquainted with the Assembly Rooms?' Thea quizzed.

'Not as much as some mothers might have hoped,' Miss Beaseley answered for him. 'And when he was present, you should have seen the lures cast his way.'

'I can well imagine,' Thea said, enjoying the discomfiture on the viscount's face. 'If I ever go to London, I shall have to see Almack's.'

'But you can't just go there,' Miss Beaseley protested, looking shocked.

'Why not?'

Miss Beaseley floundered for words. 'Well. Because…'

'Almack's is not open to anyone,' Emery explained. 'The arena is guarded by lions in the form of females known as patronesses. They grant vouchers grudgingly to enable the favoured few to enter Almack's hallowed halls.'

Thea made a face. 'It sounds dreadfully complicated.'

'Oh, it is,' he agreed.

'And you must make sure you arrive before eleven,' Miss Beaseley put in. 'Once Wellington himself was turned away because he came late.'

'Good heavens!' Thea said, her mind boggling at anyone so high in the instep as to turn away the hero of Waterloo. 'It sounds most unpleasant.'

'But it isn't, really,' Miss Beaseley said. 'Quite the contrary. And while it may seem complicated at first, these are just precautions. You wouldn't wish to associate with cits and mushrooms, would you?'

'Not to mention mere shabby genteels,' Emery drawled.

Thea felt another laugh bubble forth. 'This is all past speaking,' she said finally, 'for I don't think I shall ever go to Almack's. I don't have vouchers or the slightest notion how to get them.'

'Should that need ever arise,' Emery told her, 'you have only to apply to Lady Jersey. She is one of the patronesses and a friend of mine. Once you tell her you know me, I'm sure she'll grant the vouchers without too much of a fuss.'

Thea was surprised at his generosity and murmured her thanks, which were drowned out by Miss Beaseley's announcement that they had arrived at Sir Percy's estate.

The baronet himself greeted his guests this evening, standing at the top of the long marble stairs. Smiling expansively, he greeted Thea, bowed over Miss Beaseley's hand, and clapped Emery heartily on the shoulders— perhaps too heartily, for the viscount winced involuntarily.

'Oh, I say, dreadfully sorry, old boy,' Percy said, not appearing sorry in the least. 'The shoulder still pains you, I see.'

'Just a trifle.'

'Well, that highwayman put a good shot into you,' Percy said, his voice sounding to Emery's ears unnecessarily loud. His colour rose as he felt himself the target of the curious.

Lady Marlow had predicted that the ball would be a small affair, but Sir Percy had amassed several notable guests visiting the region, including, in addition to Emery and Marlow, the Earl of Daughtery and his brother, Captain Henry Blaine.

Neither of these men could be described as dashing or handsome, but Daughtery did boast an earnestness that some ladies might have found appealing, and the captain did appear to good advantage in his regimentals.

As is common with brothers, the two had had numerous differences of opinion over the years, but tonight a rare moment of agreement occurred. Within minutes of meeting Thea they each singled her out as the most appealing female present, almost coming to cuffs over the honour of dancing with her.

Thea, amazed to find herself the object of such intense interest, was at a loss to decide which to choose until, with the wisdom of Solomon, Amelia declared a toss of the coin should suffice. The captain's luck held and with a smile at his brother the earl, who believed that rank should have all privileges, the captain led Thea out.

Captain Blaine was not among those gentlemen who deemed it enough to dance. He preferred to speak as well, supplying his partner with the precise strategy of Wellington's victory over Napoleon at Waterloo, along with an account of his own deprivations suffered during the course of the battle.

'Military life certainly seems an arduous undertaking,' Thea commented as he paused for breath. 'I wonder that you haven't sold out by now.'

His sturdy chin jutted out a fraction of an inch. 'I intend to do precisely that, I assure you. Indeed it has been on my mind for considerable time now that Bonaparte is finally vanquished. Also I intend to take a wife.'

Thea was a little astonished at receiving such ready confidences. 'Really? When may I wish you happy?'

For the first time the captain seemed at a loss for words. 'Well, actually, Miss Campion,' he admitted, 'I haven't really fixed an interest in anyone. Until now, I mean,' he said, casting her a meaningful look.

Much to her relief, for that one look was enough to cause alarums to go off in her brain, the dance ended and the captain escorted her back to the chair where the earl was waiting impatiently for his turn.

Thea alas found the earl no great improvement on his brother when it came to dancing. And he was as prosy as they come, bespeaking a keen interest in matters political. He obviously took his duties in Parliament very seriously, and invited Thea to sit as his guest the next time the house was in session.

'I shall make it a point to speak on an issue,' he declared earnestly.

'What issue would that be?' Thea asked politely.

'Why, any issue at all.'

Her astonishment was considerable. 'Do you speak, then, on every issue, Lord Daughtery?'

'Practically every one,' he said modestly. 'I deem it important to exercise one's right and express one's opinions, don't you?'

'I suppose so,' she acknowledged, a little in awe of anyone having the capability to speak on every issue before Parliament. But midway into her waltz she discovered that the earl had and did express opinions on practically everything under the sun, from the Regent's choice of Mr Nash as his architect to the deplorable fashion of Oldenburg hats for females.

Her mind began to wander, as it frequently did when she was bored, and she found herself wondering what sort of refreshments Sir Percy planned to lay in front of his guests.

'When you come to London, Miss Campion, you must pay a call on Parliament as my guest,' he said, smiling indulgently at her.

'That is kind,' she said, not unappreciative of the invitation. 'But I don't think I shall be going to London.'

'Why not?'

'Well, I don't know,' she said, a little surprised at the question and at herself for not being able to supply a good reason. 'I'm just not going to London.'

'But you can't mean to stay here for the duration of the month, can you?' he pointed out.

'No, of course not,' she murmured, and was relieved when the dance ended.

The earl's words continued to reverberate in her brain. Why could she not go to London? And had she really meant to impose on Amelia for much longer?

As she sat later, pondering her future—provoked by the earl's innocent questions—Emery, who had abstained from dancing with any of the current country beauties present and who had already stood up once with Miss Beaseley, ambled over to her side.

'Has the belle of the ball finally realised a chance to catch her breath and rest her feet?' he quizzed, unfolding his lanky frame into the chair next to hers.

Her green eyes widened. 'Don't talk fustian, Emery.'

'Too modest by half, Miss Campion. It is quite an accomplishment to snare Captain Blaine and the earl from under the noses of several other females.' He dropped his voice slightly as he bent closer. 'A word of warning. I shouldn't turn my back on Lady Seares if I were you. She brought her niece here expressly to meet the captain. That's she,' he nodded off to the corner, 'the bran-faced chit. Might be pretty if not so freckled.'

Thea was torn between amusement and anger. As was usually the case with Emery, amusement won.

'Do stop talking so odiously,' she chided. 'You speak as though I were on the hunt for a husband, which I assure you is not the case.'

'Yes, yes,' he said complacently, 'I know your aversion to matrimony, but does Daughtery or Blaine? And for someone who doesn't wish to interest either gentleman, you certainly didn't try to fob them off.'

She stared at him incredulously. 'Fob them off? But this is a ball, after all. And,' she said, stiffening, 'I certainly didn't encourage them.'

Two of the viscount's fingers disappeared into his snuff-box. 'To certain gentlemen, no discouragement is tantamount to active encouragement.'

'Really?'

He closed his snuff-box. 'Really. And those two certainly seem fixed on you. Quite a prosy pair. All in all, the Blaines have always had tongues that ran on wheels.'

'I am not interested in your opinion of either the earl or the captain,' she said scorchingly.

'Then how about some advice on fobbing them off?' he asked cordially. 'Turn them the cold shoulder, and they'll take the hint at once. Surely a lady like you knows that gentlemen are put off by an aloof manner.'

'Are they?' she quizzed. 'And how do you know such a thing unless you receive a cold shoulder yourself, but that I won't believe. What woman in her right mind would try and fob you off?'

'Miss Beaseley did once,' he reminded her.

Amusement danced in her eyes. 'I said right mind, Emery.' A bark of laughter escaped him.

She was immediately contrite. 'That was old-cattish of me.'

'Save your apologies,' he commanded. 'Your words were on the mark.'

'Even so, it was not charitable of me.'

The viscount turned her a deaf ear, noticing now that the captain was making a strategic move in their direction. 'No doubt to try and plead for this waltz,' he said in a low voice as the musicians struck up the three-four time. 'And who is that on the right? Daughtery. Who shall outflank the other, I wonder?' He bent his head closer to Thea. 'I put my money on the captain. Oh.' A note of disappointment entered his voice. 'He is being detained by Lady Seares, who will make him known to her niece after all. And the earl has been caught between Sir Percy and young Gaylord. It seems neither will extricate himself. Ah, what's this? The captain has broken free of Lady Seares's grasp and here comes the earl as well.'

Thea was very nearly in whoops by the end of this recitation and hard put to it to maintain her countenance as the captain, huffing a little, stepped up to her.

'Miss Campion!'

'Told you so,' Emery murmured under his breath to Thea. 'The military will win.'

The captain frowned. 'You spoke, sir?'

'I was merely making an observation to Miss Campion concerning the stalwart capabilities of our military,' Emery drawled.

The captain appeared somewhat mollified by his words, but irritation descended anew on his brow when the earl, who had sneaked up on the right, seized the opportunity to entreat Thea to waltz.

'I say, Denis, I was just about to do that myself,' the captain protested.

'Unfortunately, Henry, I asked first.'

'Shall we have another flip of the coin, Miss Campion?' the captain enquired.

Thea hesitated, but Emery broke in to say that that would be unnecessary.

'I don't think the matter concerns you, Emery,' the earl declared, looking as stiff as his collar points.

'No, perhaps not,' Emery agreed affably, 'but I myself asked Miss Campion for the honour of dancing the waltz, and she and I were just about to take to the floor when the two of you came running up. Miss Campion,' he said, turning towards Thea, who had been listening to him with astonishment, 'shall we?'

Finding his hand outstretched towards hers, Thea took it and followed him. 'You see how easy it is to fob them off if you merely apply your mind to it,' he said, sliding one arm easily about her waist.

'That was an out-and-out whisker, Emery,' she retorted.

The handsome face gazing down at her was most unrepentant. 'Not entirely,' he said. 'I did intend to ask you to waltz. Or did you really wish to spend the rest of the evening having coins flipped to decide which of the pair you ought to dance with at any given moment?' She shuddered at the spectacle his words conjured up. 'You dance well,' he said then. 'That is to be expected, I suppose, since the waltz originated on the Continent.'

'Thank you, my lord. You dance tolerably well yourself.'

His smile was warm. 'I hope I move as nimbly as your two previous partners. By the by, has either of those gudgeons solicited your company for supper yet?'

'Not yet,' she said, frowning at this new problem facing her. 'Perhaps they won't.'

'Of course they will,' he declared. 'And they'll no doubt fight tooth and nail for the privilege of bringing you in to sup.' A meditative look came into his eyes. 'A mill would be enlivening.'

'Oh, Emery, stop being so disagreeable! Tell me what to do.'

'You could always choose not to eat,' he pointed out, an idea she rejected at once.

'I'm practically starving!'

His eye glinted appreciatively. 'Well, we can't let you perish from lack of food. I have it. You can go in and sup with both of them.'

She nearly missed a step in the waltz. 'The both of them? Is that what you call a solution? I'd rather hoped with neither of them.'

He waltzed her expertly the length of the room. 'That bad, eh? Well, I'd take you in myself, but I'm already spoken for by Miss Beaseley.'

'And I'd much rather not sup with Miss Beaseley or her aunt,' Thea retorted.

He gave a sympathetic nod. 'We get too much of them at Amelia's, do we not? I only hope there ain't a harp on the premises.'

'I have it!'

'The harp?' he asked, confused.

'No, Uncle Andrew.'

The puzzlement grew on the viscount's face. 'What has your uncle to do with Miss Beaseley's infernal harp?'

'Nothing, he doesn't even like music at all. Thank you for the waltz,' she said distractedly as the music ended, and she sped off to her uncle, whom she had glimpsed out of the corner of one eye.

CHAPTER TEN

SINCE Thea's uncle had always professed a keen dislike of any social affair, she was pleasantly surprised to find him at Sir Percy's ball.

'I'm not a hermit,' he replied as she pecked him on the cheek. 'I see you have been busy.'

'Now, now, Uncle Andrew.'

His eyes twinkled. 'Daughtery and Blaine caught on one string.'

'Uncle Andrew, that won't do,' she said, and cast an oblique eye about the room. The earl was beginning to step across from his side of the ballroom, and his brother was only a step behind.

'Uncle Andrew,' she hissed quickly. 'Do say you wish to sup with me.'

Mr Campion had not risen to his position as a noted scholar due to any lack of wits, and with a real appreciation for the situation, which he later deemed as great a farce as any Mr Sheridan might have penned, he fell in with his niece's plea, leaving both the earl and the captain in search of supper companions.

'When do we eat?' he asked Thea when the two gentlemen had been sent about their business.

'Immediately. I am famished,' she confessed. 'How did you get here? Where is Jonathon?'

'Out chatting with young Gaylord, I suspect. He drove me—Jonathon, I mean. And he's not so bad a whip. You may tell Emery that.'

She entered the supper-room on his arm.

'I've been doing some serious thinking, Thea.'

'Of course you have. Is it that new translation of Virgil?'

'No, I wasn't thinking of that.'

They filled their plates with lobster patties, sliced ham and asparagus tips and took them over to a table.

'I've been doing some thinking about that young man of yours and what he had to say about Jonathon.'

Thea halted, her fork half-way to her mouth. 'Do you mean Viscount Emery?' she asked incredulously. 'Heavens, Uncle Andrew, he's *not* my young man.'

Mr Campion waved away her disclaimer. 'I may have my head in an ivory tower but I ain't daft, and when I had time to ponder his words, it made sense.' He heaved a sigh. 'Jonathon is at a ticklish age, and perhaps I've overdone the thing. I may have pushed him too hard. He could do with a little town bronze.'

'You are undoubtedly right,' Thea said. She knew her uncle's words did not come easily, and she admired him all the more for admitting he could have been wrong. 'Jonathon has spent most of his life here in rural tranquillity, so it is no wonder he is so curious about life in the big city.'

'Especially London.' Mr Campion gave a sagacious shake of his craggy head. 'Practically devours all the copies of the *Morning Post* or the *Gentleman's Monthly* that we receive. He's keen to go to London.'

Thea smiled. 'When do you leave?'

Her uncle snorted. 'I wouldn't set foot in London if you offered me the presidency of Oxford!'

She looked momentarily confused. 'But why are you speaking of Jonathon going?' She laid down her fork in alarm. 'You cannot contemplate turning him, as green as he is, on to the streets there! He will wind up in some sluicery or hell.'

'Do you take me for a fool, my dear? I know all that. That's why I want you to take him to London!'

'*Me!*' Thea exclaimed.

'Yes, you,' her uncle said, chewing thoughtfully. 'Can you give me any reason why you couldn't go to London?'

'But I haven't thought of it.'

'Then think of it now,' he ordered. 'You could take in the sights together with Jonathon. Balls. Routs. Parties. Vauxhall. Drury Lane. Almack's.'

'I suppose so,' Thea said, wavering a little. 'But it would be tantamount to the blind leading the blind,' she said at last with a shake of her head. 'I haven't been to London since I was a child. And where would we stay?'

'I still have the family house,' he reminded her. 'You can have full run of it and the servants. I'll bear all expenses for you both.'

This was generosity indeed, and Thea felt sorely tempted. 'But I still won't be able to get Jonathon entry into London circles. He needs a patron, a male, which I am not.'

'He'll have one,' Mr Campion promised. 'I have a few friends left in the city. All you need do is to accompany him and be certain that he doesn't fall into mischief.'

On the face of things it seemed a simple enough task. Yet Thea continued to hesitate. 'I still think you should accompany him.'

'I don't!' her uncle replied. 'I've lost all taste for London. It wouldn't excite me at all, and it might put a crimp into Jonathon's enjoyment.'

She made no immediate reply to this and promised to think more on the idea. As the evening wore on, she could not deny that part of her was more than a little excited at the notion of seeing London. She continued to mull over the consequences of such a trip as Miss Beaseley, having no harp at her disposal, found a pianoforte instead and was duly commanded by Sir Percy to perform. She acquitted herself as ably on this instrument as she did on the harp.

'And I only hope she doesn't find a lute and begin to pluck that as well,' Emery murmured under his breath to his sister as they headed back to the ballroom after her performance.

'Too harsh, Hadrian,' Amelia protested. 'You are an avowed lover of music, and Miss Beaseley boasts many talents on several instruments. Her aunt was telling me so just the other day.'

'Amelia, if you love me you shall cease prattling of music and Miss Beaseley. The two do not mix well together,' he pointed out, and walked off.

Noticing the exchange, Thea went to Amelia's side. 'I hope you are not in his black books,' she murmured.

Amelia laughed away such a thought. 'Hadrian can never bear a grudge. He just dislikes my pointing out how wretchedly unhappy he will be with Miss Beaseley as a wife. And to make his temper even more peevish, there's Percy hinting so odiously to everyone through the evening about saving Emery from harm. Indeed, a few guests even intimated as much to me, saying how grateful my brother must be to Sir Percy.' She snorted. 'It's no wonder Hadrian is not enjoying the ball. But,' she concluded on a happier note, 'I am glad to see you are.'

'Oh, Amelia, don't start on that,' Thea pleaded. 'I believe I have borne enough.'

'The earl is the persistent sort,' Amelia said. 'He practically cornered me and demanded to know all about you and how you might be persuaded to go to London!' She paused. 'Something about a session of Parliament, I do believe.'

Thea gave a rueful chuckle. 'He invited me to listen to him speak there. And perhaps getting me to London won't be so difficult after all.'

An odd expression flitted into Amelia's blue eyes. 'Thea,' she choked. 'Do you mean that Daughtery has prevailed on you...'

Thea laughed. 'Heavens, no. Daughtery had nothing to do with it. My Uncle Andrew has proposed that I go to London with Jonathon in an effort to give him a little town bronze. I shall undoubtedly be a strange chaperon, for I've no notion how to go on. Before this evening I'd never heard of Almack's. So you see how little help I shall be to poor Jonathon.'

'Not at all. I think London shall be the very thing for the two of you,' Amelia exclaimed, snapping her ivory-handled fan shut. Her eyes glinted. 'There are such sights to see. You shall enjoy it. I just know it.'

'Even so...'

'Furthermore,' Amelia swept on, 'if it is merely a matter of not knowing where to go and how to get about, I can provide the perfect solution. A guide.'

Thea blinked. 'A guide?'

'Yes, my dear. Me!'

Thea gazed into the beaming face. 'You, Amelia? You must be funning!'

'Not at all. I've been thinking of going to London for some time. Since you and Jonathon shall be removing there, what could be more fated? I have the advantage of knowing London and can introduce the two of you about.'

The scheme as Amelia outlined it seemed attractive to Thea.

'What about Charles? Will he come too?'

'Oh, no,' Amelia replied. 'He hates the Season. He'll probably stay on here.'

Thea was stricken. 'But you can't abandon him. After all, there are still Emery and Miss Beaseley to consider.' She caught a glimpse of Amelia's face and broke into a laugh. 'Is that why you are so desirous of leaving Wiltshire?'

'Oh, no,' Amelia denied. 'Even though it is a trifle tedious with Miss Beaseley and her aunt underfoot all day long. But whatever Emery wants to do with his marriage is his business, not mine. I have washed my hands of that.' Her voice trailed off in a hush as Mrs Chester drifted over in a distracted manner to ask if either of them had seen Mr Andrew Campion.

Wondering what Miss Beaseley's aunt might want with her uncle, Thea enquired civilly as to any message she might bear him.

'The vicar mentioned that Mr Campion is troubled with the gout. Is that true?' Mrs Chester demanded.

'Why, yes,' Thea acknowledged.

A beatific smile blossomed on Mrs Chester's face. 'I have a recipe for a cure that shall put him to rights immediately. It also purges the blood, cures the grippe, and will restore him to robust good health.'

'Good heavens!' Amelia ejaculated.

'I'm not certain Uncle Andrew is ready for all that,' Thea said hastily.

Mrs Chester's eye, however, had already spotted her quarry, and, excusing herself, she sped off towards Thea's uncle. A minute later Amelia departed as well in search of Charles. She planned to lay in front of him her plans to go to London.

Left momentarily to her own devices, Thea circulated about the ballroom. She was a bit surprised when Sir Percy sidled up to her.

'Are you enjoying the ball, my dear Miss Campion?' he asked, his cheeks puffed out a little in a smile.

'It is very enjoyable.'

He beamed. 'I can't help contrasting this pleasant gathering with the time we last met.'

Her green eyes narrowed ever so slightly. 'Oh?'

'Yes.' He smiled blandly at her. 'We had the misfortune to encounter the highwayman that day, if you recall.'

'Ah, yes. I'd never forget that.'

'I shouldn't wonder,' Sir Percy agreed with an indulgent smile. 'I dare say you may have passed many a sleepless night reliving your near brush with death.'

'Actually,' she confessed, 'no.'

He seemed a trifle taken aback. 'Most females would, after witnessing so violent an encounter.'

'Perhaps so, but I don't think I suffered irreparable harm from the incident.'

Sir Percy, perceiving the hard stare she gave him, thought better of pursuing the topic of his own heroism and turned his attention to the viscount's whereabouts.

'When last I saw him, he was bound for the card-room,' she answered, and could not suppress her own curiosity. 'Why do you wish to see him?'

'A cousin of mine is going to London,' Sir Percy divulged readily enough. 'I thought Emery might recommend him to Gentleman Jack. A small enough favour, I trust, for all I've done for him lately.'

As the baronet went off towards the card-room, Thea stood thinking it a great pity that she could not witness the hostilities certain to be engendered by Sir Percy's request.

She turned her gaze from Sir Percy's stout back and intercepted her uncle's frantic appeal for help. Mrs Chester indeed had him cornered by a bay window and appeared to be pressing something into his palm which he in turn was endeavouring to thrust back at her. Thea, controlling a quivering lip, strolled up to them.

'Thea, my dear.' Mr Campion seized her hand.

'Uncle Andrew. Mrs Chester. How delightful to see you two together.'

Mr Campion, who thought nothing at all delightful in having his ear bent by a quackish female, glared at his niece.

'Did you know, Miss Campion, that your uncle suffers not only from the gout but also the grippe?' Mrs Chester asked now.

'I had no notion of it,' Thea responded, gazing at her uncle with great concern. 'It is a miracle that you are all in one piece, Uncle!'

'Hah!' Mr Campion gave an awful bark that would have daunted a lesser female than Mrs Chester.

'He won't take this recipe I wrote for him. It is the certain cure I spoke of to you, Miss Campion.'

'I shall take it for him,' Thea said, doing so. 'And serious though my uncle's afflictions may seem, it appears to me that Mr Sidney Alsgood may be in need of your skills even more than Uncle Andrew. The squire was telling me only the other day that Mr Alsgood had what appeared to be a case of influenza complicated by a suspicious consumption.'

Mrs Chester's eyes lit up at this new challenge. 'No, really? I have a cousin who has the remedy for that.' And she excused herself to beat a path straight for the unfortunate Mr Alsgood.

'Influenza *and* consumption?' Mr Campion snorted. 'Never heard such gibble gabble in my life.'

'Did you wish to be rescued from her or not?' Thea enquired sweetly. 'I can call her back if you like.'

'Good God, no,' he ejaculated.

She chuckled. 'Here's the cure she wanted you to have.'

He waved it away. 'Instead of handing me such things, tell me if you've thought any further about the London trip.'

She nodded. 'Yes. It seems Amelia is very keen to go to London and has offered me her help. So if Cousin

Jonathon doesn't object, he may find himself with not one but two female chaperons.'

Cousin Jonathon, far from objecting, was rendered inarticulate at the news that he would be shortly London-bound. His downy face, still sporting a fuzzy upper lip, lit up as his father revealed his plans. Thea herself felt excitement building at the prospect of the great city, and Jonathon, after bussing her soundly on the cheek, went off to tell his friend, Gaylord Boyle, about the treat in store.

During the closing hour of the ball, Sir Percy had finally located Emery and prevailed upon him to sponsor his cousin to Jackson's saloon. Emery acceded to the request only because it seemed too arduous to argue the point, and he hoped the cousin was a better student of science than the baronet.

As they rode back to Chumley Field he could not but reflect ruefully on his curious tie to the baronet as his two companions chattered on about London shops and modistes.

'Madame Fanchon is quite the best,' Miss Beaseley declared. 'Although,' she conceded, 'Madame Dupont is quite good too.'

'Why are you so interested in dressmakers?' Emery demanded, so suddenly that both ladies looked startled. They had forgotten his brooding presence in the carriage.

'My Uncle Andrew has asked me to take Cousin Jonathon to London,' Thea explained.

The viscount did not try to mask his astonishment. 'You? Why on earth?'

'He thought Jonathon could do with a little season-
ing,' Thea said.

'Which you will supply?' he asked ironically.

She did not blame him for his reaction. 'I know what
you're thinking, Emery, and I share your doubts. Indeed,
I told Uncle Andrew that a male chaperon would be
better. But he insisted I take Jonathon to London. Fortunately Amelia has promised us her help.'

The viscount shook his head. 'Two females and young
Jonathon. I predict nothing but a bumblebroth.'

'Don't be so pessimistic. Daughtery has promised some
help as well. And then there's the captain.'

'Ah, yes, your two swains,' he smiled. 'I am all
amazement that they left the ball without coming to
cuffs. I credit that to their being brothers.'

'Hardly a reason,' she pointed out. 'So were Cain and
Abel.'

Here Miss Beaseley intervened to ask what the Bible
might have to do with Miss Campion's decision to visit
London.

'Nothing at all, my dear,' the viscount said drily. 'I
don't think Cain or Abel even approached the rank of
a baronet, did they, Miss Campion?'

Thea choked on a laugh while Miss Beaseley continued to look confused.

'What kind of help did Daughtery offer?' Emery
asked.

'The earl invited me to listen to him when he addressed Parliament,' Thea said matter-of-factly.

The viscount reacted as any sensible man might. 'Oh,
my God! I hope you had the good sense to say no.'

'And why should I?' she asked defensively.

'Because, my poor child, an afternoon of tedium shall be the inevitable result. What sort of help did the captain offer, I shudder to think?'

'He promised to take me for a ride in the park.'

Emery's brow cleared. 'Well, that's better than being bored to tears in Parliament.'

'If you do ride with the captain,' Miss Beaseley put in, pleased that they were back on familiar territory, 'you must make sure it is at the fashionable hour.'

'Oh, yes,' Emery agreed. 'Nothing would stigmatise you as a dowd more than to appear at the park at any other time of day.'

'But if everyone goes there, then won't it be crowded?' Thea asked.

Miss Beaseley nodded. 'That's what makes it so much fun.'

'But then, how much riding gets done?'

'One doesn't ride in the park to ride, Miss Campion,' Emery informed her, 'but to be seen.'

She wrinkled up her nose ever so slightly. 'How odious that sounds. I did think it might be nice to ride there with the captain, but not if we are to be gawked at.'

'Oh, it's not odious at all,' Miss Beaseley assured her. Her face glowed. 'There is nothing the equal of sitting in the carriage of some prominent gentleman and greeting all of one's friends and admirers. And the patronesses are quite often there too.' She heaved a sigh. 'I own to having missed it more than I thought possible.'

'An error easily mended,' Emery replied at once. 'There is no need whatsoever for you to remain closeted in the wilds of Wiltshire. And you certainly need not tarry on my part. My shoulder is fully mended.'

Miss Beaseley appeared tempted, but shook her head vehemently. 'I can't just leave you.'

'Of course you can,' he said, then tried a different tack. 'I'm certain your aunt must be perishing from boredom.'

Here Miss Beaseley acknowledged that her aunt, in addition to her other ailments, had owned to a bout of homesickness, but even so she was not persuaded to leave Wiltshire.

'My place is with you, Emery, as long as you need me.' And she looked as though she meant it.

Sheer persuasion would not do the thing, Emery saw at once, and adopted a swift change in strategy. 'If such is your feeling, perhaps you would join me fishing later in the week.'

Miss Beaseley appeared floored at such an invitation. 'Did you say fishing, my lord?'

'Yes. Fishing. Poles, hooks, worms for bait,' he continued, encouraged by the slight shudder that ran down his companion's back. 'I was planning to try the streams again the day after tomorrow with Charles. You'll come with us, I hope.'

Miss Beaseley fidgeted. 'Well, I don't know.'

'You must. If only to have me demonstrate how perfectly mended my shoulder is.' Taking her assent for granted, he turned next to Thea. 'And you'll come too, won't you, Miss Campion?'

'I shouldn't miss it for the world, my lord,' she said, wondering just what lay up his sleeve.

CHAPTER ELEVEN

TWO DAYS later Emery, accompanied by Thea, Miss Beaseley and Charles, who had been persuaded against his better judgment into bearing them company, made another attempt at angling.

'I don't see why it must be so dark,' Miss Beaseley complained as they walked towards the stream.

'Fish come out when it's early morn,' Lord Marlow explained, wondering why Emery would wish to drag this female with them. It was plain as two pins that she did not wish to be there.

He caught his brother-in-law's eye and lifted a quizzical brow, but received nothing enlightening in reply. Reaching the stream at last, he declared his intention of setting up at his favourite spot and left the other three to fish wherever they liked.

'Now then, Louisa,' Emery said, 'this is your pole, line and hook. And of course your bait.' He showed her each item in turn, the last a container filled with wiggly worms.

Miss Beaseley gave the receptacle a suspicious look. 'What sort of bait?' she enquired.

'Actually, worms.'

'*Worms?*' she shrieked, dropping the container to the ground, where the worms spilled free and writhed uncontrollably on the ground.

'Oh, stop them, stop them!' she cried.

'They won't hurt you,' Emery said, scooping one of the worms up and attaching it to her hook, oblivious of her continued shrieking. 'Now, here you go. Hold on to it.'

'Hold it?' Miss Beaseley shuddered. 'I never want to touch the squirmy things.'

'Not the worm, the pole,' he commanded, and thrust it at her. 'See, that's the thing.'

Thea, meanwhile, had already baited her hook and thrown her line out. She stood down the stream, a little removed from the spectacle of the viscount and his betrothed.

'Why are you so far away?' he asked in passing.

'I thought you and Miss Beaseley might wish to have a private lesson in the sport,' she said in muffled tones.

'Such as the one we had?' he quipped.

Her eyes flew up to his, but Miss Beaseley ended this tête-à-tête by shrieking yet again, not because of a worm but because of a fish.

'You've got a nibble, Louisa,' Emery said, going to her side at once. 'Good for you.' Miss Beaseley saw nothing good in the least about her situation with the fish.

'That's the girl,' Emery called out encouragingly as the fish jumped alarmingly.

Miss Beaseley glared at him. 'Do something!' she demanded.

'Don't you wish to bring it in yourself?' he asked.

'No,' she replied curtly, just as the fish tugged and dragged her down the embankment. 'Arggh!' she shouted as the pole flew up and she found herself up to her ankles in water and mud. The sandals that she had insisted on wearing despite Thea's advice were caked with mud.

'Oh, I say, Louisa, are you all right?' Emery asked, attempting to help her out of the water.

She shook off his arm. 'No, I am not all right,' she said. 'I am wet and my sandals are ruined and just look at my dress! I hate those dreadful worms and that odious fish and I never ever wish to see another one in my entire life.'

'Quite understandable,' Emery said with quick sympathy. 'But it is not necessary to abandon the entire sport merely on account of a minor mishap.'

'Mishap!' she shrieked, sputtering water as she rose and rubbed her cheek with the back of a wet hand. 'I wish to return to the house now, immediately, Emery. I am wet and cold, and I shan't stay here another minute.'

'Now, now, Louisa,' he protested, 'won't you reconsider? You're not all that damp, just your ankles and, er, sandals. Do but consider that you've the most luck of the four of us. No one else has had as much as a nibble. That fish that got away was at least three feet long. No wonder it nearly pulled you in.'

Miss Beaseley needed no reminder of the fish or of being dragged into the stream. Having endured a wretched morning, she gave in to her emotions and stamped her foot, a difficult task given the fact that her sandal was very soaked.

'I demand to go back.'

'Very well,' the viscount said reluctantly. 'I'll tell Miss Campion and Charles.'

'There is no need to inform Miss Campion,' Thea said,

having witnessed the entire sorry incident from her position. 'I shall tell Charles what has transpired, and we shall return later. Do get Miss Beaseley into some warm clothes, Emery,' she scolded. 'We don't wish her to catch an inflammation of the lungs, do we?'

'No, indeed,' Emery agreed, and held out a hand to Miss Beaseley, who disdained it and departed in a high dudgeon.

'Peculiar sort of female,' Charles said later to Thea as they packed up their things. 'Don't know why Emery would insist on bringing her along. 'Twas obvious she didn't wish to fish.'

'No doubt he had his reasons.'

Lord Marlow shrugged and changed the subject. 'Amelia says you and young Jonathon are bound for London with her.'

Thea nodded. 'She was kind enough to offer her help to me, upon your agreement, of course.'

Charles chuckled with the genuine good will of the comfortable married man. 'I don't have a thing to do with it,' he confessed as he secured the fishing-poles to the horses. 'If Amelia wants to go to London, she will—with or without me.'

'Are you planning to come along, then, Charles? How dull it shall be for you here.'

'Shan't be so dull. I'll go to Kemble's. He invited me some time ago. Since Amelia will be busy in London, I see no reason why I can't amuse myself for a week or two. Kemble's got a new stable of Arabians. Plans to breed them himself.'

'Of course, London would be boring for Charles,' Amelia confided to Thea later that afternoon as she worked on her stitchery in the sitting-room. 'He will enjoy himself more talking of horses with Kemble.' She put down her tambour frame. 'And he is certainly entitled to some enjoyment, having endured both Miss Beaseley and Mrs Chester so heroically.'

Amelia inspected her needlework and shook her head. 'Good heavens. I can't have sewn that!'

'Where is Miss Beaseley?' Thea asked, looking on as Amelia methodically ripped out her hour's work. 'And how is she?' Miss Beaseley had not appeared for lunch.

'She is recovering from the trauma of fish,' Amelia said, making a face. 'Her aunt thinks she'll be prostrate for a week.'

'A week? Oh, no.'

'That's what I said,' Amelia confessed. 'For what can we do with her in a sickbed? And we can't go to London while she is ill, for that would look odd. Not that the two of us are so close to her, but she is Emery's betrothed unless he has recovered his senses. And I can't think what possessed him to take the creature fishing. He must have known what would result.' She came to a bemused halt as Emery strode into the sitting-room.

'Amelia? I beg pardon.' He drew himself up. 'I don't mean to intrude on you and Thea.'

'You aren't intruding,' Amelia replied. 'And you can answer a question for us. What the devil possessed you to take Miss Beaseley fishing today?'

Emery met her eyes blandly. 'She voiced an interest in the sport.'

Lady Marlow's reaction was short and to the point: 'Fiddle!'

Even Thea was bound to look askance at such an out-and-out whisker.

'Well, perhaps she didn't say so in so many words,' Emery amended with a deprecating laugh. 'But she did say she wished to accompany me wherever I went. And since I planned to go fishing, I thought she might like to come along.'

'Knowing full well what would result,' Thea said.

He shot her a look of reproach. 'My dear Miss Campion, I am no gypsy fortune-teller.'

'What fustian! You knew very well that Miss Beaseley would fly into a fit at the first sign of a fish.'

He took exception to this ringing indictment. 'A fit? On my word as a gentleman, no. I had no notion she was prone to hysteria, although I should have suspected it. She always did overplay her emotions.'

Amelia sighed. 'Hadrian, you are incorrigible. What sort of game are you running?'

'I haven't the faintest idea of what you are speaking about, Amelia,' her brother said innocently.

The following morning Miss Beaseley suddenly announced that she was stricken with homesickness, and despite Emery's earnest entreaties to stay and fish another day, she departed with her aunt for London.

Emery saw them off that morning and returned chuckling into the parlour, where he faced Amelia.

'Now I see what you had in mind,' she murmured.

'Did you want them here for the summer?' he countered.

She blenched. 'Good gracious, no. I just hope they don't think us unfeeling. Perhaps I should have entreated them to stay instead of packing off a basket of goodies for them to enjoy on the way to London. You don't think it was coming of me?' she asked with a worried frown.

'Coming?' Emery scoffed. 'Don't be a pea goose. It was charitable. You wouldn't wish them to starve, would you?'

'That's not what I mean. And well you know it.' She sighed. 'In any case, I'll see them in London myself and make amends there.'

Emery frowned. Her words reminded him of her plan to leave Wiltshire with Thea. 'Just when do you depart, Amelia?'

'As soon as I have made certain that there are enough provisions for you and Charles. That reminds me. I should speak to Hopkins on that.' Before carrying out this task, however, she paused to ask how long a stay her brother planned.

The viscount frowned. 'I don't really know. I must resolve certain matters before I move on.' He answered the question in her eyes with two words: 'Sir Percy.'

'Poor Hadrian. It still vexes you, doesn't it?'

'More than I could tell you. Does my staying here impose on your hospitality?'

Amelia dismissed this idea at once. 'Heavens, no. I just wanted to know what to tell the servants. You are welcome here as long as you wish.' With that she went off, her own mind preoccupied with preparations for her London removal. There was Hopkins to instruct, servants to despatch to prepare the London residence in Hill Street, and also the matter of the most propitious departure date.

Jonathon was eager to set off at once, but the three of them finally agreed to depart on Wednesday, two days hence, which gave them time to attend to the inevitable last-minute difficulties that would arise.

As Wednesday approached, mixed feelings descended on Thea. On one hand she was eager to see London and all the sights it boasted. On the other hand she was strangely reluctant to leave Wiltshire. This she could not comprehend. She had never been that enamoured of country life.

On Tuesday she rode to her uncle's to say farewell and found him, predictably enough, in his study.

'I do apologise for not seeing more of you, Uncle Andrew,' she said as she sat down on the library couch. 'I can't think how time has flown by.'

'Stands to reason,' he said with a laugh. 'A young lady like you has more things to be entertained by than an old man.'

Her green eyes were warm with laughter. 'You're not in your dotage yet, nor on your deathbed. And if you ever claim the latter, I shall despatch Mrs Chester to you.'

He let out a bleat of alarm. 'If you dare, I shan't speak to you again!'

She patted his hand. 'Where is Jonathon?'

'Having a carriage lesson.'

'Not with young Gaylord, I hope!'

Her uncle snorted. 'No. With Emery.'

'Has he started to teach Jonathon the reins?' Thea asked, astonished, for the viscount had said nothing of it to her.

'They started last week,' Mr Campion replied. 'He claimed that Jonathon has a sure pair of hands.'

'Emery is kind to take such an interest in Jonathon,' Thea mused.

Her uncle grunted and tapped his fingertips together. 'If it were any other man I would think he was trying to fix an interest in someone besides young Jonathon.'

She blushed slightly as he gazed quizzingly at her. 'Now, Uncle Andrew, do give up such an absurd notion. The viscount merely has a liking for Jonathon.'

'That might explain the driving lesson,' her uncle agreed, 'but not the letters of introduction he wrote to several of his London cronies, which he gave to Jonathon. I don't need to tell you what a compliment that is.'

'No, indeed,' Thea murmured, overcome by such generosity.

'I like him, Thea,' her uncle went on, his eyes fixed on his bust of Aristotle. 'And you know full well there aren't that many people in the world I'd say that about.'

She gave an affectionate laugh. 'Your opinion on mankind is well known, Uncle Andrew.'

'Then just a word of warning. Don't let him slip out of your grasp.'

'Uncle Andrew,' she protested, flushing a little. 'You are mistaken if you think there is anything between Emery and me. He is merely being kind to one of his sister's friends.'

'I have a sister,' Mr Campion informed her tartly, 'and I don't ever recall being that kind to any of her friends.'

Observing his niece's discomfiture, however, he said no more on that topic. Instead he dipped into his desk drawer and handed her a bank draft, the sum of which took her breath away.

'Uncle Andrew, this is far too much!'

'You'll be taking Jonathon about. That will cost money.'

'Yes, I know, and half this amount will do nicely. I have my own money for my own needs.'

'That will not last long once you reach London,' he warned. 'Fancy gowns and gloves aren't dagger cheap.'

'Perhaps not, but I can't take money from you. You have already been more than generous to me.'

'I owe it to you, Thea. Your father woefully wronged your mother. I blame myself. I knew the sort he was with a female and should have warned her. I didn't say a word. I've regretted that to this day.'

'You could have been wrong,' Thea pointed out, touched by his admission. 'In all probability Mama wouldn't have believed you. She was terribly headstrong herself. Nearly as bad as Papa.'

'Take the money, Thea,' her uncle urged. Since he would have been offended if she continued to refuse, she reluctantly agreed.

'I shall take good care of Jonathon,' she promised at the door.

'I know you will.' He had her hand in his. 'Thea, I hate to interfere in what doesn't concern me, and I rarely give advice...'

'Are you about to warn me about the dens of iniquity that London is rife with?' she asked with a chuckle. 'I promise not to be lured into them.'

'No,' he smiled. 'It's an entirely different matter. Marriage.'

'Marriage?' She glanced up at his angular face. 'I think Cousin Jonathon a trifle young to be thinking of a match, but if you wish me to keep my eyes out for a suitable young lady...'

'I'm not speaking of Jonathon's marriage, but yours.'

'Mine!' She stared at him, flabbergasted. 'Uncle Andrew, I have no plans for marriage.'

'That's just what has me worried. I don't mean to poke my nose into what doesn't concern me, so I'll just say this. Don't let your parents' marriage sour you on the entire institution,' he said, then kissed her on the cheek. 'Remember that.'

'I shall,' she promised.

As she rode back to Chumley Field, Thea found herself mulling over her uncle's words. Dear Uncle Andrew! She had never known him to bestir himself to offer advice on anyone's romantic affairs before. Certainly the matter must be of enough importance to cause him to abandon his usual reticence in speaking of such personal matters. And at least there was no mistaking his opinion of Emery.

But then, most people she knew did like Emery. She gave her horse a gentle nudge, still thinking of her uncle's advice. He was wrong about one thing. She did think of marriage occasionally. As a guest of Amelia's, she would have to be blind not to see Charles's obvious devotion. Ordinarily Thea did not boast a jealous bone in her body, but at times, watching Amelia and Charles exchange smiles across the room, she had felt a pang of envy. Not that she fancied Charles as a husband for herself!

The thought of that brought a smile to her lips. Still, there was something uplifting about a marriage as happy as the Marlows', which made one optimistic. Perhaps one's own marriage might be as successful. And Thea was obliged to acknowledge as she made the turn towards Chumley Field that she was not as adamantly opposed to the institution as the day she had arrived at Amelia's with Emery.

Without Miss Beaseley and her harp, the household at Chumley Field had returned to a tranquil state after the dinner hour. On Tuesday evening, the last they would spend together in Wiltshire, Thea consented to a few hands of whist, but soon found her mind wandering.

'I seem to have turned into as poor a card-player as Miss Beaseley was,' she apologised when the play concluded an hour later.

'My dear, no one can be that!' Amelia protested, stifling an enormous yawn. 'I am off to bed. It will be a long day ahead of us tomorrow,' she reminded her friend. 'Will you be coming up, Charles?'

Lord Marlow agreed that he was fagged to death and followed her up the stairs, leaving Emery and Thea momentarily alone in the card-room. For a while neither seemed inclined to speak.

'My uncle says that you have been kind enough to furnish Jonathon with letters of introduction to your friends,' Thea said, breaking the silence. 'That's so good of you. I do thank you for it.'

'Amelia could have done as well, but I thought since he is a male, the patronage of a male would go further in opening certain doors. Jonathon is a good sort of fellow. I'm certain he'll come to no mischief in London. My friends will be there to assist him and you until I can get there myself.'

She looked up, startled. 'Do you plan to come to London, then?' she asked, wondering why the answer should matter so much to her furiously beating heart.

'Eventually, yes,' he told her.

'But I thought you and Charles were going to Lord Kemble's.'

He shook his head. 'I shall stay on here for a short time until I can solve a few matters that have plagued me.'

She hazarded a guess. 'Matters having to do with Sir Percy?'

He nodded. 'As long as I'm thought in Percy's debt, I shan't rest easy. And it's no good telling me I'm not in his debt truly. Just having him think and believe it is beyond bearing. I shall have to settle the whole muddle before I leave Wiltshire, even if I'm here all summer.'

'I wish you luck, then,' she murmured, wondering if she would see him in London after all.

'And I wish you much enjoyment in London. That reminds me.' He thrust a hand into his coat pocket and extracted a small box. 'This is for you. A going-away present.'

'Emery,' she protested, 'there was no call for that.'

'Open it,' he urged.

Obediently she lifted the top of the box and found herself looking down at two white balls of cotton. 'Cotton?' she asked, raising perplexed eyes to his face.

'Yes,' he said, taking the box from her and demonstrating the proper use of his gift by putting them in his ears. 'When you take in Daughtery's speech in Parliament you must be prepared.'

She gurgled with laughter at the sight of him with the cotton sticking out of his ears. 'Just because the earl takes his duties seriously is no reason to mock him,' she said severely.

He took the cotton balls out and gave them back to her. 'My dear Thea, I take my duties seriously, too. I have given speeches in Parliament myself.'

'Have you really?' she asked, much diverted. 'Whenever did you find the time, what with your trips to the tailor, Gentleman Jack's, Manton's shooting gallery...?'

'You do think me a fribble, don't you?' he asked, giving a sad shake of his head.

'Oh, I don't think you a fribble at all,' she denied. 'But Miss Beaseley did say you were one of the leading figures of the ton and one of the prizes on the Marriage Mart!' She yawned slightly. 'Good heavens, I am a sleepyhead. I have an early rising ahead of me tomorrow. I bid you good night, Emery. Thank you for the cotton.'

'Wear it in good health,' he said.

Hopkins, coming in to clear the card table a little later, was surprised to see the viscount still slumped in a chair. The butler, wise in the ways of the Quality he served, tiptoed out, for it was plain by the look on the viscount's face that he did not wish to be disturbed.

CHAPTER TWELVE

THE REMOVAL of Thea and Amelia to London passed without incident. Lady Marlow had had the keen foresight to send her servants on ahead to open up her residence in Hill Street, where the three of them would be residing, thus sparing Mr Campion the considerable expense of opening up the family house, which had not been used in years. On their arrival, the three travellers, stained and weary from their day on the road, were most appreciative of the soothing comforts of a hot bath and hot supper.

Thea toppled happily into the bed in the chamber she had been given, worn to the bone. She was excited at being in London, and yet she felt regret that Emery was forced to remain behind in Wiltshire. She had always considered herself to have no serious interest in marriage. However, ever since she had met Amelia's brother, thoughts of marriage had flitted into her mind to tease her.

She shook off such thoughts now. Emery was as good as betrothed to Miss Beaseley. She closed her eyes and slept, but it seemed that no sooner had she dropped her head on the pillow than the curtains about the four-poster were being ruthlessly thrust aside by none other than Lady Marlow herself.

'Come, come, Thea,' she adjured, briskly clapping her hands. 'It's morning.'

Muffling a groan, Thea closed her eyes, the better to ward off the harsh rays of the sun, and dug deeper into the bedding.

'Now, none of that,' Amelia said, pulling down the coverlet. 'Jonathon has been up since dawn. I had all I could do to persuade him not to come in and wake you himself.'

'What time is it?' Thea demanded as Amelia wrestled a pillow from her.

'Nine o'clock.'

'Nine?' Thea grimaced. 'I thought no one ever rose before eleven in the city.'

'Quite true,' Amelia acknowledged. 'And we shall undoubtedly have occasion to sleep much later some other days, but not today. There is too much to plan and do. Jonathon is already chafing at the bit to get to Tattersall's and Gentleman Jack's, which are forbidden to those of our sex. I had to persuade him to wait until I could introduce him to some of Emery's friends, who would take him about. If he did venture into Tattersall's alone they would spot him at once as a green one and take advantage of him.'

She became aware that her musings on Jonathon had allowed her guest to once again fall back on to the bed, and lost no time in rousing her swiftly.

Bowing to the inevitable, Thea rose, still protesting that she was so sleepy she could be of little help in planning anything. But the day proved to be planned for them after a light breakfast. First and foremost was a morning call on Madame Fanchon's, who eyed and measured Thea until she felt a veritable country dowd in her pale green muslin frock, which had seemed just the thing back in Vienna. Just as she felt one more measurement would drive her mad, Fanchon announced that the ballgowns mademoiselle needed would be supplied at once.

Thea was too relieved escaping from the hands of the French modiste to object to the order, but later in the carriage with Jonathon and Amelia she voiced her qualms.

'Do I really need new ballgowns?' she asked. 'I have several that have scarcely been worn.'

'Of course you need new gowns,' Amelia said, looking scandalised. 'At least a dozen to start with.'

'A dozen?' Thea exclaimed, settling in against the velvet squabs. She had no doubt that Fanchon would be frightfully expensive. She felt glad that she had her uncle's draft to help pay the expense.

Gowns, she discovered, were only the beginning. Hats, gloves, shoes, sandals and reticules all had to be examined and accepted or rejected. Jonathon's needs were not forgotten either. He was soon deposited in the hands of Mr Weston, Mr Locke and Mr Hoby to be fitted with everything a young gentleman from the country might need.

While Jonathon occupied himself with these good men, Amelia pressed on with Thea on a round of calls to several acquaintances. Thea would much rather not have met anyone on this, her very first day in London, for she was still feeling the ill effects of her travels, but she did her best, smiling brightly at each hostess and leaving most of the conversation to Amelia.

'No more, Amelia,' she pleaded as they completed their fourth call. 'My head already swims with names. I only pray I shall remember half of them.'

'You needn't worry about any of them,' Amelia answered, drawing on her gloves and giving the order to her groom to set out again. 'Constance and Letitia are old friends. The only name and face you need remember is still ahead of us. Lady Jersey.'

'Lady Jersey?' Thea checked her protest, remembering Emery's description of the powerful patroness, which piqued her interest.

She was pleasantly surprised to find Lady Jersey small and spare with an inquisitive nature that was cloaked in kindness. Her nickname, Silence, Amelia revealed earlier, had come from her inability to stop speaking for any length of time.

'How is your brother, Emery?' Lady Jersey asked Amelia as they sat now in her Green Drawing Room. 'Is it true he has become betrothed to Miss Beaseley? No more than a schoolroom miss, I would have called her, for all her prettiness. What can he be thinking of? But such is always the case with hardened bachelors.' Her purple turban bobbed emphatically.

'Emery makes up his own mind, Sally,' Amelia said, not put out in the least by this frank airing of opinions. 'You should know that by now.'

'Lud, how could I forget?' Lady Jersey laughed and turned to Thea. 'I once tried to get him to be civil to a certain young lady in order to please her mama, who was a bosom bow. He turned as sulky as a bear.'

'Perhaps he just didn't wish to raise expectation,' Thea murmured.

'Perhaps.' Lady Jersey conceded this point with another bob of her turban. 'Hadrian is a good sort, which makes me wonder even more about Miss Beaseley. The chit is a ninnyhammer. He'll be bored within a week, and if he doesn't realise that, I shall tell him so when next we meet.' Having successfully concluded this discussion, she turned to a new topic. 'So you are from Vienna, Miss Campion.'

'Yes.'

'I have always wished to visit that city. They say it is so pretty.' A wistful note entered the patroness's usually sure voice. 'Of course, that would have been impossible earlier with that monster Bonaparte still roaming at will. Nothing would have induced me to go to the Continent then.'

'You would enjoy it now, ma'am,' Thea replied. 'Napoleon is exiled to his island.'

'He escaped once before,' Lady Jersey reminded them with a shake of her head. 'Napoleon and islands don't seem to mix.' She leaned back in her gilded curricle chair. 'Now then, Miss Campion, you must tell me all about Vienna. Is it true that the waltz danced here is nothing compared to the way the Viennese do it?'

The remainder of the visit passed with the patroness quizzing Thea about life in Vienna and ended with her anticipation of seeing her next Wednesday night at Almack's.

Amelia coughed discreetly. 'We'd love to, Sally, but Thea has just arrived in London. She hasn't received vouchers yet.'

'What? The vouchers? The merest trifle. I shall send them round tomorrow for you and also for that cousin of yours.'

'Vouchers on the first day! That's almost unheard-of,' Amelia said gleefully as they left the Jersey residence. 'Your success is a *fait accompli*.'

Thea swept the folds of her green walking-dress up as she settled herself back into the carriage. 'My success, Amelia?' She eyed her friend. 'I assure you my visit to London is strictly my uncle's wish. I've no interest in finding a husband.'

'You may change your mind once you have a taste of London.'

'I'd liefer a taste of food. I'm famished! Have you no plan for eating?' she enquired, and was relieved when Amelia guiltily gave the order to the groom to return to Hill Street, where they could partake of a hearty luncheon.

The rest of that first week flew by in a riot of calls on glovers, shoemakers and milliners. Thea barely had a chance to sit down and write a letter to her uncle assuring him of their safe arrival in London before she was whisked off on a call or, as became more frequent as they went about the town, entertained callers of her own.

As for Jonathon, he was in a high fettle, having found several agreeable young friends through his patronage of Mr Locke and Mr Hoby. These young men proved as horse-mad as young Jonathon, and together they passed a good many hours at Tattersall's. Since Jonathon was a sensible sort, Thea did not worry too much that he might fall into the briars.

As promised, Fanchon produced a ballgown of stunning sapphire blue, trimmed in lace about the hem, with jaconet sleeves. As Thea was helped into it on Wednesday evening by Maria, one of Amelia's servants, she gazed at her reflection in the mirror. She felt a trifle giddy at what was about to take place.

'Oh, miss, you look splendid,' Maria squealed, her plump cheeks beaming in honest pleasure. 'You're certain to take the wind out of any beauty's sails.'

Thea laughed, but she felt rather pleased at the effect herself. 'You will turn my head with such talk, Maria,' she said, sitting down to allow the maid to dress her hair in the beguiling *à l'anglaise* that she favoured. When that was done she went off in search of Amelia, who was just finishing her own toilette.

'My dear, you look splendid,' Amelia said, looking quite the thing herself in a youthful emerald-green satin.

'Fanchon's gown...'

'No, it is not the gown,' Amelia corrected gently. 'It's you. Now then, we mustn't be too late or too early,' she admonished, drawing about her the folds of her paisley shawl and searching for her fan. 'Where is Jonathon?'

The two ladies found Jonathon waiting belowstairs, looking the very epitome of male good taste in a white frilled shirt, black swallowtail, and a cravat that seemed in Thea's mind far too intricate for one so young. But since Jonathon seemed pleased with his efforts, she forbore comment.

Jonathon had also furnished himself with a snuff-box, explaining to Thea and Amelia once they were under way in the carriage that while he knew his father would deplore such a habit, it was *de rigueur* in London circles.

'So it seems,' Thea acknowledged as he punctuated his words by inhaling a generous pinch, a deed that sparked a quick and violent sneezing fit. 'But I do think you might try to inhale less vigorously, Jonathon,' she admonished.

'And you might try to avoid spilling it,' Amelia added as he wiped his watering eyes. 'Did you buy that snuff-box yourself? It looks to be a Sevres.'

'Edward lent it to me,' Jonathon said, speaking of Mr Edward Carlyle, one of his new cronies. 'He also chose the mixture for me at the Berry Brothers. I thought it a trifle dry myself, but at least it doesn't reek of Otto of Roses the way some others do!'

Thea's eyes met Amelia's in amusement. Jonathon was picking up ton ways faster than either of them could have predicted. 'Did young Edward also teach you to tie that cravat?' Thea quizzed.

'Well, I had to have something special for my first appearance at Almack's!' Jonathon exclaimed.

'It certainly is that,' Amelia murmured under her breath to Thea.

'I couldn't make my appearance in anything so ordinary as the Mathematical or Oriental,' Jonathon went on with crushing pretension.

'No, indeed,' Amelia agreed. 'But pray enlighten me. What is that configuration called? Or does it have a name?'

'Edward calls it the *Trône d'Amour*.'

'Ah yes, I have heard of it. But isn't it frightfully complicated?'

He looked pleased by her comment. 'Not once you know how to do it,' he said, giving his cravat a fond pat.

The two ladies hid their smiles as Jonathon seemed to take their admiration for granted. In no time at all they reached King Street and were at Almack's Assembly Rooms.

So this is the Marriage Mart, she thought as Emery's caustic words returned to mind.

They passed elegantly-gowned beauties and gentlemen with cravats even more complicated than young Jonathon's.

Lady Jersey was in attendance this evening, and she greeted them kindly and made them known to the other patroness present, Lady Sefton, whose good humour even withstood Jonathon spilling snuff all about himself.

Once in the Assembly Rooms, Thea was besieged with requests for dances. Mr Clarence Arbuthnot, thanks to a nodding acquaintance with Lady Marlow, was first to lead her out for the opening set, followed quickly by the Marquis of Carvey, a distinguished-looking man with a mama prone to invalidism. No sooner had Thea murmured her thanks to the marquis than she was set upon by Daughtery, a late arrival at Almack's.

The earl had seen her dancing with the marquis and squirreled her off to the refreshment-room, looking rather put out that she had not informed him of her arrival in London.

'After all,' he said, passing her a glass of lemonade, 'I thought we were old friends.'

'I didn't know where precisely you resided,' she informed him. 'And I did think it might be *de trop* for a female such as myself to go calling on a gentleman. People would be bound to talk and might think me a veritable hussy, which I'm sure you didn't wish to happen.'

'Good God, no,' he said, reacting sharply to this picture she had sketched.

'And,' she continued blithely, 'I knew that sooner or later our paths would cross in London, as in fact they have.'

'Yes, and nothing could be more provident, for tomorrow I shall speak.'

'Speak?' She looked at him uneasily over the rim of her glass.

'Parliament,' he explained with a happy smile. 'We plan to discuss the Regent's fiscal affairs tomorrow.'

'Oh, are you? How intriguing.'

This, she realised too late, was exactly the wrong thing to say to the earl, for he thereupon launched into a vigorous rehearsal of what he would say, including an indictment of Prinny and his habits of waste, detailing his views on the matter with considerable passion until he was interrupted by Captain Blaine.

'Denis, do you have no manners?' the captain quizzed. 'Boring a lady to death, and in public, too.'

The earl frowned at his brother's jest. 'I thought you weren't coming to Almack's tonight, Henry.'

'I changed my mind, fortunately for Miss Campion, who is too polite to tell you to go away. So I shall perform that deed for her.'

'Now, see here...' the earl retorted.

'Are you spoken for the waltz now under way, Miss Campion?' the captain asked, ignoring the earl.

Before she could speak, Daughtery did. 'I haven't danced with Miss Campion yet,' he pointed out heatedly.

'Small wonder,' his brother laughed. 'But you had the opportunity to ask her instead of boring her to death.'

The earl bridled. 'I wasn't boring her to death!'

'We shall let Miss Campion decide between us, just as she did in Wiltshire.'

'Oh, heavens,' Thea murmured, envisioning yet another evening of coin-tossing ahead of her, and this time in full view of London society. Unfortunately there was neither Emery nor her uncle to rescue her from the dilemma.

'I shall dance with you, Captain Blaine, since you asked me first,' she said now. 'And you,' she said, turning to the earl, who looked on the verge of a protest, 'shall have the one immediately following.' Hoping this would satisfy them both, she then gave her hand to the captain, who led her out with a triumphant glance at his brother.

CHAPTER THIRTEEN

LADY JERSEY had expressed the wish that Thea waltz at Almack's and show Londoners just how the Viennese performed it. Unfortunately the captain danced to a beat quite different from the three-four time that Mr Strauss's music dictated. Thea finally gave up trying to waltz and surrendered to following him about the room.

'Now that you are in London,' he told her as he marched up first one side of the room and then the other, 'we must have that ride in the park you promised me. Is Friday afternoon too soon?'

'Not at all. Friday is fine.' And they set the time for him to call at five o'clock at Hill Street.

'Are you really going to Parliament to hear Denis prattle?' he queried next.

'I'm not certain,' she said, hopeful that this might slip the earl's mind. But during the quadrille that followed the waltz, Thea discovered that Daughtery had not forgotten about her proposed visit to Parliament.

'It's essential for any visitor to London,' he pointed out.

Thinking that it would perhaps be best to have the deed over and done with rather than attempt to escape from it throughout her stay, she finally agreed to spend the following afternoon listening to him in Parliament.

'That is, if Amelia will allow me use of her carriage.'

The earl beamed. 'There is no necessity to wait on Lady Marlow,' he told her. 'I shall be happy to send a vehicle for you.'

'May I bring her with me?'

The earl beamed even more. 'The more the merrier,' he exclaimed, and went off looking as pleased as Punch.

Lady Marlow, observing such signs, made a beeline at once for Thea, demanding to know if Daughtery had popped the question.

Thea replied with the giggles. 'Amelia, don't be absurd!'

'Can you blame me,' Lady Marlow demanded, 'with Daughtery so puffed in the face? He is pleased about something,' she said, and directed an enquiring look at her friend.

'I told him I shall listen to his speech tomorrow at Parliament.'

Amelia recoiled in the liveliest horror. 'Thea, you *didn't*!'

Thea laughed. 'It won't be so bad.'

'My poor, poor child. You have no idea of the dreariness awaiting you.'

'No?' Thea's eyes danced. 'You shall have to advise me, for I accepted on your behalf.'

Amelia shrieked. 'On my behalf! That is *impossible*. I can't go.'

'Amelia, for two hours...'

'No, my dear, not tomorrow afternoon. I have pressing business with Lady Hunterford. She wanted me to supervise her daughter's come-out next season.'

Thea accepted this loss philosophically. 'Then Cousin Jonathon will just have to come in your stead.' She was suddenly stricken by conscience. 'Where is he? I haven't been keeping an eye on him. I do hope he hasn't fallen into the briars.'

'Not since I told him to leave his snuff-box in his pocket,' Amelia said with some acerbity. 'He spilled half its contents on no fewer than three females. Ah, there he is in the corner with young Edward, no doubt talking of cravats and horses and the stupid things gentlemen do talk of.'

'What a scorching indictment of my sex, Amelia,' a voice responded, and Thea turned along with Amelia to behold a tall, redheaded gentleman bowing at them both. Amelia let out a squeal of delight.

'Jason!' He kissed her affectionately on the cheek. 'I didn't know you were coming to Almack's.'

'If you had, would you have spoken more kindly about males?' he quizzed. 'I don't believe I know your charming friend.'

'Then you should,' Amelia said forthrightly. 'This is Miss Theodora Campion. Thea, meet Mr Jason Ludlow. Jason,' she explained further, 'is one of Hadrian's oldest friends.'

This comment sparked a grimace from Mr Ludlow. 'Not old, Amelia,' he protested. 'You make me sound like Methuselah.'

She laughed, and he smiled back at her. Thea, watching them, could not help noticing that his figure was slender but well proportioned, and his mouth had a good-humoured set about it.

'I'm happy to meet you, whatever the case,' Thea said now.

'Perhaps you won't be so happy when I say you might blame me for your cousin Jonathon's descent into sartorial splendour.'

Thea laughed. 'What do you mean? Why should I blame you?'

'Emery had written asking me to introduce young Jonathon about if our paths crossed. During our first visit to Tattersall's I introduced him to young Edward's set, and they have taken it upon themselves to transform Jonathon into a tulip. I hope he has the good sense to resist the temptation.'

'They are young yet,' Amelia pointed out forgivingly, 'and are still trying their wings.'

'Colourful wings,' Jason corrected. 'Have either of you seen Edward's cravat yet? An eye-blinding violet.'

'Too harsh, Jason,' Lady Marlow asserted. 'I recollect that you and Hadrian dressed as wildly in your youth. I am your senior, loath though I am to recall that to anyone's mind, and can vividly recall your youthful excesses as though it were yesterday.'

'I never wore a cravat like the specimen about Edward's neck,' Jason protested.

'No,' Amelia agreed, smiling before she applied the facer, 'you were more preoccupied, as I recall, with powdering your hair.'

'Amelia!' Mr Ludlow protested as Thea tried to stifle her giggles.

'Did he really?' she asked Amelia.

'To be sure, he did—along with Hadrian, of course. And the two of them spilled nearly as much powder on their hair as Jonathon has spilled his snuff.'

'Amelia, do keep your voice down,' Jason implored. 'Perhaps I ought to pay you to forget the follies of my youth.'

'The only payment you may afford me is to do something useful like waltz with Thea before those lummoxes Daughtery and Blaine corner her yet again.'

'An excellent notion,' he agreed, and promptly offered his arm to Thea, who was not displeased by the idea of dancing with him.

Thea had danced earlier, but a world of difference lay between those partners and her current one. Jason waltzed with all the skill and grace lacking in Captain Blaine, and Thea gave in to the sheer pleasure of Mr Strauss's music, leading Lady Jersey to observe to Lady Sefton that Miss Campion waltzed divinely—an opinion shared by enough people that the floor about them soon cleared. So involved was Thea in the music that it took several passes about the room before she realised that the two of them had been granted the entire floor by the others.

'No one else is dancing,' she whispered to Jason.

He lifted his head and glanced to his right and then to his left. 'So I see. They are giving you the floor. It's quite an honour.'

'It's one I could do without,' she said vehemently. 'What should I do if I stumble or miss a step?'

'Merely pretend it is a new step you've just invented,' he suggested blithely, 'or an import from Vienna.'

Her green eyes laughed up at him. 'Turn the miscue into an advantage?'

'More or less.'

Fortunately this was not necessary, for the waltz concluded with neither of them making a mistake. The applause that burst out in the ballroom made even Jason flush slightly, and Lady Jersey herself soon descended on them, clucking compliments.

'That was superb, my dears,' she said. The ostrich feather that adorned her crimson turban tickled Thea's cheek. 'You cast all the other dancers into the shade, my dear.'

'It was not all my doing,' Thea protested. 'My partner...'

'There is plenty of credit to go round,' the patroness said. She stared at the two of them for a moment. 'How very striking the two of you look together. It must be that red hair.'

'Shall we have some refreshment?' Jason asked after the patroness had gone off. 'The waltz left me with a dry throat.'

'I had some lemonade earlier,' Thea confessed, 'and it was as sour as Emery warned me it would be. He claimed the cakes would be stale, too.'

'Fortunately there is no way to spoil champagne,' he pointed out as he led her into the refreshment-room and procured two glasses for them.

She sipped it and stood with him as the guests, warmed by their exertions, flitted in and out. Above them the great chandelier swayed momentarily.

'Emery was right,' Jason said now, looking at her with a bemused expression in his eyes.

Thea turned towards him. 'Are the cakes stale, then? I would think they could offer better refreshments.'

Mr Ludlow laughed. 'I wasn't speaking of the refreshments, although the cake is stale right enough. I was merely reflecting that Emery was right about you.'

'About me?' she asked, eyes widening.

'Yes. He called you an uncommonly good-looking female. Not just in the ordinary mode. He was right.'

'Good heavens.' She spoke in astonished accents. 'Is Emery in the habit of conferring with you regarding every female he meets?'

'On the contrary,' Jason said, unperturbed. 'A closed-mouth sort, that's our Hadrian. That's what made me even more curious to meet you.'

She sipped her champagne slowly. 'Just how did the viscount tell you about me?' she asked.

'In a letter.'

'How curious. Emery never struck me as the type who would exchange letters with friends.'

'I should rather have said, in a letter of introduction that he furnished to your cousin. He added a postscript to me that you, Miss Theodora Campion, were a charming young female and he would be grateful if I kept an eye out for you until he returned to London.'

A look of mild vexation appeared in her eyes. 'I don't need a chaperon during my stay!' she ejaculated.

'Good. For I would make an odd chaperon for you!'

Laughingly, she agreed that he did not fit anyone's idea of a chaperon. But he did suit her notion of a gentleman, a view evidently shared by many females present in the Assembly Rooms. The lures that were cast his way were so numerous—and a few so audacious—that Thea blushed for her sex. She later voiced her opinion to Amelia.

'Oh, this is next to nothing,' Amelia retorted.

'Next to nothing?' Thea repeated incredulously. 'I vow one female nearly pushed Jason down into the chair next to her.'

Amelia looked diverted. 'I must have missed that. But there's been far worse, I do assure you. Only think of Caro Lamb and the way she went after poor Byron, not that he wasn't to blame for urging her on. But one couldn't in all fairness say that he did it all alone.'

A wry smile curved Thea's lips. 'I hardly put Mr Ludlow in the same category as Byron.'

'Very true,' Amelia acknowledged. 'Jason, I vow, could not compose a sonnet if his life depended on it. But he is the kindest creature. What do you think of him?'

'He certainly seems amiable enough,' Thea said, wondering what lay behind her friend's innocent question.

'And talented,' Amelia went on. 'He is also a member of the Four Horse Club, a favourite of Gentleman Jack's, and quite lucky during his play at White's and Watier's. Not that he is hard pressed for money. He has several handsome estates in Kent as well as an income annually of over twenty thousand pounds.'

Thea's eyes brimmed with laughter. 'Amelia, do you realise what you are saying?'

Lady Marlow blushed, but only for a moment. 'I know you shall say it is idiotish, but the two of you did look just the thing dancing together. And since you are in London, it can't hurt to be better acquainted with eligible men such as Jason. I know you detest the entire topic of marriage,' Amelia put in hastily, 'but Jason is a good sort.'

'I'm sure he is,' Thea murmured. 'And I don't detest marriage.'

Amelia laid a hand on her friend's forehead. 'You're not ill, are you?'

Thea's quick laughter bubbled up. 'Amelia!'

'I beg pardon, but I'm all agog. You are the same Miss Campion who once called marriage a torture chamber, are you not?'

'I never said such a thing,' Thea denied. 'I merely said I could not fathom why any sensible female would voluntarily submit to such an arrangement!'

'It amounts to the same thing,' Amelia informed her. She darted a quick look at Thea. 'Do you mean to say that now you do know why a sensible female might wish to marry?'

'The institution is not without some attractions,' Thea said, wondering what her old friend would say if she knew that she had been indulging in frequent air dreams of late of herself married to a suitable mate, and that that suitable mate had begun to bear an alarming resemblance to a certain male they both knew so well.

Lady Marlow had no further opportunity to delve into Thea's apparent change of heart with regard to matrimony, for she was being accosted by Miss Beaseley, a late arrival.

'Dear Lady Marlow, my future sister!' Miss Beaseley greeted her with an embrace. Lady Marlow shuddered, but she managed to return the embrace.

'I am overjoyed to see you in London,' Miss Beaseley went on. 'My parents are back now. Nothing could be more congenial than for you to meet them. Perhaps a small rout party? My mother was suggesting that just the other day.'

'How kind of her,' Amelia said hastily. 'But Hadrian hasn't arrived yet.'

'No, but you are here. And since you are his sister, I thought a small party.'

'No, no. We must wait on Emery,' Lady Marlow insisted, fanning herself about the face. 'It would be fatal to upstage him. He's bound to get in the mopes over it.'

Miss Beaseley appeared stricken at the thought of her viscount in the mopes. 'I shouldn't like that,' she said now. 'I confess that he has the most thunderous look when he is vexed. It sometimes puts me into a quake.'

'It shouldn't,' Thea said, her face reflective. 'Most gentlemen get that way now and then. The thing you must do with Emery in the hips is to laugh at him.'

Miss Beaseley stared at her in fascinated horror. 'Laugh at Emery? What a curious remedy.'

'It makes perfect sense to me,' Thea divulged. 'You can't help it if he's vexed. And there's no need for him to foist his ill temper on you. So it's best to keep your sense of humour.'

'But I couldn't laugh at Emery,' Miss Beaseley said, looking as though Thea had advised her to disrobe in the ballroom. 'I wouldn't dare.' She turned to Amelia, who had been following this conversation with avid interest. 'Perhaps if you think it best to wait to introduce my family to you until Emery arrives, I'll postpone the party. When will he be back?'

'Who can say?' Amelia replied, shrugging a shoulder. 'When the whim strikes, he shall return. And now you must forgive me, the two of you, but I simply must have a word with Maria Sefton.' So saying, she darted off in the general direction of the patroness.

A little puzzled by her friend's errant behaviour, Thea found her attention demanded the next moment by her cousin, who came up looking aggrieved.

'Thea,' he said with an outraged air, 'what is this I hear about you promising to bring me to Parliament tomorrow to hear a speech by Daughtery?'

'How did you get wind of that?' she asked reproachfully. 'I had planned to broach the idea to you gently.'

'Gently or not, it's out of the question,' Jonathon replied, oblivious to Miss Beaseley lurking near by. 'I am planning to attend Tattersall's. Edward says there is a new shipment of Arabians due.'

'Won't they be there the day after tomorrow?' Thea asked reasonably. 'I don't like to insist, Jonathon, but I did promise Daughtery I'd attend. And Amelia has already bowed out because of a previous engagement. And if you cannot accompany me, then I shall have to break my promise to the earl, which shall make him as cross as crabs. He's bound to think I did it deliberately, which I didn't.'

'I shall be bored to tears,' Jonathon declared.

Thea did not try to refute this. In all likelihood she would be as bored as young Jonathon. 'It may not be so bad,' she said encouragingly.

'No, indeed.' To her surprise, Miss Beaseley, who had been shamelessly eavesdropping, spoke. She blushed now as they turned towards her. 'I think it would be exciting to listen to Parliament in session.'

Jonathon studied her for a moment. 'Have you ever attended a session?'

'No,' Miss Beaseley acknowledged, 'but I have always yearned to do so, and the earl is reputed to be a powerful speaker.'

'I have an idea,' Jonathon said. 'Since I am loath to accompany my cousin and since you wish to listen to Parliament, why don't you go in my stead?'

'Are you certain you don't wish to go?' Miss Beaseley asked, looking overcome by such generosity.

'Quite sure,' Jonathon said quickly before she could change her mind. 'It's all settled, then.' He looked at Thea, who seemed startled by her sudden change of companions. 'You don't mind, do you, coz?'

It was on the tip of Thea's tongue to say that she did mind very much, but she decided magnanimously that there was no reason for two members of her family to suffer through the earl's speech. And since Miss Beaseley did appear willing to subject herself to the ordeal, Thea acquiesced to the change, wondering what Emery would think of his betrothed coming along with her to grace the halls of Parliament!

CHAPTER FOURTEEN

WHILE Amelia and Thea were hugely enjoying their first week in London, Emery experienced quite the opposite back in Wiltshire, as his situation with Sir Percy grew more vexatious with each day.

Within that week the baronet had sought a growing list of favours from him, including the appointment of a cousin to a vicarage on one of Emery's estate parishes and the sponsorship of yet another cousin in the political arena.

'How the devil do you find yourself with so many relations?' Emery demanded one morning when Sir Percy detailed the vicarage appointment.

'My family is inordinately large,' the baronet revealed with a ghost of a smile on his pudgy face. 'My father alone had twelve brothers and sisters.'

'Good God!' the viscount exclaimed.

'I don't like to ask, Emery...'

'For someone who doesn't like to ask, you do an uncommon amount of it,' Emery retorted.

Sir Percy touched his fingertips lightly together. 'Of course, if you think it too much, you needn't bother. After all, what did I ever do for you except save your...'

'Oh, very well,' Emery growled, not wishing to hear yet again the tale of how he was rescued from the highwayman's clutches by the heroic baronet.

'I knew you would reconsider,' Percy said, the self-satisfied smile back in place. 'Once you thought of what you owed me, that is.'

The black frown descending on Emery's brow caused him to return hastily to the subject at hand. 'My cousin would rather that the vicarage be large enough to support himself comfortably. He has five children.'

The glare Emery unleashed squelched any further confidence Percy might have wished to reveal about his cousin, and he made a quick exit. As soon as he was alone, Emery banged his fist down hard on the mahogany desk and stalked out, nearly colliding with Charles.

'I say, Hadrian, what's the hurry?' Lord Marlow asked, catching his balance. 'And why are you looking so no-how? Thought you might like a game of billiards.'

'No, thank you, Charles. In this temper I would smash the cue.'

'Percy been at you again?' Marlow hazarded a guess. 'Saw his rig outside.'

The viscount nodded and scowled. 'How do I put an end to it, Charles?' he demanded. 'I've talked till I'm blue in the face. The matter is hopeless.'

'Now, now, Hadrian. Mustn't say that,' Charles said, alarmed by the frustration in Emery's eyes. 'Bound to drive yourself into an attack of the apoplexy.'

The viscount slapped one York tan glove against his fist.

'I'm half-way there as it is.'

'Don't think about it,' Lord Marlow advised. 'It's bound to blow over.'

'That's what I thought at first. But Percy hasn't allowed it to blow over. In fact, he's fanned the fire. This will probably haunt me to my grave.'

'Come, play a little billiards.'

Emery shook his head. 'Later, perhaps. I feel inclined to ride off this foul mood.'

The ride proved to be an excellent tonic as Emery rode Pompeii first up one hillock and down the next, both rider and horse exulting in the clean rush of the wind against them. He forgot temporarily about Percy and his pack of infernal cousins. His thoughts wandered towards London. A pang of longing for the city took him completely by surprise, as did the lingering question of just what Thea might be doing there with Amelia.

Thinking about Thea brought Miss Beaseley reluctantly to mind, and his mood turned gloomy once again. How had he allowed Miss Beaseley and Sir Percy to make such a mull of his life? Beholden to the one and betrothed to the other.

He had left the confines of the Marlow estate and now rode easily along the country lane, allowing Pompeii his head just as a carriage driven by Dr Marsh approached. Emery turned his horse aside in the nick of time.

'Do you wish to have another accident and damage your other shoulder?' the doctor asked good-naturedly after he had come to a stop.

Emery grinned. 'I apologise. I was lost in an air dream.'

'Not a happy one, judging by your face,' the doctor said shrewdly. 'Not bad news at home, I hope?'

'No.'

'Is Lady Marlow all right in London?' Dr Marsh enquired next.

Emery had almost forgotten about his sister. 'Oh, I suppose so,' he said now. 'We had a brief note saying she had arrived and was busy settling in. You are on your way to a patient?'

'Coming from Mr Campion.'

'Not another bout with the gout?'

Dr Marsh chuckled. 'No. He wished to comb my hair for an article I had written in a medical journal.' His eyes twinkled. 'I had taken the liberty of describing a certain patient of mine in it. He took me to task, saying that he was not at all a curmudgeon.'

Emery laughed. 'Did you argue the point?'

'Certainly not. Mr Campion is entitled to his opinion, and I to my own. Give my regards to Lord Marlow and to Lady Marlow when next you see her.'

But when would he see Amelia, Emery asked himself after the doctor had driven on. He could not go to London with Percy still tied like an albatross about his neck. He turned back towards the estate, choosing to ride along one of the less-frequented paths. As he came to a lake, he dismounted, cupped his hands, and splashed water on his warm face. He stiffened abruptly as the cold, hard press of a pistol prodded his back.

'Well, well, my lord. Out for a little ride, is it?'

He tried to turn, but the gun pressed deeper, and he stiffened.

'Not yet. Hand me your purse, carefully.'

Emery reached a dutiful hand into his pocket and extracted his purse, which he tossed behind him on the slope. As the robber moved towards it, the viscount turned ever so slightly, glimpsing the masked figure out of the corner of one eye. It looked like the same bloke who had robbed him before with Percy and Thea.

'I thought you had given up a life of crime,' he said now.

'A temporary measure,' was the reply. 'You carry very little on your person today.'

'My apologies. I had not thought a huge roll of bills necessary. Travellers doubtless carry such sums, but riders out to enjoy a brisk day don't. You ought to keep that in mind when you choose your victims.'

As he spoke, Emery had turned slowly so that he was now facing the highwayman. His certainty grew that this was the same fellow. The mask, horse, and pistol all looked familiar.

'Now what?' he asked pleasantly.

'Now, my lord,' came the muffled reply through the mask, 'you will enter the water.'

Emery's head snapped up. 'I shall what?'

'Enter the water.' The pistol was now level with the viscount's chest. 'You don't think I will allow you to come after me, do you? Loath though I am to put another bullet into you, I shall take the necessary precautions. Turn round and head for the lake. Waist-high, I should think.'

The muscles of Emery's jaw worked in mute fury as he waded into the water, ruining his Wellington boots and soaking his buckskin breeches. The fleeting thought popped into his mind of how he would have to explain their condition to his valet. When he was hip-deep, he turned round. The highwayman was still there, as well as his pistol.

'A little further, my lord.'

Fuming, Emery strode in until the water was waist-high. Then he turned. The robber had vanished. Muttering an oath, Emery ran towards the shore, his movement hampered by his wet clothing. He climbed out of the lake with legs as heavy as bricks. He was soaked to the skin. Pompeii reared up as he approached.

'Easy does it, lad.' He patted the horse. 'We are after someone.' He swung his damp body into the saddle and applied his heels gently to the horse's flanks. Willingly, Pompeii took off along the path that did not lead to Chumley Field. Doubtless the robber would expect his victim immediately to seek help and a change of clothing at the house.

The viscount rode hard. To be robbed once was unpleasant. To be robbed twice by the same person was the outside of enough, and to be humiliated into the bargain was insufferable. And he would throttle the criminal if it were the last thing he ever did.

With a grim smile that boded ill for his robber, he urged Pompeii forward. Luck for once was with him, for as he made the turn along a wooded area he saw movement of a horse and a solitary rider.

'You shall have to ride harder than that to escape me,' Emery said softly.

The robber, hearing the unmistakable clatter of hoof-beats, applied his spurs to his horse. Unfortunately, even with the aid of spurs and whip, his mount was not the equal of Pompeii. Through the thickets he rushed, with Emery giving chase. Frantically he dismounted and ran into the bushes.

Emery dismounted as well and followed on foot, catching up to the culprit with a leap that threw them both on to the ground.

'Force me into the lake, would you?' he demanded.

The robber, struggling wildly clipped him a solid blow to his recently mended shoulder. The blow was stout enough to stun Emery, and the robber sprang to his feet and raced off.

The viscount recovered quickly and set off after him, lunging for his legs and bringing him down face-first into the dirt. He turned him over quickly and landed a solid facer. Then he thrust aside the mask and sat back on his heels in utter astonishment.

'Young Boyle, as I live and breathe,' he muttered.

'Don't hurt me, Lord Emery, please,' Gaylord Boyle whimpered.

'Hurt you? I ought to hang you,' the viscount roared. 'That's the punishment meted out for robbery in these parts, or didn't you know that?'

The younger man held up his hands. 'I never meant it, truly. It was simply a lark.'

'Lark or not, you're a criminal.'

'N—No. Truly, I'm not.' Gaylord stuttered in his haste to speak. 'You won't turn me over to the bailiff, will you?'

Emery's eyes hardened. 'Give me one reason why I shouldn't.'

'Because . . . I'll give you your purse back.'

Emery rose to his feet and dragged Boyle with him. The young man no longer looked like a taunting robber, but a frightened boy.

'Please, Lord Emery, I don't wish to hang,' he cried.

'Perhaps they won't hang you,' Emery said. 'A small jail sentence.'

'No, please.' Gaylord fell down on the ground.

Emery felt a flicker of disgust. 'You sang a different tune not so long ago. Stop being such a gudgeon, and get to your feet.'

Stumbling, Gaylord rose. 'Where are you taking me?'

'To your brother.'

'My brother?!' A hopeful look came into his eyes to be replaced by one of terror. 'You can't mean to tell him about this?'

'I know it is disobliging of me,' Emery drawled, 'but that is precisely what I intend to do.'

'But he'll kill me!' Gaylord exclaimed.

'Quite probable,' Emery agreed blandly. 'But of the few choices available—taking you to Percy, calling in the authorities, or hanging you myself—it seems the least wearisome.'

Silenced by this, Gaylord submitted meekly to being led on his horse to his brother's estate. Sir Percy's butler had witnessed many curious sights during his extended years of service with the baronet and accepted with nary a raised eyebrow the curious spectacle of the Viscount Emery, begrimed of face and lower body dripping wet, leading in young Gaylord, whose clothing seemed to be in similar disarray, although somewhat drier.

Sir Percy did not take as tolerant a view as his butler. 'What the devil is all this about, Emery?' he asked when he entered his drawing-room. 'You're dripping wet!'

'Yes, thanks to your brother here.'

'My brother?' Percy swivelled his eyes towards Gaylord, who hung his head.

'Your brother wished to see if my prodigious skill as a swimmer was true. He bade me swim for him. A demonstration made difficult by his not allowing me to disrobe first.'

'Emery, you must be queer in the attic. Or is this your idea of a jest?'

'Swimming in the lake fully clothed a jest, Percy? I hope not. It was a command, one I followed when your brother issued it.'

'Command?' The baronet squinted from face to face in befuddlement. Gaylord continued to stare at the carpet. 'I don't understand.'

'Let me explain, then,' Emery said. 'Your brother wanted me in water of sufficient depth to ruin my breeches and my boots but not my cravat. This was after he first relieved me of my purse!'

'Your purse?' Percy stared at his brother, consternation replacing the bewilderment. 'Do you mean...'

'Here we have the highwayman who has been terrorising the region,' Emery agreed.

'Gaylord! Is any part of this true?' Sir Percy thundered. 'Answer me, or I'll...'

'Yes, yes, it's true, all of it,' the young man muttered.

The baronet's face went from red to purple. 'You're nothing but a common criminal!' His tone brought a mulish set to Gaylord's jaw.

'And criminals hang, do they not, Percy?' Emery put in, seeing these signs of misgivings.

At the mention of the gallows, Gaylord turned even more ashen-faced.

'Emery, he's just a lad,' Sir Percy protested. 'No need to call in the authorities!'

'That lake was devilishly damp, Percy,' Emery replied, a thin smile on his lips.

'I know it was bound to be unpleasant, but still...' Percy broke off to glare at Gaylord, who was beginning to snivel. 'Be quiet, you paperskull. This is all your doing. Leave us alone!'

'Do you think, before he departs,' Emery drawled, 'I might recover my purse? It's not the money itself,' he explained, 'but the principle of the thing.'

'Here it is,' Gaylord said, quickly handing it over. 'Everything is there,' he assured the viscount.

'I should hope so,' Sir Percy said tartly. 'Now out, you gudgeon.'

Glad for a reprieve, Gaylord beat a hasty retreat, one that Emery observed with a jaundiced eye. Now that he was alone with Emery, Sir Percy seemed at a loss for words. Emery, who was damp and had no wish to bring on an inflammation of the lungs, took control of the situation.

'I could do with a glass of sherry, Percy,' he said. 'Lord knows I'm still a trifle damp.'

'Yes, of course,' Sir Percy said, glad to have something to do. He rang the bellpull and sat meditatively as a footman entered with the drinks.

'My own brother, Emery. I can't believe it,' he said finally.

'You're not calling me a liar, Percy?' Emery asked gently.

The baronet recoiled. 'Good God, no. Gaylord's full of larks, I grant you: crashing my rig and that sort of thing. But this, robbing people!' He shuddered.

Emery swallowed his sherry.

'I'll comb his hair for this, I promise you that,' Percy said, shifting his weight in the curricle chair, which creaked an ominous protest.

'I think the exigencies of the moment dictate rather more than a hair-combing,' Emery drawled. 'If young Gaylord has been gudgeonish enough to wage a personal war against the peace-loving men and women traversing this area, then he ought to pay the consequences. I recall the squire saying just the other day that highwaymen were the scourge of the kingdom and ought to be publicly flogged before hanging!'

Percy gulped. 'Emery!'

'But, I say, if he is to be hanged, why go through all the fuss and botheration of flogging him first? The gallows certainly seems punishment enough to me. And the notion of the public viewing such a spectacle always strikes me as disagreeable, although,' he conceded, 'the rabble are a bloodthirsty lot. Wouldn't surprise me at all if they turned out in droves to view it.'

He had finished his sherry and noticed that Percy had appeared to lose his taste for his glass. Gone was the smugness that was so characteristic of the baronet. Emery took pity on him.

'I shan't report Gaylord to the authorities, Percy, on two conditions.'

The baronet lifted his chin. 'Oh, I say, Emery, that's devilishly good of you. What are the conditions?'

'That he cease all such illegal activities at once.'

'I'll make certain of that,' Percy said with a grim nod. 'And the second?'

'That my not reporting him cancels any debt I may have owed you. Agreed?'

'Agreed!' Percy said promptly.

Emery eyed him measuringly. 'This means no more favours for cousins or the retelling of how you saved my life, not that you really did any such thing!'

'I understand,' Percy said with a sad nod. 'I would promise you anything. Can't have any breath of scandal attached to the family name. I'm beholden to you, Emery.'

Emery felt a pang of alarm. To deal with the baronet's obsequiousness would be almost as bad as his condescension. And he took immediate steps to nip that in the bud. 'You owe me nothing, Percy,' he stressed. 'All I ask is that you take steps to curb young Gaylord's lawless inclinations.'

'I shall take care of Gaylord and his inclinations,' the baronet promised.

Emery offered his hand, satisfied that this was the end of the highwayman episode, and went off leaving Percy to dole out the punishment to young Gaylord.

CHAPTER FIFTEEN

IN THE great House of Parliament the air was still and calm. The absence of several of the more noted members served notice that the issue under discussion was no urgent business of state. The excesses of the Prince Regent had been debated under that same roof on innumerable occasions. Most of the House of Lords had grown accustomed by now to the Regent's spendthrift ways, but one who had not and who continued to rail against Prinny's poor sense of economics was Daughtery. He had had the floor for at least an hour and seemed reluctant to yield.

The gallery where the spectators sat was some distance removed from the floor, but not far enough to render the earl's booming voice inaudible to anyone possessed of two sound ears. Thea, however, had missed hearing the earl's ringing indictment of the Regent during the last ten minutes. Overcome by ennui, her head nodded on her chest. Suddenly she jerked herself awake.

'Good heavens,' she said, conscience-stricken. 'I fell asleep again.'

'Yes,' Miss Beaseley, sitting next to her, chided gently. 'Perhaps it's due to all the excitement of being here.'

Thea, who thought excitement had nothing whatever to do with it, stifled an enormous yawn. 'Is Daughtery still speaking?' she asked, peering down at the earl's figure in the distance.

'Oh, yes,' Miss Beaseley said, nodding her head, a little breathless. 'Isn't it remarkable how he can speak so long without stopping for water or to inhale a breath?'

'Remarkable?' Thea stared aghast at the figure couched in blue muslin sitting next to her. 'I'd sooner call it tedious.'

'Oh no,' Miss Beaseley protested. 'How can you say such a thing? His voice is ever so compelling and melodious. Just listen to it reverberate against these walls! I vow I could listen to him forever!'

'Oh, heavens, don't let him hear that or we shall be here all day,' Thea implored, feeling that they were doomed to sit in the gallery all day anyway. 'I would have thought he'd have finished by now,' she complained. 'He has been speaking ever since we arrived, a full hour and a half ago. It strikes me as rather unfair that he has not relinquished the floor. What are they talking about now?'

'Still the Regent,' Miss Beaseley informed her. 'The earl is furious that the Regent wants an increase in his allowance, and he has already called him a hedonist and a libertine, not to mention a selfish ingrate and a buffoon.'

Thea's eyes widened. 'All that, and he has only been speaking for an hour and a half? What would he say if he had the whole day?'

Fortunately for everyone, that was left in the air. Several other members of Parliament who wished to get on with their lunch began to shift restlessly and voice protesting sounds. When the earl paused momentarily to riffle through some papers in hand, one of the older members saw his chance. He jumped up to be recognised by the yawning chair and made a move to adjourn. This motion was seconded and carried before Daughtery could utter a protest, and there was an ensuing stampede of the members for the exits.

Owing to the congestion in the corridors, several minutes elapsed before the earl could weave his way through the horde and into the gallery, where his guests waited.

'Did you enjoy the session?' he asked, puffing a little from his exertions.

Thea, gazing into his expectant face, searched the recesses of her memory. 'It was unforgettable,' she said finally.

The earl looked pleased. 'Good, good,' he said, mopping his brow with a handkerchief. 'I am speaking on Wednesday as well, if you would like to attend then.'

'No!' Thea said, moving quickly to squelch this invitation. 'You must not spoil me. I think an attempt to top this session would fail.'

He accepted this with becoming grace. 'Well then, what of some luncheon? I own to being a trifle hungry and rather thirsty.'

Thea, who had no doubt about the reasons behind his thirst, acquiesced to the notion of a noon meal and followed him down the stairs with Miss Beaseley.

'And how did you enjoy the session, Miss Beaseley?' the earl enquired when they were in his carriage.

'It was famous!' Miss Beaseley said, her eyes shining at him.

The earl looked gratified and puffed out his cheeks. 'That's civil of you to say that. What did you like the best about it?'

Miss Beaseley answered without hesitation. 'Your courage!'

'*Courage!*' Thea blurted out. Even the earl looked somewhat daunted by Miss Beaseley's words.

'Yes,' she said now, looking earnestly at him. 'Calling the Regent those names with no regard for what he might do to you. A total disregard for your own safety!'

'Oh, I say, I didn't do that, did I?' the earl asked, looking alarmed.

'Indeed you did,' Miss Beaseley said. 'Calling Prinny a wastrel and a pig as though he weren't the most powerful man in England.'

Daughtery licked his lips. 'The most powerful man in England,' he muttered.

'With friends in such high places that you were bound to be ostracised if they heard of it,' Miss Beaseley went on, warming to her topic.

'Ostracised?' The pallor on the earl's face increased markedly. 'Devilishly awkward that would be—for my mother, I mean,' he said hastily.

'Yes,' Miss Beaseley agreed, 'and still you spoke your mind.'

'Perhaps no one heard me,' the earl said hopefully. 'Only half the members were present today.'

Miss Beaseley laughed away such a notion. 'Not hear you? My lord, your voice resounded like a gong.'

'Yes,' Thea put in, smiling to herself at this exchange, 'but I don't think you need fear becoming an outcast, Lord Daughtery, however courageous it might have been to tempt such a fate.'

This reassured him somewhat, and by the time they arrived at the restaurant for luncheon he had recovered enough to continue airing his views on foreign as well as domestic issues. As he reached the annual market price of wool, Thea felt her appetite wane, and she pushed away the lamb cutlet resting on her plate. She was glad when Daughtery was interrupted by the approach of Jonathon with Mr Jason Ludlow.

Jonathon, garbed this morning in a striking combination of violet trousers and puce jacket, explained that they had just been to Tattersall's, where Ludlow had advised him not to purchase any of the short-boned creatures for sale.

'Short-boned?' Thea said, astonished. 'I thought you said they were champions—Arabians.'

'It is a common ruse among sellers, Miss Campion,' Jason explained. 'They find a young man interested in horses like young Jonathon here and they try to persuade him to make an ill-advised purchase. Your cousin, however, has an excellent head on his shoulders.'

'Actually,' Jonathon said truthfully, 'you pointed out the dull coat on the grey.'

'You would have spotted it yourself,' Jason said, unperturbed. 'And an adviser can only furnish advice. It is up to the other person whether to reject or accept it.' He turned to Thea. 'How was your morning?'

'Quite enlightening.'

His lip twitched, and his eyes danced. 'Did you speak the whole session, Daughtery?'

The earl glanced up from his lamb. 'Why, yes.'

'And he'll speak on Wednesday as well,' Miss Beaseley volunteered. 'Can you come then, Mr Campion?'

Jonathon, driven to the wall, cast an agonised look at Thea. But it was Jason who took pity on him.

'Unfortunately,' Jason said urbanely, 'Jonathon and I are promised to my mother on that day.' He gazed at the food on the laden plates. 'That looks good.'

'Have some,' the earl invited magnanimously, and two more chairs were swiftly produced. With the addition of the two new members of the group, conversation buzzed, and Thea was able to exchange a few private words with Jason, thanking him for persuading Jonathon not to buy any horse.

'For the cost of stabling them here would have been prohibitive.'

'It didn't take much persuasion,' Jason told her as their heads bent over a platter of strawberries. 'Jonathon evidently thinks my expertise on horses more to the point than my thoughts on fashion. I couldn't quite induce him to give up the colour violet.'

Thea laughed. With something approaching real regret she saw the luncheon come to a close. Jason and Jonathon escorted them back to the earl's carriage.

'I wonder, Miss Campion, if you would care to go to the opera with me some time soon,' Jason said.

Thea, who had never viewed the opera in London, enthusiastically accepted the invitation and they agreed that he should call on her at Berkeley Square promptly at seven o'clock on Friday evening. She sank back against the velvet squabs, thinking happily of attending the opera with Jason, and listened with half an ear to Daughtery and Miss Beaseley's earnest discussion of political matters.

Tiring somewhat of this, she shifted her gaze and attention from her companions and on to the street they were passing. At one corner, waiting for the carriages

to clear, stood a woman who looked amazingly like
Amelia. She was talking animatedly to a young companion. As the earl's vehicle drew closer, Thea rubbed
her eyes. It *was* Amelia! And her companion did not
bear the slightest resemblance to Lady Hunterford, particularly with regard to her sex, for he was a male! And,
Thea could not help noticing, an excessively handsome
male at that.

The vehicle passed, and Thea lost sight of Lady
Marlow, but she could not help wondering what her
friend might be doing with a young man in tow.

She had opportunity to dwell further on this unlikely
pairing after she reached Berkeley Square, for Amelia,
as expected, was not within. Thea went into her bedchamber, flung her straw bonnet on the bed, and thought
hard.

Amelia's life was none of her concern. And she had
always detested those who poked their noses into what
did not concern them. Yet what was Amelia up to, particularly with that excessively good-looking young man?

She sat down in front of the mirror, frowning slightly.
Amelia had been most eager to leave Wiltshire and come
to London. Almost too eager. She had practically jumped
at the opportunity the night of Sir Percy's ball.

This remembrance brought another with it as Thea
recalled now the letter from London that Amelia had
practically snatched off the plate at Chumley Field. Had
that missive come from her young companion? And was
it possible that Amelia—faithful, loving Amelia, the best
of friends—was being unfaithful to her doting Charles?

As quickly as this idea flew into mind she dismissed
it. Amelia loved Charles. Of that she was certain. But

just who was this young man, and what was he to Amelia? And why did her friend conceal the friendship, if it were indeed so innocuous?

Had Amelia wished to avoid Daughtery's speech—which Thea did not fault her for—she had only to say so in private instead of inventing the tale of an appointment with Lady Hunterford. And she would tell Amelia so when she arrived home.

Unfortunately Amelia did not return to Hill Street until very late in the day. She came up the stairs, puffing slightly and a little flushed in the face. Thea's entreaty for a quiet cose met with an affectionate but firm rebuff.

'Nothing would give me greater pleasure, dear Thea, but I am just so fatigued. I will be restored after a brief nap. I'll see you at dinner, and we can chat then unless you are dining out.'

'No, I am dining in,' Thea told her.

'Good.' Amelia smiled. 'We shall talk then,' she promised, and disappeared into her bechamber before Thea could utter another word.

No opportunity for talk during the dinner hour occurred, because Jonathon dined with them, and Thea could not raise the issue of Amelia and her strange young man in front of her impressionable cousin. So she fiddled with her food, barely tasting the poached eels and the creamed lobster. This lack of appetite prompted Amelia to enquire if anything was amiss.

'I am just not hungry,' she explained. 'We had a large meal at noon, as Jonathon can attest to.'

'And how was Parliament?' Amelia asked. 'Very boring, I suppose.'

Thea shrugged. 'No more than I expected. Miss Beaseley at least seemed to derive genuine enjoyment from it.'

'The poor child,' Amelia exclaimed, reaching for another serving of the baby eels. Unlike her guest, she seemed this evening to have an enormous appetite.

'How was Lady Hunterford?' Thea asked.

Amelia paused, her fork half-way to her mouth. 'Lady Hunterford?' she echoed, a little confused.

'You had plans to see her this afternoon, I believe.'

'Oh, that!' Amelia blotted her lips with a napkin. 'She is very much the same as usual. So starched-up and in-clined towards invalidism that I almost wished I were in Parliament listening to Daughtery's dreary speech.'

'Don't say that!' Jonathon teased. 'He's speaking again on Wednesday, is he not, Thea? Miss Beaseley might try to get you to attend. She nearly tried it with me. Luckily Jason said we were going to meet his mother.'

Amelia let out a shriek at this innocent remark. 'Did Daughtery accept that excuse?' she demanded.

'Why shouldn't he?' Thea countered.

'Because Jason's mother has been dead for a dozen years,' Amelia said in between whoops of laughter. 'How could Jason tell such an infamous whisker? It is too rich even for one of his wit.'

'Well, whatever the reason, I'm glad I don't have to attend Parliament,' Jonathon said. He wiped his chin with his napkin. 'And now you must excuse me, for I promised Edward I would meet him at White's.'

'I suppose I should be thankful it's White's and not Watier's,' Thea said after her cousin had left them.

'You won't have to worry there,' Amelia soothed. 'Jonathon doesn't lack for sense.'

'I suppose not. Yet one never knows how the city might affect him.'

'If it is his clothing that concerns you, it needn't,' Amelia hastened to assure her. 'I dare say all young men go through a peacock stage.'

'It isn't his clothing,' Thea said, carefully watching her friend. 'Nor Jonathon himself. It's just that people are different in the country from how they are in the city, don't you agree?'

Amelia shrugged a dainty shoulder. 'It seems to me that people are the same pretty much everywhere. Are you criticising London society after only a week here?'

'Oh, no,' Thea said immediately, 'but there are some things I cannot get accustomed to. For instance, I have heard it said that in London married ladies actually encourage young men to dangle after them. In fact, some are allowed to sit in their pockets. What is the word for them?'

'Cicisbeos,' Amelia pronounced. 'And they needn't be young men. Several ladies I know have had elderly ones in tow,' she divulged. She put down her fork, a little astounded at the large amount of food she had just consumed. 'My word, I ate too much. Are you finished?'

Thea nodded and followed Amelia out of the dining-room and into the small parlour. The urge to interrogate her friend was strong, but she could not bring herself to accuse her outright of misconduct.

'Are you planning to write to Charles?' she asked as Amelia settled back with a fringe she was knotting.

'Write to Charles?' Amelia turned a distracted face
her way. 'No, I plan to knot this fringe.'

'Don't you think you should,' Thea suggested. 'He's
bound to be worried about you.'

'Worried about me?' Amelia's eyes grew wider as she
looked up from the fringe in her lap to her friend. 'What
is there for him to worry about? Besides, even were I to
write to him, there's no assurance that he would receive
the letter. He's at Kemble's by now. After that, who can
predict where he will go? It is far more likely that he
would write to me and tell me his plans.' She put down
her fringe with a small frown. 'And why all the sudden
interest in communicating with Charles?'

'Nothing really, Amelia,' Thea said hastily. 'Just a
notion of mine.'

Amelia's frown turned into a quite mysterious smile.
'Did you perhaps wish me to pass along a message to
Emery from you?'

'A message to Emery?' Thea repeated incredulously.
'Good God, no.'

Amelia's smile grew more arch. 'Are you certain about
that, my dear? For if such is the case I can easily lay
aside this fringe and take up pen and ink.'

'No, don't do that,' Thea said quickly. 'I know you
are eager to finish it.'

Amelia made a moue. 'It's not that I am eager to
finish, but I am too stubborn to stop. I started it and
so I will finish it. I only hope it resembles a fringe when
I am done.'

With that she reapplied herself to the knotting, looking
so cheerful and industrious that Thea felt ashamed for
doubting her.

CHAPTER SIXTEEN

SIR PERCY BOYLE, his life of rural tranquillity now rudely shattered, departed swiftly for London, where he hoped no one would be acquainted with the story of the Wiltshire highwayman who might be unmasked as his idiotish brother. He had banished Gaylord for the duration of the summer to Cornwall. If three months with their grand-aunt did not cure him of his stupid pranks, nothing would.

In London, however, he discovered that the peace and quiet he craved was lost to him. He was pelted almost daily by one relation or another desiring a favour from Emery.

'What do you mean, no?' Mr Septimus Boyle demanded of his cousin one afternoon in Percy's library. He had just finished sketching his plans for a small vicarage, a plan the baronet had cut short.

'I should think the meaning of that would be apparent to a five-year-old,' Percy replied testily.

'But you said you saved his life. He'd be sitting in your pocket.'

'I won't apply to him again,' Sir Percy said. 'If it's a vicarage you want, you'll have to find another benefactor.'

Septimus, still muttering, was shown the door. But the lull was temporary, because the butler soon announced another cousin. Percy found himself ruing the fact that he had so many cousins.

Emery himself had returned to London, his re-appearance causing a considerable stir in his quiet household in Mount Street. Chadwick, his butler, deplored the fact that his employer had not sent word ahead so that preparations for his comforts might have been made, while Pierre, Emery's top-lofty Parisian chef, threw a Gallic fit at the inevitability of presenting the viscount with a dinner that would fall sadly short of his usual culinary standards of excellence.

Travel-stained and weary, Emery dismissed both these complainants, but his valet was not so easily fobbed off. He waited patiently in the bedchamber and greeted his employer with the look of long-suffering horror.

'Do I look that hellish?' Emery asked, rubbing a hand across his chin.

'No, indeed, my lord.' Kemp, the valet, attempted a noble recovery. 'Once or twice I have seen you looking much worse: for instance, during your recovery from the wound you received in Salamanca. I dare say when you were in the wilds of Wiltshire you did not have recourse to comb or brush or the other necessities of a gentleman's life.'

Emery accepted this indictment of country living with an appropriate laugh. 'I'll need a bath,' he told Kemp, for he could not present himself at Hill Street in all his dirt.

'That shall be a start,' Kemp agreed, giving the order for the bath to be drawn. 'And I dare say a trimming of your locks will be next.'

'You can cut it some other day,' Emery said impatiently.

His valet shook his head. 'My lord,' he insisted, 'I shall cut it this very minute while we wait for your bath to be drawn.'

'Later,' Emery countered. 'I'm in a devilish hurry. I am eager to see a certain young lady.'

'You shall look more presentable after a trimming,' Kemp said doggedly. 'Has it only been three weeks since we saw you last? You look, if I may venture to say, so unlike yourself. Was there no one present to cut your hair?' He ran his fingers expertly through the viscount's shaggy brown hair. 'On second thoughts, it was probably better that no one did deign to touch it, for they would have made a mull of it. I shall cut it for you and put you to rights at once.'

'Let it be,' Emery replied.

'My lord, it will take only a minute.'

Muttering an oath against faithful retainers, Emery knew further protest was futile, and bowed to the inevitable. 'You will be keeping a lady waiting,' he grumbled as he sat down in front of the mirror.

Scissors in hand, Kemp smiled. 'Miss Beaseley shan't mind.'

The viscount swivelled his head sharply, causing his valet to mutter a veiled oath himself as he jerked the scissors back from the viscount's neck.

'My lord,' he implored, 'do try to keep your head still.'

'Sorry,' Emery apologised. 'Why do you mention Miss Beaseley?'

Kemp smiled into the mirror. 'You can't hope to deceive us, my lord. We heard about the announcement in the *Gazette*. All of us here do wish you happy.'

'Thank you,' Emery said glumly, for this confirmed that the wretched announcement had appeared in the paper. He lapsed into silence while Kemp cut his hair and filled him in on all manner of household business, including the news that one of the upstairs maids had eloped with a footman.

'Fortunately, Chadwick found two excellent replacements.'

When Emery was finally allowed into the tub, even there he was not safe as Kemp approached, holding up a pair of boots.

'It seems odd to me, my lord, that your new pair of top boots from Mr Hoby should be in so deplorable a condition, even after a sojourn in the country.'

Emery grinned as he scrubbed an arm. 'That's the result of swimming in them, Kemp.'

His valet did not look amused. 'Jest if you like, my lord, but these boots are ruined.'

'Then order another pair. Hoby has my measurements.'

'Shall I order another pair of Hessians, too?'

'Why not?' The viscount would willingly have ordered a dozen pair of boots if it would have removed Kemp from his bathroom.

By the time he finally did present himself at Hill Street he was clean from top to toe, looking the top-of-the-trees in a coat of Bath-blue superfine, biscuit pantaloons and a pair of champagne buffed hussar boots.

Hardy, Lady Marlow's town butler, recognised him at once and greeted him cordially, expressing keen regret that her ladyship was not in.

'What of her friend, Miss Campion?' Emery asked, for it was really Thea he wished to see.

'Unfortunately, Miss Campion is out also,' Hardy replied. 'A ride about the park with Captain Blaine, I believe.'

Emery's head shot up. 'Don't tell me he is still dangling after her.'

Had anyone else ventured such an opinion to him, the butler would have frozen him at once, but Emery was different. Hardy unbent sufficiently to confide that the captain had been one of Miss Campion's most persistent callers.

'And his brother, the earl, has come round as well, as have several other gentlemen in town.'

'Hmmph,' Emery said, digesting this fact with some annoyance. 'And what of Mr Campion, young Jonathon? Don't tell me he is absent, too.'

'I'm afraid so,' Hardy said with real regret. 'On a call to Mr Weston, I believe. Something about a new waistcoat.'

Emery slapped one glove against the palm of a hand. He had anticipated a happy reunion with his sister and friends, and it was irksome to find no one at hand to greet him—not, he told himself reasonably, that any of the three could have anticipated his arrival this particular afternoon.

'Should you care to wait, my lord, there is an excellent collection of sherries in the Green Drawing Room.'

Emery grinned. 'Hardy, you are an excellent person. Tell me,' he continued once he had settled into an Etruscan armed chair with a glass of sherry in hand, 'just how are Miss Campion and her cousin faring in London?'

'By all accounts Miss Thea is a notable hit, and Mr Campion is equally well received.'

Emery scowled. 'I suppose a score of bucks and beaux are after Miss Campion?'

Hardy, while unable to furnish the exact number, agreed that Miss Campion was very popular, which came as no surprise, since she was a lovely young lady.

'And I suppose young Jonathon has acquired town ways as well?' He put his glass down on a boulle table.

A flicker of a smile registered briefly in the butler's eyes. 'I dare say you would scarcely recognise him, my lord,' he intoned solemnly.

While Emery cooled his heels in his sister's drawing-room, Thea was engaged in circling the park in the captain's tilbury. Miss Beaseley had not exaggerated the number of people present during the fashionable hour. Only ten minutes into the park Thea had already exchanged pleasantries with Lord Enright and Mr Baldwin, nodded to Mrs Drummond Burrell, and exchanged confidences with the Misses Carter, two of Amelia's friends.

The captain bore with all these interruptions with surprising patience. Indeed, he appeared to Thea a little absentminded until they happened on Miss Hightower out with her brother, whereupon the captain's stodgy face became almost animated as they spoke of the coming ball at Lady Sefton's. Thea, watching, felt a sudden jolt.

The captain had the unmistakable look of one obviously smitten, and by Miss Hightower.

By all rights she ought to have been downcast, since he was one of her avowed admirers, but her paramount emotion was relief. At least there would be no more tortuous explanations of Wellington's campaign against Napoleon.

She smiled graciously at Miss Hightower, a comely, gentle-looking young lady, enquired after her well-being, and then bade her a warm good-bye when it became essential that they move on, their vehicle having caused a halt in the lane of traffic behind them.

'Miss Hightower is a fine-looking young lady,' she said to the captain as they parted from her.

Captain Blaine stared at her as though in a fog. 'Oh, yes, indeed she is, Miss Campion. Did you ever see such radiant eyes? And her complexion?' He became aware that to sing the praises of one lady while in the company of another might be considered a solecism of the highest order and murmured a belated apology.

'Don't apologise,' she said. 'It's easy to see that Miss Hightower is quite taken with you.'

His ruddy face beamed with obvious pleasure. 'Do you really think so, Miss Campion? I've been encouraged to hope. Her father is General Hightower.'

'What an excellent stroke of fortune,' Thea replied. 'I suppose she is very interested in military strategies, since her father is a general. Have you acquainted her yet with Hannibal's strategy of using elephants against Rome?'

'Not yet. I thought I'd do so later.' He came to a halt as he gazed at Thea. 'Miss Campion, I feel I owe you an explanation.'

'Don't be absurd, Captain. There is no necessity for any such thing between friends. I'm just so pleased you have found someone whose temperament is so excellently suited to yours.'

'But you must think me a veritable coxcomb inviting you to drive with me! I didn't meet Miss Hightower until after I had seen you at Almack's, and I wasn't certain she would be here today.'

'But no doubt you nursed hopes that she would be,' she teased. He flushed to the roots of his hair until he realised she was roasting him.

'There is no point in teasing yourself further on my account,' she told him matter-of-factly. 'Cupid may fling his arrows where he will, and there is little we can do about it.'

He accepted her good wishes, and the rest of the drive continued with the two of them rather more relaxed than when they had started out. By the time his tilbury reached Hill Street she was laughing easily with him and took her leave, stepping through the doorway, chuckling softly. This measure of good humour took an opposite turn when she heard her name called.

'Well, at last, Miss Campion!'

The smile that had arisen when Thea saw Emery faded as she found his frowning figure in the hall. His arms were crossed on his chest.

'Do you know what time it is?' he demanded, looking annoyed.

As though to answer his query, the clock in the hall bonged. 'I believe it is six,' she said, counting each stroke. 'Unless the clock is in error, which I very much doubt. Hardy would have fixed it.'

'Do you always spend such protracted visits with your admirers?' he demanded. 'And where is the noble captain? Don't tell me he was too rag-mannered to see you in.'

'The captain is none of your concern, Emery,' she said crossly, wondering why he should interrogate her in such a coming fashion.

'He's still dangling after you, along with Daughtery, I suspect?'

'You suspect wrongly,' she retorted. 'The captain is quite enamoured of another female. So you see just how much you know of things. And what are you doing here, anyway?' she asked.

'Waiting for you, Amelia, and Jonathon.'

Her eyes widened. 'But surely Hardy told you we were out.'

'I chose to wait, and an uncommonly long wait it was.'

His complaint found no sympathy with her. 'Well, you have no right to cut up so stiff,' she pointed out with ringing logic, 'since I had no notion you were here. It's not as though I deliberately kept you waiting the way some females are apt to do.'

Emery said nothing. It was not so much the wait that had caused his temper to boil as the realisation that no fewer than six gentleman callers had arrived with messages, roses and assorted gifts for her, including a hand-penned sonnet. He pointed out these dubious gifts to her on the small ormolu table.

Thea took a judicious sniff of the roses and picked up the sonnet, laughing a little at the tortuous rhymes of Mr Arbuthnot, which she shared with Emery.

He unbent. 'You've evidently been enjoying London?'

'More than I imagined,' she agreed. 'And now that you're here I shall enjoy it even more. When, pray, did you arrive? And how is Charles? And whatever happened with Sir Percy? Jason Ludlow says he's back in London and has recanted the tale of his heroics.'

Emery laughed at her torrent of questions and answered each in turn, explaining that Charles was well and informing her of his encounter with the highwayman.

'In the lake, Emery?' She could not repress a laugh.

'It wasn't amusing,' he said with crushing pretension.

She laughed again. 'No, I suppose not. And young Gaylord was the culprit?'

He nodded. 'But you must be sworn to secrecy on that point. At least it took Percy off my back.' He gazed into her lovely face and realised that he had missed her even more than he had thought.

'Can we dine together?' he asked impulsively. 'You, Jonathon, and Amelia too, of course. My chef tells me he has an excellent pheasant that he was in the act of stuffing even as I left him.'

'I can't speak for the others,' Thea said, 'but I can't accept the invitation. I am bound for the opera with Mr Ludlow.'

'Opera? Jason Ludlow?' Emery's expression turned incredulous. 'You must be roasting me. He loathes music. Calls it nothing but so much braying!'

'Does he? How peculiar, then, that he should wish to attend. I shall have to ask him more about that tonight when I see him.'

He was on the verge of asking how much she had been seeing of Jason when Amelia came through the door looking breathless and excited and exceedingly youthful.

'Hadrian!' she exclaimed, catching sight of her brother. They embraced warmly.

'Well, well, Amelia,' he said, holding her off for a moment. 'You certainly look excited about something.'

She tossed him a saucy look. 'That comes from living in London, my dear.'

'You must tell me all about it over dinner tonight,' he said, inviting her to partake of the pheasant Pierre was preparing.

Sadly, she shook her head. 'I am promised to Mrs Hamilton, who is a friend of the vicar's back in Wiltshire. But do ask Thea and Jonathon.'

'I am bound for the opera,' Thea reminded her.

'Of course you are. How skittlebrained of me to forget Jason. I suppose my mind is on other things.' She turned to Emery. 'Have dinner tomorrow night with us here, Hadrian.' Taking his assent for granted, she drifted up the stairs.

The viscount stared after her in amazement. 'What the deuce has happened to Amelia?' he demanded. 'I haven't seen her in so besotted a state since the day she met Charles, which was at least ten years ago.'

His words caused a startled look to spring up in Thea's eyes. She thought fleetingly of confiding her suspicions to him, but her loyalty to Amelia was paramount. And she could not help hoping that nothing would come of Amelia's friendship with her young man.

'I dare say it is your imagination,' she said to Emery. 'Amelia seems just as she has always been to me. Now, you must excuse me as well, for I am bound for the opera, and must rest.'

'By all means. We can't have you haggard for Jason now, can we?'

He bowed and left the establishment, nearly colliding with young Jonathon on the path. At least he thought it was young Jonathon, for the transformation from country provincial to dandy was complete. The viscount resorted to his quizzing-glass and took in the magenta waistcoat, violet coat and twisted cravat. Jonathon's nether limbs were not immune either, for they were clothed in trousers the like of which Emery had never seen before.

'Emery!' Jonathon grinned from ear to ear. 'When did you arrive in London?'

'First things first, lad,' Emery replied. 'What the devil do you have on?'

'Do you like them?' Jonathon asked eagerly. 'They're Petersham trousers. They're the latest rage, according to Edward. What do you think?'

'I think they are the most ridiculous garments ever seen on male legs,' the viscount said scorchingly, dropping his quizzing-glass. 'Or female legs, for that matter.'

'I don't look that bad,' Jonathon protested. 'I showed them to Jason earlier.'

'Did you?' Emery asked. 'And he approved?'

Jonathon laughed. 'Heavens, no. He said I looked like a veritable popinjay.'

'An opinion with which I concur.'

Jonathon grimaced. 'That's what I thought, too,' he admitted. 'But Edward did say it was the latest in fashion.'

'Then let Edward wear them and look like a cake, and you change into some decent clothes and come along with me.'

'Gladly,' Jonathon answered. 'But where are we going?'

'To eat some pheasant!'

CHAPTER SEVENTEEN

THE Royal Italian Opera House seemed unusually crowded as Thea, in rose-coloured silk, weaved her way through the door, Jason at her side.

'Is it always so congested?' she asked as they finally reached the safety of his box.

'No. And Catalani is not even singing tonight,' he said, at a loss to explain the crowd.

Jason's box was situated opposite the stage, and Thea could not have wished for a better view, but she did find herself wishing as the evening progressed that her companion was someone other than Jason Ludlow. In fact she found herself wishing it were Emery, a notion that would have embarrassed her to death had it been revealed to either of the gentlemen involved.

Loath though Thea was to admit it, no matter how vexing, irksome and high-handed she found Emery, he was still the most intriguing man she had ever met. As for Jason, in manner, dress and demeanour he was everything a gentleman ought to be. But he wasn't Emery.

Jason fortunately did not appear to notice her mood of preoccupation and chatted amicably about the opera, explaining that it would be sung in Italian.

'Which unfortunately I cannot help you with,' he said ruefully. 'Languages are not my strong suit. And you?'

'Living on the Continent, one is obliged by necessity to learn the languages,' she told him with a smile.

'Then I rely on you to translate.' He paused and glanced down at her. 'Hadrian is back in town, I understand.'

'Yes, have you talked to him?'

'Not yet. But I did see his high-perched phaeton passing on the street this afternoon. Only Emery could take such a turn at breakneck speed. Anyone else would have overturned his vehicle for their pains. When did he arrive?'

'This afternoon, and in the sulks because neither Amelia nor Jonathon nor I was home to greet him. I was out with Captain Blaine.'

'Ah, yes,' he teased. 'Your devoted captain.'

'Not so devoted,' she divulged with a twinkle. 'He has thrown me over for another.'

'Thrown you over?' he said incredulously, 'I don't belive that!'

She laughed. 'It's true. For a Miss Hightower, a pretty young chit who's quite enamoured of military exploits. Now, if only I could discourage his brother!'

Jason clucked his tongue. 'Careful, Miss Campion. Next you shall be discouraging me!'

She flushed guiltily at this, but was fortunate that the curtain rose just then, diverting their attention.

As promised, the opera was long and tedious, the singers booming out their arias in Italian—at least Thea thought it sounded like Italian. By the time the performance was over, her temples were throbbing and she was glad to call it an evening. But before she could do so she was obliged to sit through the supper that Jason had ordered for them. As she sampled the grilled oysters, smelts and curried eggs, she dwelt guiltily on the fact that any other woman would be in alt at having such a splendid companion. She stole a look at him. Jason was undeniably handsome and good-humoured, everything a young lady could want, and yet she wanted Emery, who was betrothed to another. True, the betrothal was a ramshackle affair, but the deed had been done! Amelia had pointed out the announcement in one of the back issues of the *Gazette*. She did not see the viscount crying off. And she also did not see Miss Beaseley surrendering him, which left her clearly in the middle of a terrible mull.

While Thea had been enjoying the dubious entertainments of the opera, her cousin had been feasting on the promised pheasant so heartily that Pierre himself made a rare appearance from the nether regions of his kitchen to shake Jonathon's hand.

Jonathon had changed out of the Petersham trousers and into what for him was a rather sedate outfit of green waistcoat and lilac coat. Emery, thankful for small favours, kept silent on this new combination of colours. All young ones had to try their wings, and he chuckled as he recalled several absurd costumes from his own youth.

With the pheasant finally consumed, he offered some brandy to Jonathon, who was pleased by the offer. The viscount carefully poured a modest amount into the snifter. It would never do to send the young man back to Hill Street foxed.

'I've been thinking about those driving lessons we started back in Wiltshire,' he said now. 'Since I'm in London now, we can see how you'll acquit yourself in town traffic. Unless you've lost your interest in handling the reins?' Emery said, as Jonathon remained silent.

'No,' Jonathon said slowly. 'It's just that . . . Well, the truth is, sir, Jason's been teaching me a little of town driving already. We had three lessons so far.' He flushed. 'It's not that I'm ungrateful for all you taught me in Wiltshire, but Jason did offer to teach me here. And I had no idea when you might be returning.'

'There's no need for apologies,' Emery said, swirling his brandy with a smile. 'I'm pleased that Jason has taken you under his wing. What else have the two of you been doing?'

In the next hour Emery learned more about Jason than he cared to, including the fact that Mr Ludlow had escorted Jonathon to Tattersall's on numerous occasions, introduced him to Gentleman Jack himself, and sponsored him for membership in White's but not Watier's.

'He considers Watier's too rough for a green one like me,' Jonathon said. 'He's a regular Trojan, sir.'

A flicker of annoyance passed through Emery as Jonathon sang the praises of his childhood friend. In only a week's time Jason had managed to ingratiate himself into the affections of young Jonathon and probably Thea as well, judging by the invitation to the opera. True, he had asked his old chum to take the two newcomers in hand, but there had been no necessity to sit in their pockets. And he intended to tell him so when next they met.

The viscount had an opportunity to do that sooner than expected. After dinner and the departure of young Jonathon, who was promised to Mr Edward Carlyle for a night of cards, Emery felt in the need of some companionship and went off to White's. As he stood in the doorway leading into the reading-room, he heard a familiar voice at his elbow.

'Had enough of rural tranquillity, Hadrian?'

He turned. It was Ludlow, looking like every mother's dream for a daughter. Why had he never noticed before his friend's air of assurance, uncommon good looks and winning smile?

'I thought you were at the opera,' he said testily.

If Mr Ludlow heard the irritation in his friend's voice, he did not appear perturbed by it. Indeed a look of wry amusement crossed his face.

'Tsk, tsk, Hadrian. You have been away. The opera ended two hours ago. After a brief supper, Miss Campion owned to some fatigue so I deposited her at Hill Street, where she presumably went to bed. Since the night was still young I saw no necessity of emulating her and came here instead. But what, I wonder, are your reasons for coming to White's on your first night back?'

Emery shrugged. 'I felt the need for male companionship.'

'Thea mentioned that you were dining with Jonathon.'

'Yes, and what the devil did you mean by transforming the boy into a peacock any barnyard fowl would be transfixed with!'

Jason laughed. 'Barnyard fowl! That's coming it too strong!'

'No, it ain't. You should have seen what he was wearing today.'

'But you can't hold me responsible for young Jonathon turning into a man-milliner,' Jason said reasonably. 'Perhaps he is colour-blind. And I did think his taste was running a trifle better than earlier in the week.'

Emery grunted. 'He had on a pair of trousers the likes of which I'd never seen before.'

'Petersham trousers,' Jason said with a sage nod. 'They are the latest rage, according to my tailor.'

'Not for me.'

'Nor for me,' Jason agreed. He prodded his friend in the chest with a lean finger. 'However, we are in our dotage, you must recall.'

'Stuff and nonsense! You're all about in your head to speak as though we had sixty years in the dish instead of half that.'

Jason shrugged. 'Time marches on, and the truth is, Hadrian, I've been thinking seriously of marriage.'

Emery grasped his friend by the elbow and led him into a corner of the deserted reading-room, where he sat him into a leather chair.

'Marriage, for you, Jason?' he demanded.

'Yes, me,' Mr Ludlow replied.

'Who put such a besotted notion into your brain?' Emery asked, slouching himself in a chair and delving into his snuffbox. 'One of those mamas at Almack's, I'd wager.'

'No, actually, you were the one responsible.'

'I!' Emery expostulated, and demanded to know just how this deed had been done.

'Your engagement to Miss Beaseley.' Jason furnished the clue with aplomb as he stretched his own legs out towards the fire. 'It caused considerable stir hereabouts when the announcement was published in the *Gazette*. How like you to issue such an important decision while out of town.'

'I thought we were discussing your predilection to the marital state, not mine,' Emery said, not wishing to be reminded of his pending alliance with Miss Beaseley.

'So we were, so we were,' Jason said affably. 'To make a long story short, when a man like me reaches a certain age he begins to long for the simple pleasures in life— a warm dinner, slippers by the fire, a wife to rub his back.'

'That sounds perilously close to a declaration,' Emery said with a derisive laugh. Jason scratched an ear, not in the least offended.

'And whom have you selected as a leg shackle?' Emery asked politely.

'A lady, one with uncommon good looks, intelligent, charming.'

'Who by chance goes by the name of Miss Campion?' Emery asked with a wintry smile.

Jason looked over. 'By Jove, Hadrian, you must have second sight or gypsy blood.'

'There's no second about it,' Emery retorted. 'And I'd be a gypsy myself if you think I shall let you waltz away with her and stand idly by.'

'Waltz? My dear Emery, you are mistaken. A sedate march up the nave of St George's, Hanover Square, was more what I had in mind.'

The viscount ground his teeth. 'I should never let you wed her.'

Jason's eyes met his innocently. 'I fail to see what you have to do with it, Hadrian,' he said.

The viscount stared at his friend for a long moment. He had known Ludlow since they were in short coats. He was Emery's closest friend. But still there was the matter of Thea.

'Miss Campion is my concern,' he said now quietly.

'Are you warning me off?' Jason asked incredulously.

'If you wish to put it that way.'

To his amazement, Jason, far from looking vexed, slapped his knee with a hand and began to laugh. 'Good for you, Hadrian! Amelia shall be as pleased as Punch when I tell her all this.'

Emery fixed a baleful eye on his old friend. 'Amelia? What the devil are you talking about her for? I thought we were discussing your tendre for Miss Campion?'

'Not quite,' Jason murmured, struggling to regain control of himself. He wiped his streaming eyes with a handkerchief. 'Best jest I've been part of for years!'

'Jest? Amelia? What the devil is going on?'

'This was one of your beloved sister's schemes, my dear fellow,' Jason explained, obviously enjoying himself, 'aimed at getting you to show your true colours with regard to Miss Campion. And it worked wonderfully well. Amelia was convinced that if I espoused the slightest interest in Thea, you would turn dog in the manger and reveal your true feelings for her.' He grinned. 'But I own I never expected things to come to a head on your first night back. This is serious talk indeed!'

Emery worked his jaw back and forth as he took in Jason's explanation. 'A plan of Amelia's, is it? I shall slay her!'

Jason gazed at his friend with amusement. 'My dear Emery, one can't kill one's own sister, particularly when one is male. A brother can slay a brother or a sister a sister, but the town frowns on a brother despatching a sister. Besides, Amelia's plan worked. Bound to; after all, you are in love with Miss Campion!'

Emery felt a fleeting temptation to deny this, but the look Jason shot him made the denial wither on his tongue. Instead he gave a rueful shake of his head.

'Is it so obvious, Jason?' he asked, almost humbly.

'Only to those of us who have known you all your life,' Mr Ludlow soothed. 'Miss Campion is a charming young lady. You are very lucky.'

Emery glanced at his friend quickly. 'You were joking about marriage for yourself, weren't you, Jason? Your interest in Thea was a sham?'

Jason nodded. 'Although,' he quizzed, 'if I were inclined towards matrimony, I might just give you a run for your money. And who is to say that Miss Campion would choose you!'

Bright and early on Saturday morning, while the other members of the household dozed, Lady Marlow descended her stairs and set off in her carriage with her abigail. A half-hour later, seated in a small office, she gazed, transfixed, into the eyes of the man seated opposite, her hands in his.

'Are you certain, Dr Baldwin?' she demanded. 'There can be no denying it?'

He smiled. 'Facts are facts, Lady Marlow. You shall have living proof of my diagnosis in approximately seven months.'

Amelia sprang to her feet. 'I had thought and hoped...'

'If you take care of yourself, rest, and eat well, you shall be the proudest mother in the kingdom.'

Amelia's face turned radiant. 'Oh thank you, Doctor, thank you! I vow I could kiss you.'

'I shan't mind that, I assure you,' he said as she bussed him soundly on the cheek.

'You are a miracle-worker.'

'There is no miracle to it,' he disclaimed modestly. 'Once Dr Marsh wrote to me from Wiltshire asking for advice, I merely wrote back ordering him to tell you to relax and let nature take its course. And I wrote you the same recommendation. Have you informed your husband?'

'Not yet. I sent a letter to him only yesterday, telling him to come to London as soon as possible. I'd give a monkey to see his face when I tell him!'

Thanking him once again and declaring that she would take good care of herself, she left him and almost danced back to her carriage, where Jane, her abigail, waited.

'Well?' asked that worthy, who had accompanied her mistress on various trips to various doctors over the years.

'Nothing definite,' Amelia said, fighting the urge to shout the news from the rooftops. It had been on the tip of her tongue to tell Jane the truth, but Charles had the right to know first. Having a child was the fulfilment of his dream as well as hers, so he must be the very first person she would tell. Difficult though it was, she would hold her tongue for now.

Jane sniffed, making it obvious what she thought of these modern methods and modern doctors who looked no older than one of her nephews, and he hardly out of short coats!

Amelia's urge to share her good fortune was even harder to quell when she returned to Hill Street and found Thea in the breakfast parlour. But once again she remembered that Charles must be the first to know. Thea, observing the radiance on Amelia's countenance, knew with a sinking sensation that she had once again been seeing her young gentleman.

Only love could account for that glow transfixing her friend's entire being.

'Good morning, Thea,' Amelia sang out now.

'Amelia, do you have a moment?' Thea asked, coming to an abrupt decision. Someone must talk sense into Amelia, and she was the only one around to do so.

'Why, yes, of course, my dear.' Amelia sat down and poured herself some coffee, disdaining the offer of eggs and ham.

'Now, what did you wish to talk to me about?'

Thea felt at a momentary loss for words, then she screwed her courage to the sticking-point and blurted out the truth. 'Amelia, I know your secret!'

To her shock the excitement on Lady Marlow's face increased, and Thea was seized in a scented embrace.

'Oh, Thea, I am so glad!' Amelia babbled. 'You don't know how I have been bursting to tell you *everything*. And now I don't have to, for you already know. Who could have thought such a wonderful thing could be happening to me now? At my age!'

Thea pulled herself free of Amelia's arms. 'Amelia, I implore you. Stop a moment and think of what is happening.'

'I have been doing just that. Ever since I married Charles I've thought of nothing but this.'

Thea felt a trifle faint. That her friend could entertain thoughts of taking a cicisbeo earlier in her marriage had never occurred to Thea.

'No doubt I am not accustomed to London ways,' she said now, looking a little squeamish.

Amelia, intercepting the look, felt a moment's embarrassment. 'Am I shocking you with my frank speech?' she asked. 'Some I know think females shouldn't talk of such things.'

'I have cut my wisdoms,' Thea assured her blandly. 'But have you thought of Charles?'

'Oh, yes,' Amelia nodded happily. 'In fact I wrote to him last night asking him to come to London so that I might break the news to him myself.'

Thea gasped. 'You wrote asking him to come to London? Don't you think that's rather much to ask of him?'

Amelia bit her lip. 'I own he is devoted to those Arabian champions of Kemble's, but even so, a man doesn't receive news like this every day of his life.'

Thea continued to stare at her.

'And,' Amelia went on, 'I should like to deliver it in person. I had thought of writing it all out in a letter, but I've never been the letter-writing sort.'

'Aren't you afraid Charles will be overset?'

Amelia shook her head. 'Not at all. I rather suspect he'll be relieved.' She put down her coffee cup with a frown. 'I shan't like to confess this to anyone, Thea, but I haven't been a good wife to Charles of late.'

'Amelia, you needn't tell me anything,' Thea protested, not wishing to know the details of her friend's fall from grace.

'No, it's the truth,' Amelia doggedly continued. 'I have been bored and ill-tempered, and Charles knows this well. So I dare say he'll be pleased to learn of the change to come.'

Thea ate her muffin, scarcely tasting it. Was Amelia recommending the taking of a cicisbeo as the cure for boredom in marriage?

'Besides,' Amelia went on, 'Charles is a good sort, and he shan't make any trouble.'

'It appears to me that you are asking a good deal of Charles, devoted though I know he is to you.' Thea could not resist airing this opinion. 'Any husband would be a trifle unhappy at being displaced in your affections.'

'But he isn't being displaced,' Amelia protested. 'There will just be an addition in my life. Charles shall just have to learn to share me. Emma Dudley told me once that such is the case of every husband she knows who has gone through this...'

'Has Mrs Dudley gone through this herself?' Thea enquired.

'Three times,' Amelia said sunnily.

Thea choked. Three times! 'Mr Dudley must be a paragon.'

'Oh, he is, he is,' Amelia agreed. 'Which makes me hopeful that Charles shall be just as understanding.' She put a finger to her lips as she heard Jonathon's voice in the hall. 'But don't tell anyone this yet, Thea, please. Especially not Hadrian.'

'Don't worry,' Thea said, still bewildered that Amelia—staid, dutiful Amelia—was involved in an *affaire d'amour*. 'I shan't breathe a word of this to anyone!'

CHAPTER EIGHTEEN

JONATHON, retaining a wayward scrap of information given him by the viscount, announced after breakfast his intention of setting out for Bond Street and a fitting with a tailor highly recommended by Emery. Since this fitted in nicely with Thea's own plans to call on Miss Stark, the noted milliner, they set out together in Lady Marlow's carriage.

Jonathon handled the reins and demonstrated that he was an apt student of both Emery and Jason. Thea's initial qualms receded. Knowing that her cousin had dined with Emery the previous night, she asked him what they had found to talk about.

'Oh, we talked of many things,' Jonathon replied airily, very much the man of the world. 'Good food, the properties of fine brandies, and fashion, of course.'

Thea settled back, amusement dancing in her green eyes. 'You speak as though you and Emery were bosom bows, when you've met him only a fortnight ago.'

'Perhaps so,' Janathon acknowledged, 'but he didn't seem to mind the friendship.'

'Did he mention Miss Beaseley last night?' Thea asked, turning her eyes straight ahead and giving her words an offhand tone.

Jonathon looked momentarily confused. 'Miss Beaseley? Good Jupiter, no. His main concern seemed to be Jason.'

'Jason?' Thea was startled. Why would Emery be so interested in his old friend?

Jonathon, frowning as he concentrated on keeping the team of Welsh breds together as the vehicle rounded a sharp corner, nodded.

'Odd, don't you think? He also offered me driving lessons, which I had to decline since Jason had already shown me a few points on town driving. Emery himself said that to change instructors now would be disastrous.'

He punctuated this remark by pulling the carriage up very smartly in front of Miss Stark's shop.

'I shall be at Mr Davidson's,' Jonathon told her. 'When I have finished, I shall return here.'

Agreeing to meet an hour later, Thea entered the milliner's shop while Jonathon continued to tool up the street to his tailor.

Miss Stark enjoyed a well-deserved reputation as one of the best milliners in the city, and her shop was patronised by many fashionable young ladies. Each hat in her store was laid upon Thea's head along with a brief history of its inspiration and creation. Thea listened indulgently to the rambling histories, which probably were the most potent sales weapon in the milliner's arsenal.

The daring hat à la Hussar had been inspired by Alexander's trip to London, the gay Parisian bonnet by the defeat of Napoleon, and the dazzling beplumed Allegra by the chance glimpse of the Countess Lieven one day in the street. It seemed that Miss Stark had only to swivel her head to be struck by a new inspiration for a hat.

By the time Thea completed her purchases, a pair of very pretty and practical straw bonnets, she discovered a full hour and a half had gone by. Feeling guilty and ready to make her apologies to Jonathon, she stepped quickly out of the door, to find no carriage waiting. That could only mean Jonathon was still occupied with his tailor.

Since the day was clear and she remembered that the tailor's shop was only a brief distance up the street, she decided to walk and meet him there.

As she strolled, she thought back to Amelia's confession. How she hoped that Amelia would see the folly of her ways. To ask Charles to countenance a cicisbeo seemed like the outside of enough. So deep was she in thought that she became aware too late that her feet were carrying her astray. The buildings surrounding her were totally unfamiliar to one so new to London. To add to her confusion, her wanderings had made her the object of interest of several male passers-by.

Flushing at the bold looks directed at her, she attempted to find a familiar landmark by which to make her way back to her cousin. Before she did so, however, she heard her name called from behind and instinctively quickened her step.

'I said, stop. Are you deaf as well as a pea goose?' a voice demanded as Emery, with a looping stride, caught up with her.

Her initial relief at seeing a familiar face changed instantly to annoyance. 'Whom are you calling a pea goose?' she demanded.

'You,' came the prompt rejoinder as he pushed back his high-crowned beaver felt. 'Strolling in Bond Street before noon unattended!'

'That's still no reason to call me goosish. And I'm not unattended. I am with Jonathon.'

His glance sharpened. 'Even your rustic cousin would know better than to abandon you to the beaux on the strut here,' he retorted. 'And if he doesn't, I shall comb his hair for it!'

'Of course Jonathon didn't abandon me. I simply got lost after my visit with Miss Stark was finished. And if you would direct me to Mr Davidson's shop, I shan't take up any more of your precious time.'

'I'd sooner direct you to Jericho,' Emery declared, 'than to allow you to stroll there unattended.' She realised that he had her by the elbow.

'Where are you taking me?' she demanded, trying to break his grasp.

'To my phaeton.' A note of exasperation rang in his voice, and he pointed out the carriage in front of them. 'I shan't have you walking up the street to meet Jonathon.'

'Why not?' she demanded. 'Does it brand me a hussy?'

His eyes glinted in the sunlight. 'Quite probably!'

'Then I wonder that you would wish to be seen with one so sunk beneath reproach,' she retorted.

'True,' he returned blandly. 'But no doubt it shall be taken as one of my freakish whims!'

She gave an involuntary laugh at that and accepted his help into the carriage. 'I had begun to fear you had left your sense of humour back in Wiltshire,' she told him.

'Have I been such a foul-tempered ogre?' he asked, flicking the reins lightly on the back of his team.

She cocked her head as she considered the question. 'An ogre? No,' she conceded. 'But you have been rather high-handed and autocratic.'

'Ah, but that is quite different, for I have always been that!'

Her laughter warmed him, and he felt reluctant simply to bring her back to Jonathon.

'Have you seen the exhibition at Somerset House?' he asked.

'If you mean Mr Constable's paintings, I have not.'

'Good. We can go now.'

'Now?' She gurgled with laughter. 'What about Jonathon?'

'Jonathon will be happily occupied with his tailor for half the day,' the viscount said quite accurately. And a few minutes later he went into the tailor's shop and returned with the news that her cousin had cheerfully relinquished her to Emery's care.

Thea's nose wrinkled. 'Relinquish me? I don't much care for that remark, sir. As though I were no more than a load of bricks he wished to unload.'

'Ah, but such a pretty load!' Emery pointed out with a laugh, and she could not avoid a chuckle herself.

Her annoyance with him faded as they rode on and he pointed out the sights of the city, expressing regret that she had already viewed Westminster and the Whispering Gallery of St Paul's. At Somerset House she found him a good critic, pointing out the many techniques and virtues of colour in the work of Mr Constable.

'I have always felt his work a trifle gloomy myself,' Thea said later as they partook of a small luncheon at a nearby restaurant.

'You prefer more colour perhaps? Something in the line of Mr Rubens?'

She choked on her ice. 'My lord, you must know that the artist you mention painted...'

'Nudes.' He supplied the word for her with dancing eyes. 'Yes, I am aware of that. Do you mean that in your travels on the Continent you did not see such paintings?'

She truthfully admitted that she had. 'But it's hardly the sort of art that the ton would appreciate.'

'Oh, I don't know,' he said, disposing of Mr Gunter's famous ice with two bites. 'I can think of one or two who would pay a pretty price to hang such paintings in the drawing-rooms of several ladies I could mention.'

She laughed at him. 'You are abominable!'

'Too harsh, Miss Campion. Prinny himself is rumoured to own a collection of paintings the likes of which would cause a blush to suffuse even these jaded cheeks. Mine,' he said mischievouly, 'not yours.'

'I have heard that rumour,' she admitted. 'But Prinny is a libertine, and I quote Lord Daughtery, who spoke at great length on that subject in Parliament.'

The viscount appeared puzzled. 'I didn't know Daughtery had seen the Regent's collection.

She choked. 'You know he hasn't.'

'My dear Miss Campion, I am not an intimate of Daughtery, so there is no of course about it.'

'How did we ever get on to such a tangent?'

'You led us there,' he drawled. 'I merely followed suit.'

She put down her fork and dealt him a severe look. 'Of all the absurdities! I dare say if we were discussing horses, you would accuse me of introducing the topic of Lady Godiva.'

'What a refreshing idea,' he said, much struck. 'A pity I can't recall just what type of horse it was she was riding at the time. Perhaps we ought to discuss something more ordinary, such as which of us shall have that last cherry ice.'

Thea, who had a great weakness for cherry ices, sacrificed it to the viscount, confessing that she had eaten much too much.

'Nonsense. You must eat to keep up your strength. Are you sure you don't want it?' he asked, holding the plate out to her.

She wavered for a moment. 'Quite sure,' she said at last with a sigh. 'I have already consumed three of them. If I eat any more I shall resemble a cow.'

'Do you know, Miss Campion,' Emery said, making short work of the ice, 'in the short space of two hours today I have heard you liken yourself to a load of bricks and now a cow. Such modesty is quite unjustified. If you were a cow, you would undoubtedly be the prettiest one in the herd!'

His gallantry made her smile, but she wondered at such open flirtatiousness. Along the way back to Hill Street she became aware of a few haughty stares directed at the two of them.

'Are you listening to me?' Emery demanded at one point, pulling her back from her woolgathering.

'Oh, I am sorry,' she apologised. 'I was off in an air dream. You were saying?'

'I was asking you to join me at a play at Drury Lane next week.'

'Drury Lane?'

'Do you turn cat in the pan at the idea of setting foot in such a den of vice?' he quizzed. 'I assure you that even Lady Jersey herself ventures into the theatre.'

'No, it isn't that. It's Miss Beaseley.'

'Miss Beaseley?!' he ejaculated, thunderstruck. 'What the devil does she have to do with anything? I thought we were discussing the theatre.'

'So we were. But really, Emery, it won't do. You're betrothed to Miss Beaseley.'

'I need no reminder of that,' he said with just a trace of hauteur in his face.

'Then you must see that the proprieties must be observed.'

He looked deeply into her eyes. 'Propriety can be hanged!' he said vehemently. A wild surge of hope flooded Thea's breast. Was it possible that he meant to flout convention and cry off from his engagement to Miss Beaseley?

'Well?' he asked impatiently.

'Well what?'

'Drury Lane. Will you come with me?' The impatience in his voice was tempered with the smile in his eyes and the temptation was too great for her to resist.

'Yes. I should love it.'

Back at Hill Street she mulled over her feelings for Emery, finally acknowledging the truth that had been building for weeks. She was in love with Emery. But what if anything did he feel for her? He had never so much as hinted at anything other than the affection of a friend. In manner and deportment he was always friendly, almost an older brother who was prone to tease.

Brooding, she lay down on her bed to rest and fell asleep dreaming of the viscount, but it was a disturbing dream, for the lady at his side was not her but Louisa Beaseley.

Amelia's invitation to her brother to dine had been nearly forgotten in the excitement over the baby. Jonathon, however, recalled it to her mind after returning from Mr Davidson's, and she dashed, shrieking, into the kitchen to notify Gaston.

'And I do hope that Emery remembers, for I have gone through a good deal of trouble,' Amelia confided to Thea later that afternoon. 'Not to mention having Gaston throw a Gallic fit for not being informed earlier.'

Amelia need not have concerned herself, for Emery had not forgotten the invitation. He had indeed looked forward to a cosy dinner *en famille*, particularly since he would get a chance to see Thea again.

He took particular pains with his toilette even as he wondered if it would be in vain. There was no certainty that she would be present for dinner, given her six gentleman callers from the day before.

He would have to take steps to squelch these applicants to Miss Campion's hand while at the same time holding Miss Beaseley at bay. He was still absorbed in the thorny problem of Miss Beaseley as he strolled over to Hill Street. His eagerness had made him early, and Thea and Jonathon were still abovestairs. Amelia, however, was in the Green Drawing Room, looking—as he told her—even more radiant than ever.

'Oh, Emery, you shall turn my head with such flummery,' she said, pleased none the less and wishing she might divulge the real reason for her glowing face.

'I wish Charles were here to see you.'

'So do I,' she exclaimed, prompting a quizzing look from him. 'How was he when you left?'

'Well enough. Planning to go on to Kemble's for a look at the Arabians.' He took the sherry she offered him. 'Where's Thea?'

'Still abovestairs,' she said, smiling a little at his eagerness. He saw the smile and remembered her scheme with Jason.

'Don't look so pleased, Amelia,' he said now. 'Your accomplice, Jason, has told me all.'

She spread her hands wide in innocence. 'What are you speaking of?'

'And don't show that missish face to me. You know well what I am speaking of. Setting Jason on to pay court to Thea in order to make me jealous.'

'Oh, that! And here I thought you were about to divulge something far more sinister.'

He laughed. 'I congratulate you on your scheme. It was first-rate.'

She accepted this with aplomb. 'Why, thank you, my lord.' She dimpled. 'I did think it was one of my best ideas.'

'Does Charles know what you've been up to?'

'No. If he did, he'd have told me so. I did hint about it, but men can be so stupid.'

He accepted this ringing indictment of his sex with surprising equanimity. 'All the same, Amelia, I congratulate you and have every hope myself of emulating you in my marriage!'

These innocent words triggered a laugh from Amelia, but they triggered a far different emotion in the breast of one Theodora Campion, who stood just outside the drawing-room door. Thea had been on the verge of entering when she overheard the tail end of the conversation between Emery and his sister.

Congratulate Amelia on her scheme. Hope to emulate her in his marriage. Thea felt a trembling begin deep inside her body. She was no skittlebrain who had to have things spelled out for her! Emery's open flirtation amounted to no more than a scheme to offer her carte-blanche later when he married Miss Beaseley. Amelia had her cicisbeo. Presumably gentlemen had their *chères amies*.

'But this is one *chère amie* he shan't have,' she said grimly to herself, blinking back tears of rage.

CHAPTER NINETEEN

JONATHON, coming down the steps in his latest purchase—a demure russet coat over a matching set of
trousers—nearly collided headlong with Thea outside the
drawing-room door.

'Thea, aren't you going in?' he asked. 'Hardy said
Emery had arrived.'

'So he has,' Thea said, some of the colour returning
to her ashen face. 'Forgive me, Jonathon. Go on ahead.
I must fetch something from my room.' With that, she
bolted up the stairs he had just descended.

Once in her bedchamber she stood, her body trembling with rage.

So Emery thought her no better than a high flyer, did
he? And to think she had believed differently. A harsh
laugh caught in her throat. It was infamous. And it was
a stroke of fortune that she had discovered his true intention before she had behaved like a perfect moonling
towards him.

A momentary blush suffused her cheeks as she thought
of the girlish dreams she had entertained earlier in the
day. Emery no doubt had been entertaining dreams of
an entirely different stripe about her.

'Propriety be hanged,' he had said only this morning.
And so it would with Miss Beaseley as his wife and she
as his *chère amie*!

Thea's cheeks burned as she dwelled on such an intended insult. He would pay for it if it were the last thing she ever did. But how? She could not share the humiliation with anyone! Her closest male relative in the city was Jonathon, who was no match for Emery in any affair of honour. No, she would have to settle the matter herself: repay his insult with insult.

'Thea, are you all right?' Amelia asked from outside the door. 'Jonathon said you might be ill.'

'Ill? What an idiotish notion.' Thea forced a cheerful note into her voice and a smile to her lips as she came out of her bedchamber. 'Merely because I forgot to check if my shoes matched this dress, which of course they do. I can't think what a shatterbrain I am becoming.'

Amelia laughed with relief. 'I'm so glad. Nearly everyone is in the throes of the influenza, so they say. Come, my dear. Emery has been champing at the bit to see you. Such impatience. It is a real tribute to you.'

Thea's smile turned bitter. His lordship would be biting more than a bit before she was through with him!

'Here she is,' Amelia said when they entered the Green Drawing Room together.

Emery, who had been listening tolerantly to Jonathon's account of his first meeting with Davidson, lit up at the sight of Thea. She looked as beautiful as ever in a topaz-coloured gown with lace sleeves.

'My dear Miss Campion, if this is the work of those cherry ices, I would recommend one a day for you as for Lord Petersham,' he said, kissing her hand.

Only by a herculean effort did Thea resist snatching her hand away. She longed to box his ears.

'Cherry ices?' Amelia's voice was incredulous. 'I never heard of Petersham being fond of ices, Hadrian. You must mean tarts, and not cherry tarts but apricot tarts.'

'What has that to do with Thea?' Jonathon asked, looking bewildered.

'Emery and I had lunch together,' Thea divulged. 'We consumed a great number of cherry ices. Or at least I did. And I am grateful I didn't have the stomach-ache.' To go with the heartache, she thought grimly.

'Cherry ice,' Amelia said, a speculative gleam in her eye. 'Now that you mention it, I find myself with a sudden liking for it. And do you know what would go superbly over it? Chocolate sauce!'

This suggestion sparked looks of revulsion in her guests.

'Chocolate sauce?' Jonathon ejaculated. 'Lady Marlow, you can't be serious.'

'I shall give the order to Gaston,' Amelia said, proving that she was serious indeed. 'He had ordered ices from Mr Gunter's for tonight. I can probably persuade him to whip up a chocolate sauce to go with them. I shall tell him to make a large amount in case the three of you change your minds.'

'I won't,' Emery said, shuddering at the idea of such a concoction.

'She must be daft,' he said later after Amelia had gone off to give the order to her chef.

'I think Amelia is just as she always has been,' Thea replied coolly.

'Any female who would eat cherry ices with chocolate sauce over it ain't all right.' Jonathon uttered his opinion, a view that Gaston evidently shared, for the three of them could soon hear an angry Gallic voice emanating from the nether regions of the kitchen.

Amelia, however, emerging unscathed from the encounter ten minutes later, blithely assured them that Gaston was hard-pressed for time tonight but had agreed to have the treat ready for tomorrow.

She turned to her brother. 'So if you care to come by then and try it, Hadrian.'

'Good heavens, no,' he expostulated. 'And before I lose my appetite completely, when do we eat?'

No sooner was the question out of his lips than Hardy appeared with word that dinner was waiting their pleasure in the small dining-room, where they adjourned to sample Gaston's culinary delights—including a full roast duckling, turtle soup and tiny French cakes. The two men ate heartily, exchanging opinions about horses, clothing and snuff, the last a subject of keen interest to Jonathon.

Amelia was an amiable but abstracted hostess, a mood that also affected Thea, Emery thought, for she seemed curiously changed from their last encounter, only hours before. Even as he bent an encouraging ear to Jonathon's sartorial difficulties, he wondered about Thea's mood.

'I have eaten too much,' Emery groaned at last when they moved from the dining-room to the Green Drawing Room. 'I shall have to work it off tomorrow lest I die of dyspepsia and gout and all the vile ailments gluttons are prey to.'

'How do you plan to work it off?' Thea asked.

'I might take Pompeii for a run in the park tomorrow morning,' he said, and, remembering her love of horses, invited her to join him.

Thea's first impulse was to refuse, but one look at his hopeful face sparked a new idea. She accepted.

'Is eight too early?' she asked.

The viscount, who considered nine and ten early enough, was surprised, but supposed that for a change he could rise early. And if it meant seeing Thea, he would do so willingly.

'Eight will be fine,' he said.

'Good,' Thea smiled. 'I shall see you here, then.'

Amelia, pleased that the viscount and Thea were getting reacquainted, offered him brandy and one of Charles's prize cigars. He accepted the brandy but declined the cigar.

'Thank heaven,' Amelia murmured. 'Cigars smell so. How any man can actually smoke such a thing is beyond my comprehension.'

'I'd sooner snuff myself,' Jonathon said, a little miffed that the cigars had not been offered to him. Remembering that he had not acquired the knack of taking snuff, he sought advice from the viscount on this facet of his education.

'My dear boy, don't tell me Ludlow hasn't shown you how.'

'As a matter of fact, I thought of applying to him,' Jonathon confessed. 'But he might think me a veritable gudgeon, whereas...' He hesitated as Emery lifted a quizzical brow. 'I don't mind if you think me a gudgeon,' he said naïvely.

Much touched by this display of trust, the viscount took out his snuff-box and demonstrated the proper method of flicking it open with the barest touch of a thumbnail.

'There are those who favour the one-handed method,' he said, demonstrating it, 'but I prefer two hands. One shouldn't like to spill the mixture.'

'No, indeed,' Jonathon murmured. 'I do that often enough as it is.'

'Then you insert two fingers and take the merest pinch; too much inevitably sparks a fit of sneezing. And then...' He lifted it up to his right nostril and inhaled delicately.

'Oh, first rate, sir,' Jonathon exclaimed. 'Brummell himself could not have done better.'

'Before you heap such lavish praise on my head, you'd better try it yourself,' Emery said, laughing and holding out the snuff-box. Jonathon took a judicious pinch and inhaled.

'Not bad,' the viscount said critically, 'but you might take a trifle less and not inhale it quite so vigorously.'

By the time he said adieu, Jonathon had managed to win his approbation in the taking of snuff, much to the amusement of both ladies present.

It was kind of him to show Jonathon how to master the art of snuff-taking, Thea admitted that night as she prepared for bed. One would never suspect that he was anything but what he seemed: a doting friend eager to help them in London. However, she knew differently. She blew out her candle and drew the coverlet up to her chin, feeling rather pleased with what lay in wait for the viscount the following morning.

At the godforsaken hour of seven on Sunday morning, Emery rose from his bed. For no other female, he told himself as he rubbed the last traces of Morpheus from his eyes, would he do such a thing. Leading his second hack, he rode over to Hill Street, still struggling with a yawn.

'Good morning, Hardy,' he said when the butler opened the door. 'Is Miss Campion ready?'

The butler looked doubtfully at him. 'Miss Campion? I believe she is still abovestairs, my lord.'

'I shall wait.'

'Yes, certainly. But I think I must warn you that it may be a considerable wait. Miss Campion has adopted the town habit of not rising before ten.'

Emery stared at the butler. 'Do you mean to tell me she's still asleep?' he demanded. 'Impossible!'

The servant's brows raised a fraction of an inch. 'My lord, Miss Campion has stayed in bed well past ten on several past occasions.'

'I don't mean that. I mean she can't be asleep today of all days. We're riding in the park. I invited her only last evening.'

'I could be wrong,' Hardy conceded.

'Quite probable,' the viscount said with a nod. 'I dare say it happens to the best of us, Hardy. Despatch one of the maids to see when she will be ready.'

Hardy, acceding to this request, dispatched Betty up the stairs. The maid, peeking in, found Thea with eyes shut and coverlet drawn over her shoulders. She looked to be fast asleep. Unsure what she should do next, she crept out and back down the stairs, where the viscount waited, one boot tapping impatiently on the bottom step.

'Well?' he asked.

She shrank back involuntarily. 'Miss Campion is asleep, my lord.'

'Asleep?' He looked dumbfounded. 'Wake her up. We're to ride this morning.'

'Yes, my lord,' Betty said, and scurried back up the stairs. But once she was in Thea's room, she hesitated. It was one thing for the viscount to command that she shake Thea awake; it was quite another to actually do the deed. Fortunately for her peace of mind, she was spared the necessity of making this decision, as Thea's eyes fluttered awake.

'Oh, Miss Thea.' She pounced quickly on these signs of life. 'I am so glad you are awake.'

'What is it, Betty?' Thea asked, yawning and preparing to dive back beneath the coverlet.

'It's Lord Emery, miss. He's downstairs asking for you.'

'Asking for me?' Thea said, a little confused, then she smiled as she remembered the ride they had planned. 'What time is it?' she asked mildly.

'A quarter past eight. I shall help you to dress.'

'That won't be necessary, Betty,' Thea said, declining the maid's helping hands. 'Tell Lord Emery that I am still asleep.'

'Miss Thea!' The servant looked shocked 'I did tell him that before, and he ordered me to wake you up.'

'He did?' Thea exclaimed, rather annoyed that Emery would issue such a command. 'Then you may tell him I have fallen asleep again.'

'But he'll merely send me back to rouse you. He seemed to think you had an important appointment with him. I overheard Hardy say something about riding in the park.'

Thea sat up in the bed. 'Betty, tell the viscount for me that I am obliged to him, but I have changed my mind. I shan't wish to accompany him on that ride we had planned.'

Betty's usually placid face went several shades pinker. 'Miss Thea!'

'You heard me, Betty,' Thea said firmly.

'Yes, miss,' Betty said, and then went out of the room and down the stairs, fearing the explosion that would undoubtedly ensue.

'Well?' Emery asked as she appeared. 'Is Miss Campion awake?'

'Oh, yes, my lord,' Betty said quickly.

'Good. I only hope she can change into a riding-habit without too much delay. I don't like to leave the horses standing for long in this wind.'

'I don't believe there will be any riding-habit, my lord.' Betty ventured this timid opinion.

He swivelled his head towards her. 'What do you mean by no riding-habit? She can't mean to ride in her nightdress!'

'No, of course not,' Betty said, her mind boggling at the image his words conjured up. 'Miss Campion directed me with a message for you. She has changed her mind.'

'Changed her mind?' the viscount repeated incredulously.

'I believe, my lord,' Hardy interposed, much to Betty's relief, 'that such is the prerogative of the female sex.'

Emery snorted. 'I hadn't believed her to be such a ninnyhammer. Are you certain she knows I am the one asking for her?'

'Oh, yes, my lord. I told her so myself,' Betty said. 'And she still seemed unwilling to rise. That's when she ordered me to be sure and tell you that she's changed her mind and won't be riding after all.'

Emery glanced up the banister, feeling a temptation to have Miss Campion repeat those words to his face. But since propriety dictated that no gentleman other than one's nearest and dearest could invade a lady's boudoir, that route seemed closed to him.

Quite obviously Thea did not wish to ride with him. Then why the devil had she jumped at his invitation last evening?

'Perhaps she is ill,' he said, reluctant to believe that she was deliberately provoking him.

Betty, however, scotched this notion, divulging that Thea did not appear sick, merely a trifle sleepy, which was only to be expected so early in the day.

'You are still welcome to wait, my lord,' the butler intoned discreetly. 'Until Miss Campion feels the inclination to rise.'

Emery twisted his lips bleakly. 'No, thank you, Hardy. I know full well when my presence is undesired.' With that he turned and stalked out.

A cold fury whipped through him as he rode Pompeii back to Mount Street, still leading his second hack. One look at his thundercloud face, and Chadwick swallowed his salutation and avoided any mention of breakfast. In his experience, Emery would be holing up in his bookroom until his temper cooled.

True to his butler's expectation, Emery strode into his library, pulling off his York tan gloves, which he then threw into the fire—a sight that would have smitten Kemp to the core!

Was there ever such a female? Who did she think she was? No woman had ever dared to treat him so scurrilously. And had she not hidden away in her bedchamber he would have told her so point-blank. But it was so unlike her to resort to such missish ways.

Pivoting, Emery flung himself into an armchair. She must be ill, despite Betty's words. Or else, why the sudden change of heart about their ride? He had thought her unlike the usual female in the ton, who delighted in playing one gentleman against the other. So what was she up to now?

He was still brooding over this when Chadwick entered an hour later. The viscount looked up with a frown.

'I won't be needing breakfast.'

'Yes, my lord, I thought not. But you have a caller, sir.'

A grim smile came to Emery's lips. Had Thea come to apologise for her treatment of him?

'Male or female?' he snapped, rising from his chair.

'Why, female, sir.'

Chadwick had no opportunity to utter another syllable, for Emery shot out of the library and into the Blue Drawing Room, coming to a rigid halt when he perceived that his visitor was not Thea, as he had hoped, but Miss Beaseley, with her aunt.

'Oh,' he murmured, 'it's you.'

Realising that this was not the most gallant of greetings, he made a quick recovery. 'Chadwick didn't tell me that it was you.'

'I know it must be a surprise,' Miss Beaseley said, wringing a lace handkerchief between her fingers. 'And I dare say you think it odd of me to call like this. But I had heard you were in London for the past three days.'

'Two, actually,' he drawled. 'I came late on Friday afternoon.'

'So I thought I might visit you. And I did bring along my aunt.'

'So I noticed,' Emery said, smiling at Mrs Chester, who did not return that smile but directed a rather peculiar look of her own at him. He felt a guilty pang, aware that he should have paid a call on Miss Beaseley earlier. It had slipped his mind.

'I told Louisa that she needn't be concerned about calling on you like this,' Mrs Chester said as she sat down on the Egyptian couch with Miss Beaseley, 'since the two of you are betrothed.'

'I need no reminder of that, ma'am,' Emery said with an autocratic sniff, which had the desired result of silencing Mrs Chester.

He turned towards her niece and forced a smile to his lips. Amelia had mentioned her eagerness for him to meet her family. No doubt she was here to press such an issue. His mind dwelled fleetingly on such a family gathering, the hands to be shaken, the names to be sorted out. He shuddered.

'How have you been?' he asked now, a question that seemed to agitate Miss Beaseley, for she jumped when he addressed her.

'Been?' she repeated. 'Oh, I have been quite stout. And you, my lord? Your shoulder?'

'As fine as fivepence,' he said.

These few words appeared to have exhausted Miss Beaseley's conversational skills.

'Have you called for any particular reason?' he asked a trifle impatiently.

'Any particular reason?' Miss Beaseley seemed to function as an echo this morning. 'No, we were just passing by and thought to stop and see how you were. But now we should be going.'

'But, Louisa,' Mrs Chester protested, 'you haven't told him . . .'

'Told me what?' Emery asked, looking from face to face. He had enough of confused riddles for one day. 'Is there something you wish to tell me?' he asked sternly.

Miss Beaseley gave her head an emphatic shake. 'We should be going.' She all but pushed her aunt out of the door.

Relieved to see her go, Emery succumbed to the notion of breakfast and went in to the breakfast parlour, wondering what the London air had done to the females he had known. His sister had developed a strange appetite for cherry tarts and chocolate sauce. Miss Campion had changed from a female of sense to a flirtatious ninny-hammer, and Miss Beaseley had made the unheralded transformation from prattlebox to mute!

CHAPTER TWENTY

ONCE Emery had left Hill Street, Thea abandoned her pose on the bed, but delighted little in her victory over him. Betty had supplied her with the full details of the outrage he had manifested, and while one part of her rejoiced that he had received his comeuppance, another part was strangely discomfited.

Her conflicting emotions stayed with her throughout Sunday and well into Monday evening. She, along with Amelia and Jonathon, was promised to the Seftons for an event that had been anticipated with more eagerness than usual.

The patroness had a reputation as one of the premier hostesses in the kingdom. Thea, however, scarcely noticed the crush of carriages outside the Seftons' home nor the dazzling display of flowers—orchids!—that had been shaped into a heart through which each guest passed.

'You are in a lachrymal mood this evening,' Jason observed during one of her dances.

'I'm sorry.' She gave a guilty start. 'I am not myself tonight.'

'From what Hadrian tells me, you were not yourself yesterday morning either,' he said blandly.

Her eyes met his, and she could not suppress her curiosity. 'What did he say about me?'

'Merely that between Saturday night and Sunday morning you had lost your fascination with riding,' Jason said diplomatically. 'I told him he must have done something stupid to have you fly into a sudden pet, but of course he is too much of a gudgeon to remember what it is.'

Her laugh was close to a sob.

'So tell me,' Jason went on with a kindly look. 'What has he done? I promise to relay the message to him. The role of peacemaker is unfamiliar to me, but I trust I can function well enough to help you both to sort out this coil.'

'You are very kind, Jason,' Thea replied, for there could be no doubt about his genuine wish to help. 'But truly you can't be of any use.'

'Let me try,' he suggested. 'What, pray, has Emery done?'

There was no earthly way Thea could divulge to a gentleman like Jason just what Emery's intentions had been towards her. So she merely shook her head and hoped he would not press her. Although he looked disappointed he did not pursue the point, and she was glad when their dance ended and Daughtery took his place as her partner.

The earl's politics seemed easier to tolerate this evening than Jason's kindness. Daughtery himself seemed rather less garrulous than usual, an occurrence that would have piqued her interest if her own thoughts had not been so absorbed. The two danced in an amicable silence, which ended when she caught sight of Emery's tall figure striding about the ballroom.

She had not dreamed that he would appear at the Seftons' ball. Amelia had assured her that this was precisely the type of affair he loathed and would view any appearance there as a penance. But there was no mistaking him. He was, she was bound to admit, the most elegant man in the room. He was also staring pointedly at her through his quizzing-glass.

Her temper mounted as he made her the object of his scrutiny. She would give him something to look at through that odious glass of his. Thinking thusly, she smiled dazzlingly up at the earl, who was so overcome by this change in behaviour that he gaped at her with real concern.

'Are you feeling at all the thing, Miss Campion?' he asked.

'Oh, yes,' she said, smiling as they danced near the viscount. 'I am enjoying myself, aren't you?'

'Well, yes, I suppose so.'

'How was your speech today at Parliament?' she enquired, conscious that the viscount had put down his glass and stood with arms crosssed on his broad chest.

Daughtery had brightened at her mention of Parliament. 'Oh, first-rate,' he said, and with that for an opening proceeded to enlighten her with just what had been said in the hallowed house that morning.

While Thea was listening to this, Emery was mulling over her apparent fascination with the earl. Was it possible she had thrown him over for Daughtery? An absurd idea, but stranger ideas had taken root in the heads of females. As he mused further on this unlikelihood he found his sister at his elbow.

'Hadrian!' she exclaimed, looking quite elegant in a ballgown of spider-white gauze with matching pearls sewn in the hem. 'I never thought I'd see you here! You consider Maria Sefton's parties penance of the highest order.'

'Good evening, Amelia. I had not intended to come, but I changed my mind—which is a prerogative of my sex as well as yours.'

Amelia gave him a sympathetic smile. 'In the mood to mend your fences with Thea?'

He scowled. 'If I only knew what to make up for! Anyway, it's she who owes me the apology.'

'Thea has been acting most peculiarly of late,' Amelia revealed now, watching her dance by with the earl. 'She turned rather frosty even with me the other day. Perhaps she feels the awkwardness of her position. You are still betrothed to Louisa Beaseley.'

'I need no reminder of that, Amelia,' he said with a trace of hauteur discernible in his handsome face.

His tone would have squelched anyone but his sister, who merely bade him not to get on his high ropes. 'And what caused that thunderous scene between you and Thea? Betty was nearly scared witless by you. It's a pity I wasn't at hand to see it for myself, but I was fast asleep, having consumed too many ices the night before.'

'I wonder that you could even sleep, Amelia, with some of the vile concoctions you want to eat nowadays. And it wasn't so thunderous a scene, for Miss Campion fights her battles from a distance. She didn't even have the gumption to leave her bed and face me.'

'She's left it tonight,' Amelia pointed out. 'And if you do wish to know why she is in the hips with you, I'd suggest that now is as good a time as any to discover why.'

Emery, thinking the matter over after Amelia had glided off, decided that she was right and crossed the room quickly to Thea's side, where he bowed and solicited the honour of her hand in the next waltz.

'I'm afraid that my cousin Jonathon has that honour, my lord,' Thea said stiffly, and turned to smile on Jonathon, who was approaching.

'But I'm quite willing to relinquish it to Emery,' Jonathon said when the viscount had appealed to him for help.

'You may relinquish it,' Thea said coldly, 'but perhaps I shan't grant it.'

'That doesn't surprise me,' Emery returned. 'You doubtless find it uncomfortable to face me. I dare say if a maid were near, you would make her refuse your partners tonight.'

'You are not my partner,' she snapped, 'and if you wish the dance so much, we will.'

With meticulous courtesy he led her out on to the floor. 'Isn't it odd how one can think he knows a person, and yet at the last moment discover something untoward about him or her?' he remarked.

An enigmatic look transfixed her face. 'You take the words right out of my mouth, my lord.'

The scornful note in her voice jolted him. 'Why the blazes are you so angry with me?' he demanded, abandoning all pretence.

She tossed her head back. 'Ask Amelia.'

'Amelia?' He nearly trod on her foot. 'What has she to do with anything?'

Her green eyes flashed. 'You and she are brother and sister, after all. You must share the same view of life and people.'

'Let me have the word with no bark in it, Miss Campion,' he demanded. 'Unless'—his eyes narrowed—'your courage deserts you as it did yesterday morning when you hid cravenly in your bedchamber rather than face me.'

'I was not dressed to receive visitors,' she said stiffly.

'Will you be similarly indisposed to dress on Thursday evening?'

She frowned. 'Thursday? What happens then?'

His smile tightened. 'We were to go to Drury Lane,' he reminded her. 'I see that it has slipped your mind. How fortunate that I am here to remind you. Now you can tell me ahead of time whether you shall have the headache or whatever excuses females dream up nowadays.'

She flinched. 'I do not dream up excuses, my lord.'

'My apologies.' His tone was ironic and his eyes glinted. 'Perhaps you will merely have changed your mind, which, as Hardy told me, is the prerogative of your sex. Only, I do wish you would change it a little sooner and spare me the burden of appearing a total cake!'

'And what would I have resembled had I allowed you to go on with your odious scheme?' she blurted out.

The viscount had reached the limits of his endurance. 'What a farrago of nonsense this is, Miss Campion! You are undoubtedly the only female of my acquaintance who could find something sinister in a ride in the park.'

'I didn't mean that . . .' she said hoarsely.

'What about Drury Lane?' he asked coldly, as she did not elaborate further on what she meant. 'Would you still be going?'

'On one condition.'

He lifted an eyebrow. 'Which is?'

'That you invite Miss Beaseley to join us,' she said in dulcet tones.

'Are you daft?'

'On the contrary,' she said scorchingly. 'I *was* daft, but I have regained my wits.' And as the waltz came to an end, she did not wait for him but stalked away, leaving him alone, the target of much curious interest.

The habitués of Manton's shooting gallery shook their heads the next morning as they surveyed the viscount's shooting. It was obvious that Emery's mind was not on the target, for he had missed the bull's eye each time, and by a far wider margin that anyone there could recall. It was not at all usual for a crack shot like him.

Among those observing the viscount's errant ways with a pistol was Lord Daughtery, who had gone to Manton's expressly to find Emery, knowing it to be a favourite haunt. He had intended to speak to the viscount the night before at the Sefton's, but after Emery's tête-à-tête with Miss Campion, the viscount had bade an early adieu.

Anyone possessing a halfpennyworth of sense would have been warned off by the rigid stare in Emery's eyes, but the earl was no great barometer of perception.

'Good morning, Emery,' he said now.

The viscount, caught in the midst of reloading his pistol, glanced up with some annoyance and surprise. As a rule, no one interrupted him when he was shooting, particularly when he was shooting badly. He managed to throw a curt nod at the earl.

'Your mind is not on your shooting today,' Daughtery commented.

'So it would appear,' Emery replied. He fired again. Much better. A bull's-eye.

'Emery, I think we should have a talk,' Daughtery said, staring at the target.

The viscount grunted. 'Talk away.'

'It seems we share a certain admiration for a certain young lady.'

The viscount lowered his pistol arm. So Daughtery had an interest in Thea, did he?

'Yes,' he said mildly. 'I believe you've even taken her to Parliament.'

'You act as though it were a gaming-hall,' Daughtery said, rising to the defence of the halls he loved.

'Don't be idiotish. You're free to bore whomever you like with your speeches. But, I remind you, I have a claim to the young lady you so admire.'

'That may change,' Daughtery replied stiffly.

The viscount turned and glared at the other man. 'I give you fair warning, Daughtery. Leave it alone.'

'You are in no position to dictate what I should do or not do,' the earl replied, puffing out his cheeks in annoyance. He was an earl after all. Emery was merely a viscount.

Emery nodded now. 'You are quite right. I never dictate to coxcombs or fools. It's a waste of time.'

The earl turned crimson. 'Take those words back.'

'Which?' the viscount asked blandly. 'Coxcomb or fool?'

'Take it back, Emery, or'—Daughtery swallowed here—'I shall seek satisfaction.'

Emery was so surprised that he nearly dropped his pistol. 'Do you mean a duel, my good fellow?'

'If need be, yes,' the earl declared.

'There is no need to resort to that,' Emery protested. He was much the superior in swords and pistols and had no wish to prove it. 'I'll take my words back,' he said, willing to compromise, 'but only if you promise to quit plaguing that young lady we know.'

'I'd never promise any such thing!' the earl declared.

'Then,' the viscount said, rather astonished at the events that had just unfolded, 'I suppose we shall have a duel.'

'A duel with Daughtery—are you foxed or merely touched in the old cockloft?' Jason Ludlow demanded in his Albemarle Street establishment. His mood was somewhat surly, since he had been roused from a sound slumber by his friend, who was now pacing furiously in his library.

'What the devil are you duelling over? He's not the type to give offence. A bit of a bag pudding, I grant you, and as prosy as they come...'

'We are duelling over Miss Campion.' The viscount paused in his pacing.

Jason rubbed his eyes. 'A female? Good Jupiter, that's positively Gothic!'

'I don't care what it is,' Emery snapped. 'He wouldn't promise to stay away from Thea, so I lost my head and called him a few names.'

Ludlow peered over at his friend. 'What sorts of names?'

'Coxcomb and fool, for a start.'

Jason doubled over with laughter. 'I happen to agree with your opinion, Hadrian, but really, must you resort to duelling?'

'I don't need a peal rung over me. Just tell me if you'll stand second for me,' Emery said with mounting impatience. 'If not, I shall have to rouse someone else from a sound sleep.'

Jason held up a deprecating hand. 'If you do, you shan't have a friend left to you. I suppose I remember the form well enough,' he said, accepting the role the viscount had thrust upon him. 'I haven't had a duel myself in years. Are you using pistols or swords?'

'Pistols,' Emery answered.

Jason gave an approving nod. 'Good. Swords slash so. We'll need a surgeon to tend to Daughtery when you're finished with him. Or do you plan to kill him outright?'

'Don't talk rubbish,' Emery snorted. 'Find the best surgeon you can.'

'Of course,' Jason said, rubbing his hands. 'Now, when and where?'

'Tomorrow. Paddington Green. At dawn.'

Jason, after first deploring the impossibility of getting all the details of an affair of honour straight in a mere twenty-four hours, threw himself into the task with his usual boundless energy. His day passed quickly as he met with the earl's seconds to discuss the weapons, arranged for a doctor who would take care to stanch the flow of blood—and knowing Emery's skill, a good deal would undoubtedly flow from Daughtery—and, most importantly, kept a cloud of secrecy over the entire event to come lest someone such as Thea or Amelia got wind of it.

At six o'clock on Wednesday morning, Emery, accompanied by Jason, who was complaining bitterly about the necessity of rising so early, reached the Green. Daughtery, pacing with a cloak about his shoulders, was already there with his grim-faced second, who knew only too well their opponent's skill with a pistol. The only hope for his man was to pray that Emery's aim might be a little off.

A snowy-haired gentleman, the only other witness present, was introduced as Dr Callum. As the duelling pistols were examined and accepted by the seconds, Emery made a last attempt to end the matter.

'You can call a halt to all this, Daughtery,' he said mildly. 'Just promise me...'

'I promise you nothing,' the earl said, taking off his cloak. 'No one dictates to me about any lady I choose to court.'

'Then I have no choice,' Emery said with a shrug. If the earl was bent on a duel, a duel he would find. His eyes drifted speculatively over Daughtery's lanky body as he wondered where to plant a small but disabling wound that would be enough to stun him and cause him to drop his weapon, but not serious enough to cause a cessation of breath and life.

While he was mulling over the earl's curious anatomical properties—he seemed more bone than flesh!—a hack approached the Green and stopped. The door flew open, depositing Miss Beaseley on to the Green.

Her face was as pale as the cream-coloured redingote she wore.

'Thank goodness I have come in time!' she exclaimed.

'Good God, who told her about this?' Emery demanded.

'Not I,' Jason murmured.

'You shan't duel. You shan't!' she cried.

'My dear Louisa . . .' The viscount began to speak, but he felt his words withering on his tongue as Miss Beaseley ignored him and flung herself headlong into the earl's arms.

CHAPTER TWENTY-ONE

SEVERAL seconds elapsed before Miss Beaseley detached herself fully from the earl's bony chest.

'Louisa, I told you not to come,' Daughtery said, gazing ardently into her eyes.

'I had to, Denis. I couldn't stand by and let you be killed.'

'I shan't be killed!' he insisted. 'I am a good shot.'

'Oh, I know you are!' She retrieved this slip at once. 'But Emery is better.' She turned, perceiving the dumbfounded expression on the viscount's face, which had nothing to do with the fact that he was more than rather superior to the earl in pistols.

What was Miss Beaseley doing at Paddington Green? And why had she hurled herself on Daughtery's chest?

'Louisa . . .' Emery said now, attempting to delve into the mystery of her appearance.

Miss Beaseley shrank from his touch. 'You shan't get me to the altar, Emery! I don't care if we have announced our betrothal in the *Gazette*. I love Daughtery, and he loves me,' Miss Beaseley went on, oblivious of the inarticulate gurgle that came from the viscount's throat. 'Nothing you do can persuade me to wed you.'

'Persuade you to wed me?' The viscount almost choked on the words. He shook his head. 'Louisa, are you trying to tell me that you and Daughtery . . .'

'Yes.' The earl spoke up. 'And despite your prior claim to her, I shan't stop seeing her, in the way you wanted.'

'My prior claim to her,' Emery echoed as enlightenment dawned at last. 'Good God, you were speaking of Miss Beaseley yesterday morning at Manton's!'

Daughtery looked aggrieved. 'Naturally of Miss Beaseley. Who else could there be?'

'I know you must think it bad of us,' Miss Beaseley put in hastily, 'but I couldn't help myself, Emery. I've been in love with Denis ever since I first heard him speak in Parliament!'

'They say that politics makes strange bedfellows,' Jason murmured under his breath to Emery.

'And jealousy makes cocklebrains,' Emery muttered back. He turned to Miss Beaseley, who had taken this opportunity to reattach herself to the earl's bosom. 'But why didn't you tell me of your tendre for Daughtery?' he demanded now. 'I should have released you from our engagement at once!'

'I did try to tell you the other day when I called with my aunt, but you looked as sulky as a bear. I couldn't get the words out.'

'My apologies!' he bowed. 'Had I been slightly more civil, I should have spared us all considerable distress.'

'Indeed you would have,' Miss Beaseley agreed. 'I even thought of eloping. But Denis thought that rather drastic. He thought to speak to you man-to-man, only of course the two of you would choose to duel instead.'

'A difficulty that has been resolved with your help,' Emery said at once, suddenly aware that with his engagement to Miss Beaseley dissolved, he was free at last to marry Thea. That was, if she allowed him the opportunity to tender a proposal!

* * *

A half-hour later, Thea descended the Adam stairs and came to a rigid halt as a gentleman came through the door.

'Charles!' she exclaimed before lowering her voice to a hush. 'What are you doing here?'

'I live here, remember?' Charles replied, rather put out by such a greeting. He handed his coat, hat and portmanteau to Hardy. 'I got a letter from Amelia telling me to come here at once. She's never interrupted me before, so I know the issue must be pressing. Do you know what's it about?'

Thea could not bring herself to dissemble in the face of his worried eyes. 'Yes,' she spoke softly. 'But I'd much rather you heard it from Amelia.'

'Well, where is she?'

'Upstairs, but you can't go up!' Thea said, stepping in his way.

'And why not?' he asked, rather affronted by his guest's issuing commands to him concerning what he could and could not do in his own residence.

A wave of pity for the unsuspecting gentleman in front of her swept over Thea. 'Charles. Poor, dear, devoted Charles! Believe me, I know well what you are going through.'

'Do you?' Lord Marlow asked affably. 'I'm glad, for I certainly don't!'

'Come into the breakfast parlour,' she coaxed, leading him in as she spoke. 'Have some coffee and something to eat. Your Gaston has buns nearly the equal of Sally Lunn's. Do have one.' She held out a plate of the buns.

Charles, who was a trifle hungry after his long journey, resisted nobly. 'I'll eat after I see Amelia.'

'But you may not feel like eating then,' she warned. Tears suddenly sprang into her eyes. 'Oh, why did this have to happen to you?'

'There, there,' Charles said uneasily. Why his appearance should suddenly spark a show of the vapours in Thea was beyond his understanding. She had not struck him as the vapourish sort, but then one never did know about females.

'Charles,' Thea said, once again taking command of herself, 'I'm sorry. There is no point in turning into a watering-pot. I just want you to remember that I am on your side. Should you need any help at all, you have only to ask.'

The portentous note in her words alarmed him. 'I say, Thea, Amelia ain't ill, is she?'

'Not in the sense you mean.'

Before he could respond to this, which hinted of dire straits indeed, Emery strode in unannounced, his great multicoloured driving-cape flung over one shoulder. Charles brightened. He would get some sensible answers from Hadrian.

'Hadrian!' He greeted his brother-in-law with relief.

'Hello, Charles,' Emery said distractedly. 'Thea, I must speak to you.'

'Later,' she ordered. 'Can't you see I am comforting poor Charles?'

Since Lord Marlow boasted an income of nearly twenty thousand pounds annually, Emery was surprised to hear him so described, as was Marlow himself.

'Thea,' Lord Marlow expostulated, 'I insist you tell me what is going on.'

'Have some coffee,' she insisted.

'I don't want any. I want Amelia!' His protests were in vain as she thrust a cup at him.

'Thea!' Emery, having come this far, was prepared to declare himself even in Charles's presence.

'Do you want some coffee too?' she asked.

'No, blast it, *I want you!*' he roared.

Thea blenched. 'Emery, really...'

'I know this ain't the proper mode, but I've thought of nothing else since I met you. And since of late you seem determined to hide from me when we meet, I must take advantage of seeing you here.'

Charles coughed discreetly. 'I say, Hadrian, p'rhaps I should leave. Not the right thing to be present when a fellow makes love to a female.'

Thea sniffed. 'You needn't go, Charles! Emery is not making love to me.'

'No,' the viscount agreed. 'I had rather thought I was making you an offer.'

Thea gasped, then reached for the nearest object—a pitcher of cream—which she dashed full into Emery's face, blinding him temporarily.

'Here,' Lord Marlow came swiftly to his brother-in-law's aid, 'what sort of madness is this, Thea? No call to get disagreeable just because Emery is offering you marriage.'

'He is not offering me marriage,' Thea said hotly. 'He is offering me *carte-blanche.*'

'What?' Lord Marlow dropped the handkerchief he had been applying to the viscount's face and peered down at him. 'I say, Hadrian, that's deuced out of character for you.'

Emery broke free from Charles's ministrations. *'Carte-blanche?'* he said thickly, glaring at Thea. 'Where the devil did you get such a besotted idea?'

'From you and Amelia!' Thea replied.

'Amelia?' Charles ejaculated.

'Amelia?' Emery frowned.

'Yes, Amelia,' Thea declared.

'Are the three of you gossiping behind my back?' a gay voice enquired as Amelia came into the breakfast parlour. 'Charles, my love, how wonderful to see you. Hardy told me you had arrived.' She pecked him on the cheek and turned next to her brother. 'Hadrian, is there any more cream for my coffee, or has it all been deposited on your shirt?'

'Here, take mine,' Charles said, handing her his cup. 'I don't want it.'

'Thank you, my dear. And if you would just hand me that jar of strawberry jam, please.'

He looked puzzled, but passed it obediently to her, flinching when she put a dollop of the jam into her coffee and stirred it.

'What a cosy group this is,' Amelia said brightly. 'And it's not even eight o'clock yet!'

'Amelia, you don't mean to drink that, do you?' Charles asked, a look of horror on his face.

'It's rather good,' Amelia said, smacking her lips as she sipped it. 'You must try it.'

'I'd sooner chew on laurel leaves!' he retorted.

'But that's poisonous,' she exclaimed.

'Exactly my point!'

She squeezed his hand. 'Dear Charles, how I have missed you. I suppose you are on pins and needles to know why I summoned you away from Kemble's.'

'Amelia,' Thea interrupted, not wishing to view Charles's humiliation at first hand, 'don't you think Emery and I should leave?'

'Of course not, Thea,' Amelia replied. 'Emery must know some time, and I should like you all to share the news.'

She turned back to her waiting husband as Thea steeled herself for the inevitable bombshell.

'Charles,' Amelia announced, 'I am going to have a baby!'

'What? Amelia, my dear!' Charles exclaimed, enfolding her in his arms.

'So that explains the cherry ices and the chocolate sauce,' Emery said, glad to have a reasonable explanation for his sister's exotic tastes.

'Have you been to a doctor?' Charles asked Amelia.

'Yes, the new one recommended by Dr Marsh. And I must own, he looks so young, but he knows all the latest developments. And I have been very discreet about seeing him, for I didn't want any of your family here to catch sight of me. They might have been disappointed if it had been futile. Indeed, the only one who did suspect what was happening was Thea.' She paused and beamed happily at Thea, who had been riveted by the announcement.

Amelia was going to have a baby! She had been meeting her doctor surreptitiously, not a cicisbeo after all.

'That is good news,' Charles said, calling for champagne, after first eliciting Amelia's solemn promise not to put strawberry jam in it.

Emery, who had observed Thea's stupefaction in the bubbling excitement, seized the opportunity to hustle her out of the breakfast-room. 'For I do think Charles and Amelia should be allowed some private moments together, don't you?' he asked, leading her to a small parlour.

'Yes, yes, of course,' she agreed, still in somewhat of a fog. 'Amelia is going to have a baby, Emery.'

'So she says.'

'A baby,' she repeated, 'not a cicisbeo.'

His brows lifted. 'Cicisbeo? Our Amelia?'

She gave a rueful laugh. 'I know it sounds idiotish.'

'No more idiotish than my offering you *carte-blanche*,' he said blandly. She blushed as she recalled her accusation.

'I have been guilty of many things, Miss Campion, but never of offering you *carte-blanche*.'

'Yes, I realise that now,' she said, stricken. 'But, you see, I can explain. I thought Amelia was bent on taking a cicisbeo, since she was being so secretive about meeting a man. He must have been her doctor, I realise now. And then you congratulated her on her scheme one evening and even announced your wish to emulate her. So I thought the two of you... Oh, I dare say it was stupid of me. But what other scheme could there be?'

'The scheme,' he explained, 'was Amelia's little plan to make me jealous of Jason, who was being so attentive to you. And, by Jove, it worked.'

'Oh,' she said in a small voice, feeling suddenly very shy.

His eyes were bright. 'Make a female an honourable offer, and see what results!'

'Honourable? But you are still betrothed to Miss Beaseley, Emery, unless you've cried off.'

'I haven't cried off,' he told her.

She was conscious of a disappointment. 'Oh.'

'I have been jilted,' he said, watching her carefully.

'Jilted?' she exclaimed. 'By Miss Beaseley? You must be hoaxing me.'

He shook his head. 'Believe me, no gentleman jokes of such a thing.'

'But why?'

He rubbed his jaw ruefully. 'It seems she prefers another in my place. Daughtery.'

'Daughtery?' Thea sank into the velvet settee. 'She must be daft.'

He laughed. 'No, merely engrossed in politics. Fortunately I discovered their tendre before I was obliged to shoot Daughtery.'

She laid one hand on her breast. 'Shoot him?'

'Yes. In our duel.'

'Duel? Emery, I don't quite understand.'

He smiled at her tenderly. 'No, of course not. But there will be time to discuss that after we have settled more pressing matters.'

She felt his arm stealing about her waist. 'Such as?'

'Such as our wedding.'

'Our wedding? I have not said I will marry you,' she reminded him.

'No,' he agreed affably. 'You have merely said that you would not accept *carte-blanche* from me, and I should wring your neck for even thinking that. Instead of which...' He kissed her firmly on the mouth.

Thea, responding instantly to the kiss, shivered slightly and burrowed deeper into his embrace. He pressed his lips against the side of her throat.

'You must marry me,' the viscount said minutes later as they sat still entwined on the settee, 'if only to spare me the considerable humiliation of being jilted by one female and refused by another all in one day!'

She laughed. 'How could any female refuse such an inviting offer?'

'Easily. You have only to ask Miss Beaseley.'

Her fingers traced the line of his jaw. 'I shan't do any such thing! She might change her mind.'

'As is the prerogative of your sex,' he teased as he dropped a kiss on her nose. 'I love you, Thea.'

'And I, you, Hadrian.'

They were engaged in demonstrating quite enjoyably the truths implicit in this statement, to each other's mutual satisfaction, when Lord Marlow burst in.

'I say, Thea...' He came to a halt, realising that the usually meticulous viscount was sporting a crushed cravat, and Miss Campion appeared rather dishevelled in his arms. 'Oh, I say, I'm sorry, Hadrian.'

'Come in, Charles,' Emery invited him with a wave of a hand. 'Thea has just accepted my offer. We were celebrating.'

'So I see,' Lord Marlow replied. 'I'm glad about your engagement, I mean. But, Thea and Hadrian, you must both help me with Amelia.'

'Amelia?' Thea looked up with alarm. 'She hasn't taken ill from all the excitement!'

'No, no,' Marlow quickly assured her, 'but she speaks of putting honey on her eels.' He shuddered at the image. 'And then she's going to eat them! I really don't think I can stomach seven more months of this. Strawberry jam in coffee I might see, but not honey on eels.'

'No indeed,' Thea agreed, giggling, and the three of them went off to acquaint Amelia with their happy news and to dissuade her from any more culinary experiments!

Mills & Boon

WINTER
COMPETITION

How would you like a
year's supply of Mills & Boon Romances ABSOLUTELY FREE?
Well, you can win them! All you have to do is complete the word
puzzle below and send it into us by 30th June 1989.
The first five correct entries picked out of the bag after that date
will each win a year's supply of Mills & Boon Romances (Ten
books every month - **worth over £100!**) What could be easier?

```
C W A E T A N R E B I H
H R I C E R W O L G M Y
I F R O S T A O E L U Y
L N I B O R U D R I V Y
L B L E A K B W I I N F
T O G L O V E S E A R R
S O S G O L R W I E T E
T T C H F I R E L R O E
S K A T E M Y C I K S Z
I Y R R E M I P I N E E
N A F D E C E M B E R N
N C E M I S T L E T O E
```

Ivy	Radiate	December	Star	Merry
Frost	Chill	Skate	Ski	Pine
Bleak	Glow	Mistletoe	Inn	
Boot	Ice	Fire		
Robin	Hibernate	Log		
Yule	Icicle	Scarf	**PLEASE TURN**	
Freeze	Gloves	Berry	**OVER FOR**	
			DETAILS	
			ON HOW	
			TO ENTER	

How to enter

All the words listed overleaf, below the word puzzle, are hidden in the grid. You can find them by reading the letters forwards, backwards, up or down, or diagonally. When you find a word, circle it, or put a line through it. After you have found all the words the remaining letters (which you can read from left to right, from the top of the puzzle through to the bottom) will spell a secret message.

Don't forget to fill in your name and address in the space provided and pop this page in an envelope (you don't need a stamp) and post it today. Hurry - competition ends 30th June 1989

Only one entry per household please.

Mills & Boon Competition, FREEPOST, P.O. Box 236, Croydon, Surrey CR9 9EL.

Secret message _____

_____

Name_____

Address_____

_____

_____

_____ Postcode _____

COMP5